"You thinking I'm some sort of hero?"

Griffin asked flatly. The sooner he disabused Nora of that notion, the better. "For all you know I was itching for a fight and got lucky enough to find one."

"You were protecting me," she insisted.

"You've been nothing but a pain in my ass since you walked into my garage, you know that?" Maybe his harsh words would change her mind, keep her away.

She walked closer to him, then stopped and laid the flat of her hand lightly on his chest.

"I'm sorry," she said, as she rose onto her toes, "but I really feel like this is something I have to do."

He looked at her, unable to see more than the flash of her eyes, feel her moving ever closer to him. He shook his head once, a quick, decisive no. A warning. A plea.

She ignored them all. "Brace yourself," she said, her breath washing over him, "this might hurt."

And she brushed her lips against the uninjured side of his mouth.

Dear Reader,

One of my favorite things about being a writer—other than working in my pajamas if I so choose—is getting inside my characters' heads. I love developing their personalities, figuring out their wants and desires, their secrets and fears and, best of all, discovering what they need to grow to become their best selves.

Most of the time, I'm completely in charge of my stories. I have a very clear idea of who my characters are and how I want them to behave. Before I wrote even one page of the first book in The Truth about the Sullivans trilogy, I knew the Sullivan sisters. Layne is honest, controlled and responsible. Tori is independent, clever and charming. And baby sister Nora? Well, she was supposed to be a nice counterbalance to her confident sisters—smart, sweet and a bit shy. Someone who doesn't look for confrontation, who weighs all her options before carefully making a decision.

You'll notice I said *supposed to be.*

From the moment she stepped onto the page of *Unraveling the Past,* Nora let me know I had her all wrong. Oh, sure, she's smart. Very. And while she's warm and generous, I'm not sure I'd call her sweet. She also says exactly what's on her mind and leaps into situations without considering the consequences.

Best of all, she keeps cynical Griffin York on his toes, never acting or reacting the way he thinks she will. He returns the favor by pushing her out of her comfort zone and challenging her to see herself as her own person instead of just one of the Sullivan girls.

I had a great time writing *On Her Side* and getting the chance to revisit the town of Mystic Point. I hope you enjoy the story!

I love to hear from my readers. Please visit my website, www.bethandrews.net, or drop me a line at beth@bethandrews.net or P.O. Box 714, Bradford, PA 16701.

Happy reading!

Beth Andrews

On
Her Side

BETH ANDREWS

HARLEQUIN®
entertain, enrich, inspire™

Recycling programs
for this product may
not exist in your area.

ISBN-13: 978-0-373-71794-1

ON HER SIDE

ABOUT THE AUTHOR

Romance Writers of America RITA® Award winner Beth Andrews has never purposely destroyed a car, rode on a Harley or started a barroom brawl. Thank goodness she gets to live vicariously through the characters in her books! Her goals for the year of walking three miles each day, and making every recipe in the dessert cookbook she got for Christmas, go together like diet Coke and a large order of French fries. Beth and her two teenage daughters outnumber...oops...*live* with her husband in Northwestern Pennsylvania. When not writing, walking or eating, Beth can be found texting her son at college. Learn more about Beth and her books by visiting her website, www.BethAndrews.net.

Books by Beth Andrews

HARLEQUIN SUPERROMANCE

*The Truth about the Sullivans

Other titles by this author available in ebook format.

For Hannah

ACKNOWLEDGMENT

Special thanks to Assistant Chief Mike Ward of the Bradford, PA, Police Department.

For Hannah

ACKNOWLEDGMENT

Special thanks to Assistant Chief Mike Ward of the Bradford, PA, Police Department.

ABOUT THE AUTHOR

Romance Writers of America RITA® Award winner Beth Andrews has never purposely destroyed a car, rode on a Harley or started a barroom brawl. Thank goodness she gets to live vicariously through the characters in her books! Her goals for the year of walking three miles each day, and making every recipe in the dessert cookbook she got for Christmas, go together like diet Coke and a large order of French fries. Beth and her two teenage daughters outnumber...oops...*live* with her husband in Northwestern Pennsylvania. When not writing, walking or eating, Beth can be found texting her son at college. Learn more about Beth and her books by visiting her website, www.BethAndrews.net.

Books by Beth Andrews

HARLEQUIN SUPERROMANCE

1496—NOT WITHOUT HER FAMILY
1556—A NOT-SO-PERFECT PAST
1591—HIS SECRET AGENDA
1634—DO YOU TAKE THIS COP?
1670—A MARINE FOR CHRISTMAS
1707—THE PRODIGAL SON
1727—FEELS LIKE HOME
1782—UNRAVELING THE PAST*

*The Truth about the Sullivans

Other titles by this author available in ebook format.

CHAPTER ONE

IT WAS THE RARE—and what her sisters would probably describe as blessed—day when Nora Sullivan was struck speechless. But try as she might, she couldn't articulate any of the thoughts flying through her head. Not after the bombshell Layne had oh-so-casually just dropped.

Luckily her other sister, Tori, had no such problem. "What did you say?"

At the head of the table, Layne tightened the band around her long, dark ponytail. "I asked you to pass the Italian dressing."

Tori shoved the bottle at her. "Before that."

"You mean when I asked if you wanted a beer?" Layne soaked her salad with the dressing, releasing the scent of olive oil, vinegar and seasonings, then licked a drop off the side of her thumb. "Because there's some in the fridge."

"No, smartass. What did you say after that?"

"Oh. You mean that Ross and I are seeing each other?"

"Yeah," Tori said, taking a big bite of her pizza before reaching for a paper napkin from the pile in front of her, "that's what I thought you said."

How could they both be so cavalier? Nora wondered as Layne dug into her salad. This wasn't just huge, it was momentous. Shocking. And possibly the dumbest, most reckless thing Layne had ever done.

"Wait, wait. I think my head's going to explode." Nora pressed her palms against her temples in case her brain went *boom!* and splattered over their dinner. "You're sleeping with your boss?"

That was so wrong on so many levels, and so unlike her usually cautious sister, Nora didn't even know where to start. Though she was pretty sure *Have you lost your freaking mind?* was as good a place as any.

"Isn't that against the law?" Tori asked as she got a beer out of the fridge and twisted it open.

"He's my superior officer," Layne said dryly, picking out a second slice of cheese pizza and setting it on her paper plate. "Not my brother. And there are currently no rules against departmental relationships."

Nora speared a cherry tomato from her salad with her fork. "Well, gee, if there aren't any written rules against it, we should all hook up with our bosses and damn the consequences."

Tori dropped the cap from her beer into the trash can. "Considering my boss is a woman, and our father's girlfriend, I guess I'm out."

"This is serious."

"Please. Cancer is serious. Kids going hungry is serious. This is sex between two single, consenting adults. What it should be is fun. Hot. And, if they're doing it right, and often enough, exhausting." She sipped her beer and sat back down, wiggled her eyebrows at Layne. "So, is it any of those?"

Nora deliberately set her fork down so she wouldn't be tempted to stab Tori in the hand. Breathing deeply, she centered herself. "Look," she said to Layne, "Chief Taylor seems very…capable—"

Tori snorted. "Just how every man dreams of being described in bed."

Nora's lips twitched and she had to clear the humor from her throat. "I meant at his job. God, get your mind out of the gutter." And capable did aptly describe the big, silent, watchful police chief. "But that doesn't mean you should risk your career for…for…"

"A few rounds of slap and tickle?" Tori interjected helpfully.

Reaching across the table, Layne plucked the beer from Tori's hand and took a long drink. "Whoever said sisters are one of the nicest things to happen to anyone never met you two."

"Hey, I'm on your side." Tori took her beer back. "I don't blame you for wanting some good times with Chief Taylor. He's completely hot. All controlled and commanding and in charge." She gave a little shiver that, if it'd been any other woman, would've looked like a convulsion. But with Tori it was just sexy. "Plus he has a top-notch ass."

"I'll be sure to mention to him you think so."

Tori grinned sharply and shook her hair back. The caramel highlights in the dark, shoulder-length strands caught the setting sun as it streamed through the French doors. "Oh, I'd be more than happy to pass that information on myself," she said in a seductive purr that went perfectly with her tight dark jeans and off-the-shoulder yellow top.

She would, too. Of that, Nora had no doubt. Tori was confident and sensual and used to men falling at her gorgeous feet. Layne, while more reserved, was no less beautiful. When Nora was younger, she'd envied her sisters for their long legs, dark hair and sharp features. Until she'd realized being blonde and curvy had its own rewards.

Like the ability to get away with just about anything because you were pretty and looked as if your head was filled with pink cotton candy, happy thoughts and sugarcoated dreams.

Nora may not be as brazen as Layne—who bulldozed her way over opposition—or as inherently sensual as Tori—who flirted and charmed her way into getting what she wanted—but she was smart.

Smart enough to have learned long ago to forge her own way instead of following in her sisters' footsteps.

Bobby O, Layne's black Rottie/Lab mix with floppy ears and a squared off snout, nudged the side of Nora's thigh then dropped a worn tennis ball at her feet. She kicked it softly so that it rolled across the wooden floor into the family room. Bobby raced after it, his tail wagging furiously as he skidded to a stop, taking the burgundy-and-brown throw rug with him.

"I'm having a hard time processing this," she said. "Have you considered what could happen to your job, your reputation, once this gets around?"

"Of course I have," Layne said, as if a few of those brain cells Nora had tried to hold back earlier had seeped out anyway. Which was crazy. Because anyone who knew Nora would never accuse her of being stupid. And her sisters knew her best. "I just… I think he's worth the risk."

"Wow." Stunned, Nora sat back. "You… He… Wow. Wow."

"Very articulate."

"Sorry, but you've never been big on the whole relationship thing before."

Any relationship. Layne was a rock, an island in their

family. Nora had always thought she preferred it that way. After all, while Nora and Tori shared secrets and clothes, good times and bad, Layne maintained her distance. But maybe that had less to do with her wanting to be alone and more to do with how she'd cared for her sisters from such a young age, had set their bedtimes and helped with homework. Had given them attention, love and, when needed, discipline. Things their father hadn't been around enough to do, their mother was too selfish to do.

Nora wondered if Layne would ever forgive their parents for being so much less than perfect. If she'd ever stop resenting her sisters for needing her.

Layne tore her pizza crust into small pieces. "I tried to ignore my feelings for Ross, hoped that if I pretended I didn't care, whatever I felt for him would go away. But it didn't work. Today he stopped by and I realized what a coward I was being by not taking a chance on him. On us. I don't know what's going to happen—with our jobs or this relationship—and that terrifies me, but..." She brushed the crumbs from her fingers. "I'm not willing to let him go."

"Look who realized she can't control everything," Tori said, lifting her bottle in a toast. "I thought this happy day would never come. But I doubt the only reason you invited us over for an impromptu pizza dinner is to share with us that you finally have a sex life."

"I wanted to tell you before it got around town."

Tori picked a carrot slice out of the salad on her plate and popped it into her mouth. "And?"

Sighing, Layne pushed her plate aside. "And I wanted to talk to you about Mom's case."

"Did something happen?" Nora asked, hope rising

that after three weeks the Mystic Point Police Department finally had a lead. "Did they find Dale?"

"No." Layne got to her feet and began to pace, Bobby on her heels, the ball in his mouth. "There have been no bank or utility records in his name, no credit card statements, payroll information or tax returns filed. It's as if he ceased to be when he left Mystic Point."

"Why don't you quit chewing on whatever it is you have to say," Tori suggested, "and just spit it out?"

Layne stopped, gripped the back of her chair with both hands. "We have to face the fact that we may never find him."

A roaring filled Nora's head. If they never found Dale York, they'd never punish the man responsible for their mother's death.

"So he gets away with murder?" she asked incredulously, her fingers curling into her palms. "No. Unacceptable."

"It's more than likely Dale skipped the country all those years ago. Or he's dead. The truth is, even if we did catch a major break and find him, the chances of getting a conviction are slim to none. We have no concrete evidence linking him to Mom's murder and no eyewitnesses."

Layne was using her reasonable *I'm Assistant Police Chief and therefore know better than you* tone. Nora wanted to toss her salad in her sister's face, rub Ranch dressing into her hair. God, how dare she stand there so poised and rational? This wasn't just another case they were discussing. This was their mother. She'd never understand how Layne could stay so detached.

Not that she'd question her sister about it. She'd done that once, the night they'd discovered their mother was dead. She'd never seen Layne so angry with her. So hurt. She'd never felt so guilty for causing that pain. Nora never made the same mistake twice.

"You're just giving up?" Tori asked Layne.

"The case will remain open—"

"But you don't believe Dale will ever be found."

Layne met Tori's gaze, then Nora's. "No. I don't. As much as I want to see that son of a bitch brought to justice, we have to realize that this isn't some police show on TV. Not every case gets solved. Real life isn't fair. It isn't easy, tidy or guaranteed to end happily."

"I think we're all familiar with those concepts," Nora snapped. She sure didn't need her sister reminding her of them. But despite the realization that life sometimes sucked the big one, Nora did her best to maintain a positive outlook, to hold on to the hope that no matter how rough the waters got, there'd be smooth sailing ahead.

That motto, combined with a healthy dose of optimism and a natural, sunny demeanor that bugged the hell out of her sisters—a nice bonus—made it possible for her to become a fairly well-adjusted adult, despite being abandoned by her mother. She'd done her best to maintain that healthy balance even after she and her family discovered everything they thought they knew about their past had been a lie. Valerie Sullivan, their beautiful, charming, imperfect mother hadn't left her husband and daughters to run off with her lover eighteen years ago.

She'd been murdered.

Brutally attacked and then left to rot in the woods outside of town where her remains were found over three weeks ago. And though the police had little to go on in the way of evidence and the most likely suspect hadn't been seen or heard from in eighteen years, Nora fully believed justice would be served. The truth, after all, always wins out in the end.

She'd make sure of it.

"You need to talk to his son again," Nora said. "Make him tell you where Dale is."

Layne gave her a look of exasperation mixed with indulgence. As if Nora was a precocious seven-year-old instead of an intelligent adult with a damn good suggestion. "Ross has already questioned Griffin and his mother and I spoke with Griffin about it when I ran into him a few weeks ago. Neither one of them have heard from Dale since he left town."

"So they claim." But what if they were lying?

Layne crossed her ankles and leaned back against the large, granite-topped center island, one of the few changes she'd made to their childhood home after she'd bought it from their father five years ago. "What would you have me do? Get out my rubber hose and beat the information out of them?"

"Maybe you haven't asked in the right way," Nora said.

"I asked in the only way I know how and it didn't work so don't think you'd have better luck."

Nora widened her eyes. "Did I say anything about my speaking to either of them?"

"You didn't have to." This from Tori. "It's written all over your face."

Nora started to lift a hand as if to wipe her expression clean but then slowly lowered it. Sent a bright smile at her gorgeous, overbearing, irritating sisters. "Now you're both just being paranoid."

Layne and Tori exchanged a long look. Nora hated when they did that. It was as if despite their many, many differences, they still had the ability to read the other's mind. "Stay out of it," Layne told her.

"More importantly," Tori added, "stay away from Griffin York. He is nothing but bad news. Do you understand?"

"First of all," Nora said as she rose and began clearing the table, her movements fluid despite the anger starting to sizzle in her veins, "save that mother tone for Brandon. I'm way past the age where it'll work on me." Not that it had worked on her twelve-year-old nephew lately, either. He was still mighty pissed at Tori for divorcing his father over six months earlier. "Secondly, what on earth gave you the crazy idea that I planned on speaking with Griffin York?"

"Because you always think you can succeed where mere mortals have failed," Layne said.

Tori nodded. "Because you fully believe you can charm what you want out of anyone."

Since both of those statements were true, Nora did her best to project sweetness and light and innocence. "I'm flattered you two think so highly of me. But honestly, you don't have to worry."

"Just promise us you won't do anything stupid," Layne said, watching her carefully.

Nora laid a hand over her heart. "I promise."

An easy enough vow to make. She didn't do stupid. But she did do whatever she had to in order to get her own way. If that meant facing down big, bad Griffin York, then so be it.

GRIFFIN CLIMBED DOWN from the tow truck and reached back inside for a copy of the day's *Mystic Point Chronicle*. Tucking it under his arm, he grabbed his cup of take-out coffee and sipped it as he shut the door. The cool, early morning breeze ruffled his hair, brought with it the briny scent of the ocean as he walked toward the garage.

Though the tow truck and building both carried the name Eddie's Service, they—along with the quarter acre lot they sat on, the tools and equipment inside the garage and the monthly small business loan payment—were his. All his.

It gave him a jolt, as it always did, to see it. To realize what he'd accomplished with little more than a high school diploma and a talent for taking cars apart. An even bigger talent for putting them back together again.

Surprise and pride mixed together to make that bump in his belly, along with a hefty dose of pure satisfaction that his father had been wrong.

He wasn't worthless.

Which was a hell of a lot more than he could say for Dale York.

More than that, Griffin had made a place for himself in this small town despite his last name and his father's reputation. Now, for good or bad, he was a part of Mystic Point. But that didn't necessarily mean he was accepted there, that he belonged.

Didn't mean he wanted to be either of those things.

Typing in the code on the security system's keypad, he waited while the bay door rose. Across the street, the Pizza Junction, a long building with a flat roof, was dark, the sign reading Sorry, We're Closed hanging at an angle on the glass door. Next to it, the pounding beat of some synthesized dance tune threatened to shatter the windows of Leonard's Fitness. Why people needed Marty Leonard, with his overdeveloped muscles and penchant for tight, bright running shorts—*short* running shorts—to tell them how to exercise and what they could and couldn't eat, was beyond Griffin. Then again, he'd never been much of a joiner.

Or one to take orders well.

Inside the garage, he flipped on the overhead lights before turning on the iPod in a docking station in the corner. Aerosmith's "Deuces Are Wild" floated through the sound system he'd rigged throughout the building so that when he stepped into his office, Steven Tyler's voice met him.

Tossing the paper aside, he sat behind his cluttered desk and did a quick check of the day's work schedule: four oil changes and two inspections this morning, plus Kelly Edel was to bring her Expedition in for new tires. That afternoon he'd work on Roy Malone's ancient Chevy's transmission and, if that alternator cap he'd ordered last week came in, he'd be able to get George Waid's precious Trans Am finished.

He stretched his arms overhead then picked up his coffee, took a sip. Not a bad workload for a Monday. Barring any unforeseen emergencies, mishaps or time sucks, he'd start his week on schedule and be out of here today by five.

One corner of his mouth lifted. His days never went according to plan. There were always flat tires, fender benders, overheated engines or breakdowns to deal with. Hell, some days he dealt with all of them and then some.

He loved every minute of it.

He ran a successful business. One that had far exceeded the expectations he'd had when he'd bought out Eddie Franks five years ago. He knew what people thought when they saw him. That he was trouble. Dangerous. Like his old man.

He'd gotten tired of trying to prove them wrong. Had long ago stopped caring what other people thought.

So he'd kept to himself, kept his head down and worked his ass off. Now they brought their vehicles to him because they trusted him to keep their minivans and SUVs and pickups and sedans running safely. And they came back because he was damn good at his job.

That was enough for him.

He heard a car pull into the lot. Frowning, he checked the Kendall Motor Oil clock on the wall. Kelly was early, he thought as a car door slammed shut. No skin off his nose—unless she expected him to fit her in earlier than scheduled.

But when he stepped out into the garage, it wasn't a middle-aged, overweight mother of two walking toward him.

It was a blonde. A young blonde in a light purple dress that wrapped around her waist in a wide band, the skirt flaring out slightly and ending above her knees. Her legs were bare, her feet encased in a pair of pointy toed high heels the color of sand. She'd pulled her hair back into some sort of twist, showing off a delicate neck and a pair of diamonds glittering at her ears.

He narrowed his eyes. There was something…familiar…about her. Something more than his seeing her around town—though in a town the size of Mystic Point most everyone looked familiar.

But then it clicked and he realized who she was. And he could make a damn good guess why she'd come.

"Well, well, what do we have here?" he asked softly as she stepped inside. "A Sullivan in my shop. Has hell frozen over? Or is it just the end of the world as I know it?"

Instead of scowling—the reaction he'd expect from

a Sullivan—the blonde blushed, pink spreading from the small V of skin visible at her chest, up her throat to her face. But her eyes stayed on his and she even smiled as she approached him.

"Griffin York, right?" she asked, holding her hand out. "Hi. I'm—"

"I know who you are." His coffee in one hand, he shoved the other into the pocket of his jeans. After a moment, she slowly lowered her arm. He raked his gaze over her. She was pretty—in an angelic sort of way. He'd never been much for angels. Or Sullivans. "You're Layne and Tori's sister."

Her megawatt smile dimmed a fraction. "Actually I usually go by Nora. Seems easier for people to say."

He lifted a shoulder. "You having car trouble?"

She blinked. "What? Oh, no. No," she repeated, holding on to the strap of her purse as if it was a lifeline, "my car's fine. I—"

"Then I guess there's no reason for you to be here." He nodded toward the parking lot where her silver Lexus blocked the entrance to his garage. "See you later, Nancy."

"Really? That's the best you can do?"

"Not sure what you mean."

"Yes, you do. You're trying to prove to me that I'm so unimportant, you can't even be bothered to remember my name." That damn smile was back to full power, as if he amused her to no end. "Aren't you clever to target my tender feelings that way? Is this the point where I'm supposed to take my broken heart and scurry away?"

Studying her over the rim of his cup, he sipped his coffee. "That sounds about right."

"Sorry to disappoint you," she said, and he wondered how she managed to convey such sincerity when she sounded as far from sorry as humanly possible. Must be that face of hers. Someone who looked like she kept a spare halo in her pocket could get away with quite a few sins before anyone realized she was like every other poor slob walking the earth.

Flawed, untrustworthy and only out for herself.

"I'm not ready to leave yet," she continued. "I was hoping I could talk to you about your father."

He figured that's why she'd come, but hearing her say it still gave him a twinge of guilt, of nerves, both of which pissed him off. He wouldn't be held accountable for his father's mistakes or his crimes. Wouldn't feel responsible for them.

"You don't always get what you want," he said smoothly, rubbing the pad of his thumb along the faded scar under his jaw. "That was one lesson the old man taught real well."

Tossing his coffee cup into the trash, he walked over to the car on the lift, his stride unhurried, his movements easy as he opened the driver side door. But when he reached inside, he gripped the keys tightly, cranking them so hard the engine whined in protest.

The back of his neck heated. He gave the steering wheel a sharp rap with the side of his fist. Damn it. Damn *her*. This was his place. She had no right to waltz in here, looking all untouchable and superior, and bring up his bastard of a father.

Ducking back out of the car, Griffin walked to the shelves along the far wall without so much as a glance to see if she'd left or not. He took down a funnel and tossed it on the rolling cart next to the plastic jug he used to store old oil.

Blondie couldn't change the rules because she had a bug up her ass about something. He never set foot in the Ludlow Street Café, the restaurant her father's live-in girlfriend owned, where her sister Tori worked. Even back in school when he and Tori were in the same grade, Layne two years ahead of them, he'd kept to himself. He never, ever, stepped over the invisible line that had kept the Yorks and the Sullivans separated for the past eighteen years. Pretending the other family didn't exist—let alone that they lived in the same town—had worked pretty damn well for both the Sullivans and him and his mom.

Had worked until Valerie Sullivan's remains were found outside the old quarry, proving she hadn't taken off with his father like everyone in town had believed. Bringing up the very real possibility that his father had killed his lover before he'd left Mystic Point.

And just like that, Griffin and his mother had been yanked back into the past. The police chief had wanted to know if they'd heard from Dale, if they had any idea where he was, how he could be reached. They hadn't and they didn't, but that didn't stop the rumors from flying. Wouldn't stop people from remembering that his mother had once been married to the man suspected of Valerie's murder. Reminding them all that Griffin was his son.

"I spoke with my sister yesterday," the youngest Sullivan said, standing in the middle of his garage as if nothing short of a dynamite blast would move her. Which he was starting to seriously consider. "The assistant police chief?"

He shut off the car and slammed the door shut. "Not interested."

"Layne said you claim not to know where your father is," she continued as if Griffin's words had floated in one ear and out the other without meeting so much as one working brain cell as resistance. "Is that true?"

"I thought you were the smart Sullivan sister," he said, pressing the button to raise the car on the lift.

She crossed her arms, for the first time looking uncomfortable—and wasn't that interesting? "I don't see what my IQ has to do with—"

"But in case you're not as bright as they say, let me make myself very clear." He tapped his fist against his thigh as he closed the distance between them, stopping in front of her. Though she wore two-inch heels—and he topped off at five-ten—she still had to tip her head back to maintain eye contact. "I've already been questioned by the cops. And no matter how many times you or your sister—*the assistant police chief*—ask me, the answers aren't going to change."

"But you—"

"So unless you're having car problems—and are prepared to pay me to fix those problems—there's really no reason for you to be here. And nothing for us to talk about."

Inhaling deeply, she sent a beseeching glance at the ceiling, as if asking the heavens from whence she came to grant her patience. "I think we got off on the wrong foot here."

"Do you?" he murmured, figuring only an idiot would miss the calculation in her blue eyes. And the intelligence behind them.

He'd been called many things in his life, but never an idiot.

"How about we start over?" she asked, holding out her hand again. "Hi, Griffin, I'm Nora. It's nice to meet you."

For a moment, he almost believed she was as innocent and harmless as she looked with her perfect face, guileless charm and dry sense of humor.

She was good, he'd give her that. Damn good.

He enveloped her warm hand in his, noting the relief, the triumph that crossed her expression. But when he held on past what was considered the polite amount of time for a simple handshake, that relief turned to unease. The triumph to confusion. He felt no small amount of satisfaction from that unease. And he had no problem using it against her.

"How about this?" he asked quietly, tugging her toward him until she was so close he could smell her light, clean scent. Could hear the soft catch of her breath. Her throat worked, her eyes widened as they met his. "You walk yourself out of my garage, get into your car and drive off my property. Or—"

"Or what?" she asked, yanking free of his hold, her face flush. "You'll toss me over your shoulder, throw me into my trunk, hook my car to your tow truck and drag me out of here?"

He could easily imagine himself doing the first and wished he could figure out a way to make the second idea work without going to jail for it. "Not that I have anything against those suggestions, but no. I won't do anything."

She smirked, reminding him of how Layne had looked a few weeks back when she'd tried to arrest him for the dubious crime of being Dale York's son. "That's what I thought."

No, she thought she had him firmly by the balls. And all she had to do to keep him in line was squeeze.

"I won't do anything," he repeated. "I'll let the Mystic Point Police Department do it for me."

She blinked. Then she laughed. Bright, tinkling

laughter that filled the cavernous space of the garage and seemed to echo back at him.

He was in hell.

"Keep that sense of humor," he said. "It'll come in handy when they take your mug shot."

"Come on," she said as if inviting him to share in the joke. "You're not going to call the police."

"I'm not?"

"Why would you? It's not like you and the Mystic Point PD have a strong relationship based on mutual trust and admiration."

Because he was Dale York's son. Because he'd been a wild and rebellious kid and was an adult who didn't take shit or back down from anyone.

"I'm a tax paying, law-abiding citizen," he pointed out, not getting so much as a parking ticket since he turned eighteen and realized he'd be following his old man's footsteps straight to prison if he didn't keep his nose clean. Watching her, he took out his cell phone. "Make sure to duck when they put you in the back of the squad car. Wouldn't want to hit your head and mess up that fancy hairdo."

"While I'm sure that's excellent advice—and comes from your own personal experience—I don't need it. It's not illegal to have a conversation with someone. Unless, of course, you know something about the law I don't?" she asked in a sweet, condescending tone that grated on his last nerve.

He raised his eyebrows. "You always have that ego, or did it come with the law degree?"

"It's not ego. I just meant—"

"I know what you meant." She wanted to prove how smart she was—so much smarter than him because she went to some fancy college while he was lucky to finish high school. So much better than him by virtue of her last name. "And I don't care what the cops do with you. Arrest you for trespassing, cite you for loitering or give you a ticket for being a pain-in-the-ass. Doesn't matter to me as long as they get you out of my hair and out of my garage."

Biting her lower lip, she regarded him warily as if trying to figure out if he was serious. "Okay," she said with a decisive nod, "if that's the way you want it—"

"It is," he assured her, mimicking her somber tone.

"Fine." Her sigh was very much that of a poor, put-upon female forced to deal with a brainless, tactless male. "We'll do things your way. But for the record," she said, wagging her finger at him like some librarian to a naughty schoolboy—never one of his favorite fantasies, "let me just say I'm not happy about this. Not one bit."

"Life's tough that way. Best get used to it."

"Thank you for those words of wisdom," she said so solemnly he didn't doubt she was messing with him. "I will endeavor to keep them in mind."

Endeavor. Jesus. Who talked like that?

She strode away, her back rigid, her arms swinging like one of those women he saw power-walking in Hanley Park each morning.

Except, she didn't march her irritating self out the door. She brushed past him, crossed to the long shelf behind the lift and stared at the tools there as if trying to figure out which one went best with her outfit.

A prickle of trepidation formed between his shoulder blades. What was she up to?

Finally she grabbed a small crowbar and held it up as she walked toward him. "I'm borrowing this."

His muscles tensed, and the prickle morphed into an itch of warning. Not of physical violence—though he didn't doubt this piece of fluff was capable of it. Everyone was. But that whatever she planned on doing with that crowbar was going to piss him off but good.

"You plan on beating me over the head for not talking to you?" he asked mildly, his hands at his sides, his weight on the balls of his feet in case he had to defend himself.

"Of course not," she said, passing him by without taking so much as a swing. "That would be a little overkill, don't you think?"

She walked into the sunshine and he figured his skull was safe—for now. Unable to resist, he followed her, stopping to lean against the door frame as she marched up to her car, raised the bar over her shoulder like a batter ready for a grand slam—and swung hard. Her headlight exploded in a spray of glass. Pieces clung to her dress, sparkling against the dark material. More rained down onto the pavement.

And people thought he was dangerous.

"Lady," he said, straightening, "you've got a sparkplug loose up in that head of yours."

She strolled over to the other headlight and took it out as well. Cocking one hip, she studied her handiwork for a moment then started whaling away at the grill, the clang of metal on metal setting his teeth on edge.

She didn't have the strength to do much damage to the grill, though she gave it her best shot—no pun intended. But what she lacked in muscle, she made up for in enthusiasm. She grunted with exertion, her hips swaying in time with her swings, the hem of her dress lifting to show a few more inches of her thighs.

He might have enjoyed the sight if he didn't want to wring her pretty neck.

Griffin glanced behind him. He could go back inside, close the door and pretend this whole bat-shit crazy episode had never happened. He was tempted, sorely tempted to do just that. But he had customers scheduled to arrive soon and traffic was picking up along Willard Avenue. It was only a matter of time before someone noticed what the psycho blonde was doing.

And wonder what he'd done to drive her to it.

He stormed over and grabbed the bar on one of her upswings, plucking it from her hand. "Knock it off," he growled, frustration eating at him, making him think about taking a few swings at the vehicle himself. "You're going to hurt yourself."

"I'm done anyway," she said, breathing hard. Her cheeks were flushed, her eyes bright—with temper? Or insanity? "Now, let's go inside so we can discuss how you can help me track down your father."

CHAPTER TWO

GOOD LORD, but Griffin York was beautiful.

His hair, a rich shade of chocolate-brown, fell past the collar of his T-shirt in tousled waves and yet did nothing to soften the sharp line of his jaw, the harsh slash of his cheekbones. His brows were thick and drawn together as he studied her warily, his green eyes flecked with gold. He had a slight dimple in his chin, broad shoulders, a flat stomach and muscular arms.

Beautiful and, she realized, pissed off.

What a crying shame. Someone that pretty shouldn't scowl so much.

"You," he bit out, "are a crazy person."

Nora's hands stung from the reverberations of hitting the car with the crowbar, her heart raced from her exertion. "Not crazy. Just determined."

Although, she thought with a glance at her poor car, she might plead temporary insanity. But it had felt surprisingly good—in a therapeutic way—to hit something after all the trauma and drama of the past few weeks. After the frustration of realizing the local police couldn't, or wouldn't be able to bring Dale York to justice.

"You keep telling yourself that," Griffin said in his gravelly voice.

She hooked her pinkie under a strand of hair stuck to her temple, narrowed her eyes at him. Okay, she was trying to be fair here. She didn't know enough about Griffin to judge him, to dislike him as her sisters did. To mistrust or fear him because he had a less than stellar reputation.

Yes, she was trying to be fair and he wasn't making it easy.

"You said that unless I had a problem with my car, there was nothing for us to talk about." She gestured to her car. "Well, I have a car problem now."

His gaze went from her to her car and back again. "What's to stop me from kicking you out of here anyway?"

"Oh, let's see. How about integrity? A latent sense of decency? Or maybe everyone is right about you. Maybe you are just like your father."

His jaw worked, his mouth a thin line, and for a moment, she regretted the low blow. But a good attorney knew not only which questions to ask, but which argument to make to get the win.

And there was no win she wanted more than to see Dale York spend the rest of his life behind bars for her mother's murder. But first, she had to find him.

"You want to talk," Griffin said tightly. "You'll have to do it while I work." Then he turned and walked back into the garage.

The man put a new spin on the word *stubborn*.

Luckily so did she. And so far, she was ahead of the game since he'd stopped threatening to call the cops on her. Not that the police would really arrest her. But they would send someone out to check what was going on, which meant Layne would find out Nora was there.

And she wanted to keep that little tidbit of information to herself for...oh...forever. Or longer.

Inhaling deeply, she shook the glass fragments from

her dress. Looked at her car once more. She winced. She'd only had it a few months. It'd been a gift—an extravagant, thoughtful gift—from her aunt and uncle upon her graduation from law school. Maybe her family was right. Maybe she was a bit impulsive from time to time.

But at least she got the job done. And that was all that mattered.

Not seeing Griffin in the garage, she headed toward the direction he'd come from when she'd first arrived. She found him in a cramped office searching through the piles of paper on a metal desk. She scratched her elbow. Great. She was probably breaking out in hives from this mess. How did he get any work done?

"Nice office," she lied, crossing to check out a yellowed calendar on the wall. Pursing her lips, she studied the photo of a brunette with huge, curly hair, melon-size breasts and a teeny, tiny black bikini, sprawled across the hood of a white Lamborghini. "May 1987, huh? I take it a memorable event happened that month you like to be reminded of?"

He straightened, resentment and anger rolling off of him like waves crashing onto shore. "Knock it off."

"Knock what off?" she asked with a smile as she tucked her hands behind her back. God only knew what sort of flesh-eating disease lingered on these surfaces.

He waved a hand in the air. "Your whole Little Miss Sunshine routine."

"Routine?"

"Yeah, your act where you pretend there's some sort of holy light shining down on your head while you shoot rainbows from your ass. Knock it off because I'm not buying it."

Bristling, she ground her teeth together behind her grin. "It's not an act. It's called being pleasant. Friendly."

He swept up a black bandana from the desk. "We're not friends."

"No kidding," she muttered. Which was fine with her. She had more than enough friends already. She certainly didn't need to add one bitter, antagonistic, angry, *rude* man to the list. And if he couldn't be bothered with social niceties, then he could kiss her rainbow-shooting ass.

Jerk.

"Where's your father?" she asked, no longer caring if she sounded haughty or demanding.

Setting his foot on the seat of the chair behind the desk, he laid the bandana on his jean-covered thigh and quickly folded it into a strip. "As I've already told Chief Taylor, and your sister, I have no idea."

"You must have heard from him at some point during the past eighteen years."

"Not even once."

What could she say to that? They'd never heard from their mother and had never thought anything other than she hadn't cared enough to contact them. Of course, now they knew she'd been dead all those years, but before the truth had come out, no one had questioned Valerie's lack of communication with her family. Did Nora have any right to doubt Griffin now?

"Let's back up a bit here," she said, digging a small notebook out of her purse. She tucked it under her arm and searched for a pen. "We'll start at the—"

"I'm not sure how much clearer I can be. I don't know where he is."

Damn it, why was it she could never find a pen when she needed one? Giving up she gingerly picked up a pen from his desk, held it between the tips of her fingers. "I believe you."

He shook his hair back and put the bandana on, tied it behind his head. "You have no idea what that means to me."

Not much if the sardonic lift of his mouth was anything to go by. So much for her thinking he'd be more receptive to helping her if he thought she was on his side.

"Whether or not you are aware of your father's current whereabouts is irrelevant," she said, "because I've hired a private investigator to track him down." But instead of sounding certain and resolute, she came across as smug and, she hated to admit it, slightly obsessive.

"Industrious little thing, aren't you?" he murmured. She didn't take it as a compliment. "What does your family think of that?"

"They're all for it."

He set his hands on his hips, the faded material of his green T-shirt pulling tight across his muscular chest. "You'll give lawyers a bad reputation lying that way, angel."

Angel. Well, it was better than Nancy. Even if he did say *angel* the same way normal people said *tapeworm*. Still, the only reason he refused to call her by her given name was to prove he couldn't be bothered to remember it.

That it bugged her was her own damn fault.

And what was up with him reading her so easily? How could he possibly know her family had no idea she'd hired a P.I. from Boston? Not that she planned on keeping that information from them indefinitely. She had every intention of telling them. After Dale was found and arrested for her mother's murder.

"The more background information the P.I. has," she said, ignoring her unease, her guilt at keeping a secret from her family, "the easier it will be for him to do his job." Swinging her purse onto her shoulder, she took the notebook in one hand, held the pen poised over the paper. "Does your father have any living relatives? Anyone he may have sought out after leaving Mystic Point?"

The dark fabric of the bandana made his eyes seem lighter. Colder. "I get what you're after, and I guess I can even understand where you're coming from—"

"Hooray," she said, her tone all sorts of wry.

"But I can't help you."

"You mean you won't."

He scratched under his jaw. "Either way, the end result's the same."

"If you're uncomfortable discussing this with me, you can talk to the P.I. directly." Her words were rushed. Desperate. "Just give him five, ten minutes of your time, answer a few quick—"

"No."

She shook her head. "But you can help us. It's the right thing to do."

And that meant everything to her. Doing what was right. What was best for others.

It was one of the many things that proved she was the exact opposite of her mother.

"I'm not interested in doing what's right," he said so simply, she had no choice but to believe him. To resent him for it.

"If you won't help, maybe your mother would be willing to give me some answers."

He edged closer to her, his expression hard, his eyes glittering. Wishing she still had the crowbar—just in case—she stepped back, held the notebook over her furiously pounding heart. "You stay away from my mother."

She didn't mistake his quiet words for a request or even an order. They were a warning, a challenge as subtle and soft as the summer breeze.

Pulling her shoulders back, she forgot her nerves, her momentary fear of him. She never backed down from a challenge. "But you and your mom may be able to help find Dale. Isn't that what you want?"

"It's not really a question of what I want," he said, watching her carefully. "This—you being here, hiring some Sherlock Holmes wannabe to waste his time and your money searching for the old man—it's all about what you want."

"He needs to pay for what he did to my mother," she said through her teeth.

Surely even someone as cocky, as solitary as Griffin could see why he should help her. How important it was.

"Even if you do find him, there's no guarantee he'll be convicted of anything. Trust me, the best thing that could happen for everyone is for Dale to remain missing. Leave the past alone." He glanced at the clock on the wall. "Now, I have work to do. Which means we're done."

She gaped at his back as he walked away. "Have you suffered a recent brain injury?" she called, but he kept going.

She didn't move. Couldn't, not with her thoughts spinning, panic strangling her. He meant it. He wasn't going to help her. And she wasn't going to be able to persuade him otherwise. He was too cynical to charm. Too sharp for her to outwit.

She bit the inside of her cheek. It wasn't supposed to go this way. She never failed. Never. Had never gotten anything less than an A in any subject, had reached every goal she'd ever set for herself, from getting the lead in her sixth grade's production of *Our Town*, to making the varsity softball squad as a high school freshman, to graduating law school at the top of her class.

But Griffin refused to be swayed in his position by her passion for truth, justice and the American way, her sense of morality or sparkling personality.

It was as if she'd stepped into some weird dimension where she didn't get her own way.

She couldn't say she liked it here much.

She drummed her fingers against a bare corner of Griffin's desk. She had two choices: she could stay and keep bashing her head against the wall that was Griffin York's stubbornness.

Or she could cut her losses and get the hell out of there before any damage was done. She thought of her car, her stomach turning with nausea and regret. Make that before any serious, irreparable damage was done. She'd back off, regroup and strengthen her case before trying again.

And when she came back—and she would—Griffin wouldn't know what hit him.

Out in the garage, Griffin stood under the car on the lift, his back to her. He reached up and did something under the car, the muscles in his upper back contracting under his taut shirt. Warmth suffused her, settled in her lower stomach. She ignored it.

"I have to get to work," she said as oil ran into the funnel and dripped into the plastic jug. "Why don't we continue this conversation at a more convenient time? How about dinner tonight? My treat," she added quickly in case he thought she was angling for him to pay.

He wiped his hands on a stained rag and stuck it into

his back pocket as he slowly faced her. "You asking me out?" His rough voice was low and amused. "Because if you are..." He scanned her from head to toe, one corner of his mouth lifted in a sardonic, insulting smile. "I'm not interested. Not even for a free meal."

"Ouch," she murmured, unable to stop her cheeks from heating even though going out with him was the last thing on her mind. Yes, he was all walking sex appeal and mysterious and gorgeous, like a fallen angel come to tempt her to the dark side. But she was quite content living in the light, thanks very much.

Unlike her mother.

Besides, her family would lose their minds if they knew she'd breathed the same air as Griffin York. She couldn't imagine their reactions if she dated the man.

She sighed dramatically. "Hopefully I'll survive the heartbreak of your callous words, but if you're sure there's nothing I can say or do to change your mind about talking with the P.I...."

"There's not."

That was what she was afraid of. Damn him. "Then I guess there's nothing left for us to discuss—"

"I told you that fifteen minutes ago."

"Except when you think you'll have my car repaired."

His brows drew together. "You expect me to fix your car?"

"Yes, how silly of me," she said, pulling her cell phone from her purse, "to expect a mechanic to perform car repairs. What a ludicrous idea." She opened her phone and brought up the calendar function. "So when should I come back to pick it up?"

He looked at her as if she'd asked when a good time was for her to return and burn his business to the ground. "You are some piece of work."

Again, not a compliment. "Yes, well, be that as it may, I need my car fixed and I'd like to hire you to do it." She couldn't take it to her usual garage. Not when it was so obvious someone had damaged it on purpose. And wouldn't that be fun to explain? "Unless you have a problem taking money from me because I'm a Sullivan?"

"I never have a problem taking someone's money for doing my job. I have a problem with people coming to my place and harassing me about things that are none of their damned business."

"Your father is my business and has been since he and my mother decided to get together. But if it'll make you feel better, I promise not to *harass*—and I take exception to that term—you about anything. You fix my car, I'll come back when it's finished, pick it up and pay my bill. As long as the work is done satisfactorily, of course."

"I do quality work." Though the words were said calmly enough, she couldn't help but feel as if she'd offended him.

"I'm sure you do," she rushed out, realizing she'd sounded a bit snotty. And superior. "Which is why I'd like you to work on my car. So...do we have a deal?"

DID THEY HAVE a deal? Griffin wasn't sure. He didn't trust her. She was too unflappable. Too freaking cheerful.

She was a Sullivan.

At least she'd been up front about wanting to drag him into her crusade to find his old man. A noble cause, sure. But Griffin wasn't some knight in shining armor. He didn't do noble. He put in ten hours a day at the garage, six days a week, stayed out of the trouble that had seemed to follow him wherever he went as a kid and kept his nose out of other people's business.

And expected others to do the same for him.

Besides, it wasn't his problem if the cops couldn't find Dale. That they didn't have any evidence to charge him with Valerie Sullivan's murder.

Not that Griffin thought for one moment that Dale was innocent. He'd seen firsthand the kind of violence his father was capable of. His old man was a criminal, a con man who could adapt to any situation, become anyone. But underneath his exterior, he was nothing but an animal. He brushed off civility as easily as most people batted away a fly, disregarded rules in favor of following his own self-serving instincts.

Only the strong survive, boy.

Dale's sneering, hate-fueled voice filled Griffin's head. His stomach clenched as if Dale could reach through time and punctuate his statement with one of his stinging slaps.

Griffin rubbed his fingertips across the stubble on his chin. A reminder to himself he wasn't some skinny, scared kid anymore. But though many years had passed since Dale had left town, Griffin was sure his father hadn't changed. He'd always be dangerous. Violent. And God help anyone who stood between him and what he wanted. He hoped blondie knew what she was doing by going after Dale.

But it wasn't Griffin's job to warn her or protect her from his old man. He'd tried once to save a woman from Dale. Tried and failed. Better to leave people to their own devices and foolish decisions.

"Come back Friday," he told her. He may not want to save her from herself but that didn't mean he couldn't take her money for doing his job. "Your car should be done by then."

"That long?" she asked, looking put out, as if he'd delay the job to mess with her.

"I have to order parts," he said shortly. "They take a few days to get here but if you don't like the timeline, you're free to go somewhere else."

"Wow, business must be booming, what with that charming way you have with the customers."

"Friday," he repeated because his business did just fine despite him not wasting time chatting with customers, pretending to be someone he wasn't.

He had enough work to keep him busy—more than enough. Yeah, he made a fraction of what that lawyer uncle of hers probably raked in during the year but Griffin was his own boss, paid all of his bills on time and even had a little cash left over at the end of each month.

For someone who'd spent most of his childhood slipping out of towns in the middle of the night, his old man running from the cops, creditors or other crooks, his current situation was close to perfect.

"Call first to make sure it's done," he said, going back to the oil change. He didn't want her showing up and giving him grief if the parts didn't get there in time.

Nodding, her fingers flew over the buttons on her phone. Probably one of those fancy models that did everything but wipe your ass for you. She tossed it back into that huge purse of hers then glanced around. "Which car should I use?"

"For what?"

"For transportation," she said as if he was the one who needed to be fitted for a straitjacket instead of her. "I'll need a vehicle to drive while my car is being worked on."

"Guess you should've thought of that before you went all PMS on your headlights." He put the cap back on the oil pan. "You want something to drive? Try a car rental agency."

"But I have to be to work in—" she checked the slim, fancy watch on her wrist "—fifteen minutes. Could you at least give me a ride downtown?"

"No."

"No?" she squeaked as if she'd never heard the word before.

"I'm not a taxi driver. And, thanks to you, I'm already behind on the day's work."

"What do you expect me to do?" She slammed her hands on her curvy hips, tugging the top of her dress lower, exposing more of the creamy skin on her chest. He jerked his gaze back to her face. "Walk?"

"I don't care if you fly. I'm not driving you."

"B-but...it's at least two miles from here."

He considered that. "More like two and a half."

"I'm in heels," she snapped.

He shouldn't feel so much pleasure at finally ruffling her feathers, but what the hell? He was about as far from a saint as you could get. He sure wasn't above enjoying her discomfort. Not after she'd done nothing but irritate him since walking into his place.

"And you're down to thirteen minutes," he pointed out. "You might want to get going."

She glowered at him. He couldn't help it. He grinned.

"What," she asked imperiously, "is so funny?"

"You and that glare." Two high spots of color appeared on her cheeks but instead of making her look indignant, she just looked cute. Cuter. If that was possible. "Sorry to break it to you, but you're about as intimidating as a magical fairy."

"A...fairy?" she repeated, about choking on the word, her arms straight, her hands fisted.

Hoping it would piss her off but good, he winked at her. "*Magical* fairy. A sparkly one. Floaty. You must get eaten alive in court, huh? Maybe Layne could give you a few lessons on how to be a hard-nosed bitch."

She lifted her chin. "I will not allow myself to be dragged into some ludicrous argument over fairies—"

"Magical fairies."

Her mouth flattened. "Or my sister. I will see you Friday." She whirled on her heel and sashayed away.

He waited until she reached the door before calling out, "Hey, angel?"

She stopped but didn't turn.

"The next time you feel the need to pound on your car," he continued, "you might want to think about slashing a tire instead. It would've been easier and you would've saved yourself a lot of grief and about a thousand bucks."

Her back went so straight he was surprised her spine didn't audibly snap. Her head held high, she walked out into the sunshine.

He could've sworn he heard her mutter something that sounded suspiciously like "Crap."

There was no way she'd make it to work in time. Even if she ran—and he couldn't imagine her so much as jogging in that dress and those heels—she'd still be late.

He shrugged. Not his problem. *She* wasn't his problem.

But he still had the strangest urge to call her back, this time to tell her he was messing with her, that he'd drive her into town. Because he wanted to. Contemplating how big of an idiot that would make him, he deliberately went to the back of the garage for a case of oil.

So she had to walk. Big deal. It was only a few miles, the sun was shining and it was still cool enough for a brisk, morning trek to be refreshing instead of sweat inducing. And she had a cell phone. She could always call one of her sisters or a friend to pick her up.

From the moment he'd realized who she was, he'd wanted to get rid of her. And now he had his wish so there was no reason to waste time wondering if he should've handled the situation, handled her, differently.

She was out of his hair, out of his personal business, at least until Friday. He'd just be grateful for small favors.

CHAPTER THREE

FIVE MINUTES LATER, Nora shifted her weight from her left foot to her right as she waited on the sidewalk in front of Pizza Junction. She'd grabbed her briefcase and laptop from the backseat of her car before stomping off Griffin's property.

She couldn't stop thinking about how he'd looked at her. As if she was an annoying mosquito barely worth the time and effort it would take to swat her away.

What an ass. Her lips tightened. A rude, blatantly antagonistic ass.

Maybe her sisters, her father and pretty much the entire town were right about him. He really was trouble. The kind she'd do best to avoid.

A familiar red Jeep pulled up and stopped in front of her. She opened the passenger side door and climbed in.

"Hey," she said to her cousin Anthony. "Thanks for getting me."

"No problem," Anthony said with a smile that had his dimple winking. "Being without a car sucks."

"True." Especially when it was due to your own stubbornness and stupidity. She set her briefcase and laptop case on the floor, then rolled her window down a few inches. Spotting something sparkly in the cup holder, she picked it up. "I always imagined you as more of a dragonfly guy," she said, holding up the butterfly barrette.

He glanced at it. "Funny."

She patted his leg. "Don't be embarrassed. Holding on to a keepsake from your girlfriend is sweet. As long as it's not underwear. That's just weird. And pervy."

"It's not a keepsake," he said, his expression hard, his hands strangling the steering wheel.

She blinked at the vehemence in his tone. And then it hit her. Which girlfriend the barrette must've belonged to. Jessica.

Damn that girl.

Nora curled her fingers around the barrette, the edge biting into her palm. "Want me to see she gets it back?" she asked quietly.

He lifted a shoulder as his phone buzzed, which she took as an affirmation. He checked his text. "Hold on a sec," he told her then responded to the message, his fingers flying over the keys.

He kept his head down, the sun turning his curly hair gold. He was handsome and charming, smart and funny and used to having the world by the tail. He was also honest to a fault and young enough to believe everyone else was, too. Until a slip of a girl lied to him.

Anthony, twenty-one and about to start his senior year at Boston University, had gone out with Chief Taylor's niece Jessica a few times. Until he'd found out that the girl who'd claimed to be a student at Northeastern University was really only a high school junior. He'd been humiliated and furious at being tricked.

But Nora wasn't sure what upset him most: that Jess had lied to him...

Or that he'd had to let her go.

Now Jessica—who'd moved to Mystic Point when her uncle been granted custody of her—would undoubtedly be around the Sullivans more thanks to Layne and

Ross hooking up. They were in for some awkward family holiday celebrations this year.

Nora had warned Layne that her involvement with her boss would cause problems. People really should listen to her more.

"Sorry about that," Anthony said, tossing his phone back into the console then pulling out onto the road. "What's wrong with the Lexus?"

"I had a small fender bender," she said, deciding not to tell him about Layne and Ross. Let Layne break the news to him herself. "I'm going to have to have a headlight—" or two "—replaced."

Not quite a lie, just not the whole truth. And really, whoever said omission was the same as lying never went to law school.

The next time you feel the need to pound on your car you might want to think about slashing a tire instead. It would've been easier and you would've saved yourself a lot of grief and about a thousand bucks.

Yes, Griffin had made a valid point. One that had run through her head about a dozen or so times since she'd walked out of his parking lot. She'd been a bit... rash with the headlight-smashing episode.

But really, it had made a much bigger impact than if she'd let the air out of a tire.

"You want to hear something weird?" Anthony asked, sliding her a look, one hand on the steering wheel, the other tapping along to the classic rock song playing softly through the speakers.

She flipped the visor down and checked her hair. Smoothing back a loose strand, she turned this way and that, before snapping the visor shut, satisfied her unleashing hell on her car hadn't done any serious damage. "Weird like it being eleven after the hour every time you check the microwave clock? Or alien gives birth to Elvis's love child weird?"

Pulling to a stop at a red light, he faced her, his blue eyes serious and she was reminded that though she'd tried to deny it for years, he wasn't a kid anymore.

"Weird like guess what I saw in the parking lot of Eddie's Service station when we passed it? Your car," he continued before she could answer. "Why would you have Griffin York, of all people, work on your car?"

She shrugged, but the movement came across as irritated instead of casual. "Why shouldn't I take my car to his garage? From all accounts, he's a good mechanic."

Anthony stared at her as if she'd just admitted the story about Elvis's alien baby was true and she was the mother.

The light changed and he pulled ahead. "What's going on, Nora?"

"I told you, I had a bit of car trouble." She snapped her lips together realizing she'd sounded defensive even to her own ears. "Look," she said, using her mellowest tone, "this isn't a big deal. And, really, it shouldn't matter where I take my car to get fixed."

"It shouldn't," he agreed, "but it does. Especially when you're doing business with the son of the man suspected of Aunt Val's murder."

"Dale York is suspected, yes. But it's not fair to hold Griffin accountable for his father's sins. They're not the same person, no matter that they share DNA. You, of all people," she said gently, "should understand that sons aren't clones of their fathers."

He flushed. "This is different than him following his father's career path." Like Anthony had done with his own father. But he'd confided to Nora he wasn't sure he wanted to go into law. "It's not just who his father is, though that's part of it," Anthony admitted as he pulled into the private parking lot of Sullivan, Saunders and Mazza, the law firm where they both worked—she as an associate lawyer, he as an intern. "Griffin is not exactly a model citizen."

"Speculation," she said breezily, unbuckling her seat belt and reaching down for her things. "Rumors based on who his father is."

"More like based on who he is and how he acts." Anthony reached into the back for his laptop. "I heard he beat the hell out of a guy down at the Yacht Pub all because he didn't like how the man was looking at him."

She refrained—barely—from rolling her eyes. "And I heard it was a tourist who'd had too much to drink and was looking for a fight. A fight Griffin didn't give him, obviously, as no charges were filed against him." She climbed out and shut the door. "You can't believe everything you hear, which is why a good attorney doesn't take anything into account other than what they can prove," she said, softening her subtle rebuke with a gentle hip check. "And the fact is that Griffin is an excellent mechanic."

"I still don't like it," Anthony grumbled, stopping at the doors to the building. "What're Uncle Tim and my dad going to think when they find out about this?"

"They're not going to think anything because there's no reason for either of them to know." She squinted up at him—why everyone in her family had to be taller than her, she had no idea. "I love you. I do. If I had a little brother, I'd want him to be fairly similar to you."

He grinned, all confident charm. "I am pretty awesome."

She shook her head but couldn't help but smile in return. "That you are. But I don't want you to worry about me." She had more than enough people doing that in her life already. "Let's not make a major issue out of this."

His eyes narrowed as if he could somehow see inside her head and discern fact from fiction. "Are you sure all you want from York is his mechanical skills?"

"Absolutely." The lie caused only the slightest twinge of regret. Sometimes the greater good called for a bit of subterfuge.

"Fine," he said, sounding as put out as he used to when he was a teenager and she refused to buy him beer. "I won't say anything—"

"To anyone."

"To anyone," he repeated dutifully as he held open the door for her to enter the building. "But that doesn't mean they won't find out."

She doubted that. It wasn't like her taking her car to Griffin's garage was some juicy tidbit of gossip. Besides, the rumor mill was already busy enough talking about her mother's death, Dale's mysterious disappearance off the face of the earth and her family's past. Soon they'd be all atwitter about the police chief and assistant chief hooking up.

Such was life.

You couldn't live in a small town and escape rumors and speculation. When the remains were found, her mother's past had been dug up, her family's personal business printed in the *Chronicle* along with the day's weather report and the scores from last night's men's softball games.

It'd never bothered Nora, not in the same ways it had her sisters or her father. Probably because she'd been so young when her mother had disappeared. Or maybe it was because she'd understood at an early age that she couldn't escape the gossip so instead, she'd decided to give the town something to talk about. Good things. Positive things. They could talk, but she'd made sure they did so on her terms.

It was easy enough. She'd just been herself. And in doing so had found herself elected homecoming queen and earned the spot of valedictorian of her high school graduating class. Her successes had carried over into college and then law school and she had no reason to think any of that would change now that she worked at her uncle Kenny's law firm. She was used to the spotlight.

She had to admit, she rather enjoyed being all lit up that way. Call it an inflated ego, but she did so love shining bright for all to see.

But maybe this one time she could slip under the radar.

Anthony followed Nora into the cavernous foyer, with its expensive tile floor and high ceilings. She waved at the firm's receptionist, Jodi McRae, as they passed and went down the hall toward their offices.

Nora stopped outside her closed door and moved her laptop to the hand already holding her briefcase. "How about lunch today?" she asked. "My treat for you picking me up."

"You sure it's a thank-you gesture and not a bribe for my agreeing to keep my mouth shut?"

"Who says it can't be both?"

"I do hate to say no to a good bribe, so yeah. Okay."

"Great. You choose the restaurant. Thanks again for the ride."

Inside her tiny office, she shut the door behind her and leaned back against it. Chewed on her lower lip. She had some big decisions to make. She'd crashed and burned with Griffin, had gone down in a spectacular blaze of glory all because she'd underestimated him.

Pushing away from the door, she tossed her purse onto the chair in the corner then crossed to her desk and set her laptop down. She was supposed to drive down to Boston Thursday for her first meeting with the investigator one of her friends from college had recommended. But that wasn't going to happen since her car wouldn't be ready until Friday. Guess she should have thought of that before she started swinging that crowbar.

Besides, without Griffin's help, without the information he could provide, would a P.I. be able to track down Dale? What were the chances someone in the private sector could do so when the police had failed?

She toed off her shoes, began to pace in front of her desk, the low-pile, pewter carpet rough against her bare feet. Maybe Griffin's refusal to help was fate's way of telling her to back off. Maybe it was her salvation.

She shut her eyes and could've sworn she heard the Hallelujah chorus. She could blow off this whole idea right now by calling the P.I. and telling him she changed her mind.

Wouldn't everyone be thrilled if she decided to finally be the meek, mild-mannered girl those who took her at face value expected her to be? The girl her family had long ago stopped hoping she'd turn into. One who didn't make waves, didn't cause problems and kept her mouth shut. Who sat back and let her older sisters and father take care of everything. Who trusted things would somehow magically work out with no help, input or manipulation from her.

Yes, she could do that. And she would. Right after she gave herself a lobotomy with a cereal spoon.

Trust me, the best thing that could happen for every-one is for Dale to remain missing. Leave the past alone.

Griffin's words floated through her mind...strength-ened her resolve. She dug her phone out of her purse and placed a call.

"Good morning," a perky female voice said. "Thank you for calling Hepfer Investigations. How may I help you?"

"Uh...good morning." She cleared her throat. "This is Nora Sullivan. I have an appointment with Mr. Hep-fer Thursday at five." Her fingers tensed on the phone. "I'd like to reschedule."

"Of course, Miss Sullivan. What day works best for you?"

"Actually I'd like to offer Mr. Hepfer twice his nor-mal consultation fee if he can meet with me in Mystic Point. Today."

Leave the past alone?

No way in hell.

"Afternoon," someone called later that day as he walked into Griffin's garage.

Griffin rolled out from underneath the Impala he was working on, sat up and nodded. "Can I help you?" he asked.

The man, Jimmy if the script written on the left of his blue uniform shirt was anything to go by, held out a clipboard. "I just need you to sign here and tell me where you want it."

Griffin glanced at the clipboard then got to his feet and wiped his hands on the rag he kept in his back pocket. "I never sign for something I didn't order."

"This Eddie's Service?" Checking his paperwork, Jimmy frowned. His stomach hung over his belt, strained the buttons of his shirt. "At 1414 Willard Avenue?"

"Yeah."

"And you're Griffin York?"

"That's right."

"Then it's your delivery," Jimmy said mulishly, holding out the clipboard again.

This time Griffin took the paperwork, skimmed it. He had no idea why his name and the garage address were listed under delivery recipient. "I didn't order a '69 Firebird," he said, handing the clipboard back. "And I haven't been hired to do a restoration on one."

Jimmy scratched his round head, knocking his hat off center. "Says here—" He flipped a page, scanned it. "The owner's name is Tanner Johnston. He a customer of yours?"

"No," Griffin said. Tanner Johnston. Hadn't he always known the quiet, seemingly harmless ones were who you had to look out for most? "Not a customer."

"I gotta call my supervisor." Jimmy's face was red and sweat dotted his upper lip and brow. Guy looked like he was one heavy breath away from a heart attack. "See what he wants me to do."

Griffin lifted a shoulder. "Suit yourself."

While Jimmy pulled out his cell phone, Griffin went outside, too damned curious not to. Squinting against the bright afternoon sun, its warmth beating down on his head, he crossed the lot toward a shiny blue truck bearing the name of a towing company from Boston on its side.

Hands in his pockets, he circled the back of the truck where the remnants of what could possibly have been, at one time, a red—or maybe orange—Firebird sat on two front bald tires. The body looked like it was held together with rubber bands and a prayer. There was no rear end, no front grille and it looked as if the car had been overrun by leaves and possibly squirrels. He hopped onto the back of the truck, peered into the interior. Gutted. Seats, carpets and dash.

He eyed the hood. Opened it warily. Sighed. No motor. No transmission. He let the hood shut, brushed off his hands.

A tan minivan pulled slowly into the lot, creeping to a stop at the back of the truck. A moment later, Tanner Johnston, star center for Mystic Point's varsity basketball team, unfolded himself from behind the steering wheel.

Tanner shut the door and studied Griffin. Christ, but he hated when the kid did that, looked at him as if he could read his mind. See into his very soul. Gave him the creeps.

"Hey," Tanner said, walking toward Griffin in his usual easy pace. The only time the kid moved fast was on the basketball court.

Griffin crossed his arms and leaned back against the Firebird. Hoped it would hold up under his weight. "Something you want to tell me?"

Tanner stopped and tipped his head back to maintain eye contact with Griffin. He nodded slowly once. "I bought a car."

"Don't delude yourself. You bought a pile of scrap metal."

He lifted a shoulder. "It'll look better when we're done with it."

Griffin froze. Aw, hell. This was worse than he'd thought. "We?"

At his quiet, deadly tone, Tanner dropped his gaze

to the ground. "I thought you could help me fix it up," he mumbled to his high-tops.

"What made you think that?"

Tanner's shoulders hunched, his head ducked even farther down as he muttered too low for Griffin to hear.

"What?"

The kid raised his head, a blush staining his smooth cheeks. "I said because we're brothers."

Scowling, Griffin stared at the kid. Tanner was tall and lanky with light brown hair and their mother's green eyes. He was a good-looking kid. Popular despite his quiet nature. Smart and athletic.

He was, in every way that mattered, Griffin's complete opposite. Polite. Thoughtful. He didn't break the rules, didn't even try to bend them. He'd been raised by two parents who loved each other and him. By a father who rarely raised his voice and would never even think of raising his fist. By a mother who'd somehow found the courage to trust in love again, who hadn't had to shield him from another man's wrath by succumbing to it herself.

They may be brothers but they had nothing in common except a shared mother and their eye color. And despite Tanner's best efforts to get them to bond, Griffin wanted to keep it that way.

"No," he said then dropped lightly to the ground and headed back toward the garage.

"Why not?" Tanner asked, catching up to him.

"Because I'm running a business here, kid. Not a charity."

"I could pay for it," Tanner said after a moment. He slid in front of Griffin, walked backward. "For the parts and stuff. And your labor."

"You can't afford it."

Though even he wasn't that big of an asshole to charge his teenage brother for working on the kid's car. But Tanner didn't know that.

"I could pay you back a little at a time," he insisted quietly. "Like a loan. Or I could work here and you could take it out of my wages."

"And have you around all the time? No thanks."

The kid's face fell. Shit. Griffin tipped his head side to side until his neck popped. He wanted to apologize, to tell Tanner he hadn't meant it. But the kid was smart enough to recognize a lie when he heard it.

"You and your dad can work on it," Griffin said brushing past him. "I'll tell the tow driver to take it over to your place."

"You can't," he blurted, looking guilty as hell.

"Why not?"

"You just can't."

"Not good enough."

He walked away but couldn't miss the sound of Tanner's loud sigh. "I sort of already told Mom and Dad you'd agreed to help me fix it," he admitted.

"And why would you *sort of* tell them that?" Griffin asked, not sure he wanted to hear the answer.

"I had to. They didn't want me to buy a car at all so I had to convince them it wouldn't be that much to get a junker and fix it up…" Tanner lifted his shoulder again in that careless shrug. "But they didn't get on board until after they found out you were all for it."

"Except I'm not."

"Mom's really excited," Tanner told him solemnly. "She keeps talking about what a great experience this will be, for the two of us to do this together."

Griffin grabbed the back of his neck. Wished he could seize Tanner by the throat instead, maybe give him a few shakes. But that was too reminiscent of how his old man would've reacted.

Besides, Griffin didn't want to hurt the kid. Just make him pay for putting Griffin in this situation. Their mom was probably doing backflips at the idea of her sons bonding over carburetors and exhaust fans.

He could walk away. All he had to do was tell Jimmy, who watched their little family drama with no small amount of interest, to take the car over to the Johnstons' house. Or, better yet, back to Boston. It would serve Tanner right if he lost out on the tow truck fee.

Yeah, he thought, exhaling heavily. He could do that. Sure, his mother would be disappointed, but she was used to that from him. It was how they worked. She continually pushed him for more than he was willing to give, and in return he made it clear she wasn't getting it. No sense changing the dynamics between them now.

But if he walked, Tanner would have to admit the truth to his parents. Hey, if you broke the rules, you had to be prepared to face the consequences. And knowing his mom and stepfather—having been punished by them many, many times during his own teen years—those consequences would be major. At least to a seventeen-year-old.

Nothing less than the kid deserved for lying.

But he was watching Griffin with such freaking hope in his eyes, saying no to him would've been like kicking a newborn kitten in the head.

"How much did you shell out for it?" Griffin asked, nodding toward the Firebird.

"One thousand."

"You were screwed," he said flatly. "It's not worth more than a couple hundred. Hope you have some cash left for the restoration."

For the past three summers, Tanner had worked down on the docks with his father. It wasn't an easy job and he didn't get to hang out at the beach all day like his friends, but it did pay well.

"Mom and Dad said I could use a total of five thousand on the car," Tanner said. "The rest of my wages are being saved for college."

Four thousand dollars wasn't nearly enough to get the job done, but it'd make a good start.

"Here's the deal," Griffin said, unable to believe he was actually agreeing to this. Pissed that the kid had backed him into a corner this way. "We work on it Monday, Tuesday and Wednesday nights and Sunday afternoons. I'm not putting any time in on it on my own. If you're not here, the work doesn't get done. In exchange," he continued when Tanner opened his mouth, "you'll clean up the garage and do anything else I need done around here. You can pick your own hours but you'd better put in at least twenty a week or the deal's off. You hear me?"

Tanner nodded like a bobblehead doll. "Yeah, yeah. I hear you. It's a deal."

And then he grinned, slow and easy, like he'd won the lottery and a night with the hottest cheerleader in his school.

"Enjoy this moment," Griffin told him. "Because that was for working on the car. The deal for me not ratting you out to your parents is going to cost you even more."

"You'd blackmail your own brother?" he asked, sounding merely curious.

"Don't think of it as blackmail. Think of it as me kicking your butt for dragging me into this in the first place. The way I see it, you have a choice. You can take my punishment. Or we can tell Mom and Roger you lied and tricked them. Your choice."

Griffin imagined Tanner was having visions of himself spending the rest of the summer grounded. Or worse, completely losing his driving privileges.

"What do I have to do?" Tanner asked.

"You are now in charge of all yard work and exterior maintenance at my house for exactly one year."

"Huh?"

"You'll mow the grass, do the trim work. In the fall you can rake leaves—"

"You never rake your leaves."

"Well, they'll get raked this year, won't they? You can also clean the gutters. In the winter I'll expect my walk and driveway cleared each and every morning before I go to work."

Tanner gave him a long look. "That's fair."

It wasn't. It was overboard and Griffin had the feeling Tanner knew it. Or maybe he knew Griffin had been trying to get him to back out of their deal, which would then let Griffin off the hook.

Now he was stuck, for the second time that day, with a deal he didn't particularly want and that his instincts told him would somehow come back to bite him on the ass.

"THERE'S A GENTLEMAN here to see you," Jodi told Nora over the office phone. "He won't give his name."

Jodi's tone was disapproving, either at the audacity of the man showing up five minutes before the office was to close or because he hadn't shared his name or the reason for wanting to see Nora.

Jodi did love knowing everything that went on in the office.

Nerves jumped in Nora's stomach. He was early. When she'd spoken with Mr. Hepfer that morning, he'd told her he probably wouldn't make it to Mystic Point before six. She'd asked him to meet her at the office instead of her house or a local restaurant so she could claim he was just another potential client, should anyone ask.

"Thanks," Nora said. "You can send him in."

Setting the phone down, she hurried across the room and opened the door then raced back behind her desk and took the small mirror out of her top drawer. She freshened her lipstick, did a quick hair check then tossed the mirror back inside.

She sat. Stood. Sat again. Then jumped to her feet when she saw him round the corner. She froze, her polite smile sliding from her face.

Because the man walking toward her looked nothing like the picture of the balding, retirement-age man on Hepfer Investigation's website. Trepidation filled her.

He was an older, harder version of Griffin.

Not the P.I. she'd hired, she realized numbly. Which was fine, as it seemed she no longer needed him to find her mother's ex-lover.

Dale York had found her instead.

CHAPTER FOUR

NORA'S BREATH LOCKED in her chest, made each inhalation painful. Panic-inducing. She'd wanted this moment, wanted to face this man down but now that he was here, her body was frozen, her mind numb with terror.

She couldn't take her eyes from Dale as he slowly crossed her office, his confident stride bordering on predatory. She'd only seen his face once—a grainy photo the *Chronicle* ran the day after her mother's remains were found, but there was no mistaking him.

She'd spent the past eighteen years thinking about him. Wondering what kind of man he was. Hating him. She'd expected him to be taller. Her father was tall. Tall and kind and honorable. A good, decent man who'd worked hard to support his family, who'd always taken care of them.

But her mother had still chosen this man over her husband. Over her daughters.

She'd paid for it with her life.

As a kid, Nora had always imagined Dale as some sort of monster. Huge and dark and deadly. Now she saw he was just a man. Not so huge, but still dangerous.

Despite his age—he had to be closing in on sixty—his short hair was still thick, the dark strands threaded with silver. His shoulders were wide, his waist narrow. He was handsome, she was forced to admit. With his sharply angled face and smooth-shaven jaw.

It was easy, so pathetically easy, to see why her mother had been attracted to him.

What she didn't get, what she'd never understand, was how her mother could love him.

He stopped in front of her desk, his expression hard, his brown eyes cold. Nora's mouth dried. Fear coated her throat. Made it impossible for her to speak, to get any words out. Words that should've put him on the defensive, made him wonder and worry. Made him realize he faced a worthy and formidable opponent.

All she could do was stare. And wonder if Griffin had been right.

Trust me, the best thing that could happen for everyone is for Dale to remain missing. Leave the past alone.

"If it isn't little Nora Sullivan," Dale said, his deep voice tinged with some accent she couldn't quite put her finger on. Her skin crawled as his gaze drifted lazily over her face, sexual and appreciative. "All grown up, I see. I'm Dale York."

"I know who you are," she said, barely above a whisper. Her scalp prickled, her breathing quickened. She gripped the edge of her desk, held on when her knees threatened to buckle. "You're the man who killed my mother."

"Now, is that any way to greet an old friend of Valerie's?" He winked. "I never laid a hand on her. Not unless she wanted me to."

Her stomach churned sickeningly. "Wh-what are you doing here?"

Why had he come back to Mystic Point now, risking arrest? What kind of game was he playing by seeking her out?

"I'm here to do my civic duty." Hitching up his dark slacks, he sat in the chair across from her, looking like a successful salesman instead of a cold-blooded killer. "I would've come sooner but I was out of the country and didn't hear about Valerie's death—and that the local police department wanted to interview me—until a few days ago. But before I talk to the new police chief, I wanted to see you. Offer my condolences on your loss."

"You *want* to talk to the police?"

"Of course. I want to do anything I can to help them find out who hurt Val." He studied her, like a fox watching a rabbit. "I never would've pegged you for one of Valerie's girls," he murmured, reclining in the chair as he linked his hands behind his head. His arms were well muscled, his biceps flexing against the sleeves of his dress shirt. "Now your sister, the cop, I knew she belonged to Val the moment I saw her. But you're as far from your mother as light is from dark. Guess you take after your daddy. Except you didn't take after his career, did you? Followed your uncle's footsteps there."

All her nerves, her fears at having her mother's killer sitting calmly across from her, flew out of her head. He'd seen Layne? He'd been watching them?

"What do you know about my sister?" she asked hotly. "Or me?"

He smiled slowly and those nerves spiked. "You'd be surprised," he said softly.

She covered her cell phone with her palm, feeling somehow stronger, safer having it in her hand so that she could call the police in a second if he threatened her. When in reality, all she had to do was yell and a half a dozen people would come running. Including her uncle. "You really expect anyone to believe you're here because you want to help in my mother's murder investigation?"

"Why else would I come back?"

She didn't know and that was what worried her. "You won't get away with it."

"That so?" he asked, watching her with his hooded gaze, his damn smirk.

Realizing her knuckles were white from gripping the desk and her phone so tightly, she let go and tucked her hands behind her back. Damn it, she should be the one in charge of this conversation. Should be controlling it and keeping him on edge.

Instead she felt off balance and inadequate. And that was unacceptable. She refused to let this man, with his flat eyes and cocky grin, get the best of her. He'd taken her mother away from her and her sisters. She'd do whatever she had to in order to make him pay for that.

Pressing her lips together, she inhaled deeply and held it for the count of five. When she spoke again, she was more composed. "Yes, that's so. Because I will do everything in my power to make sure you're brought to justice. I won't rest until you're convicted of my mother's murder."

He didn't even blink. "Is that a threat, baby girl?"

Her blood ran cold. *Baby girl*. The nickname her mother used to call her. Bastard.

"It's a promise," she said, hating how her voice shook, how sick she felt at the reminder that her mother had shared so much of herself with this man. "One you'll have plenty of time to think about when you're serving a life sentence in state prison."

Shaking his head, he sat up. "That's a nice fantasy you've spun for yourself. But it's going to be tough for anyone to get a conviction against me when there's no evidence connecting me to Valerie's murder."

"There will be." There had to be. They had to find something, anything that would help the case against him.

"You go right on believing that," he said as he stood. "But it's not going to happen."

A lump formed in her throat. Oh, God, he was right. Unless new evidence surfaced, or he confessed, the police would have no reason to arrest him, to even hold him. He'd come back because he knew the chances of him being charged with murder were slim to none at this point.

For the first time since they'd discovered the truth about what happened to her mother, Nora was afraid. Terrified Dale would walk away a free man when it was all said and done. And that there would be nothing she could do to stop that from happening.

"You're upset," he said in a soothing tone that made bile rise in her throat. "That's understandable. But I didn't come here to argue with you. I came back, voluntarily, to give my statement to the police." He stepped forward and though her desk separated them, she jerked back, bumping into her chair. "Since it looks like I'll be in town for a little while, maybe we'll see each other again."

With another of those disturbing winks, he walked away. At the still-open door he faced her. "And, baby girl? Be sure and tell your father I dropped by to see you."

"Do you want anything else?"

As with every other time she'd stopped by Tanner's booth during the past hour, Jessica Taylor's gaze stayed somewhere on the wall above their heads as she spoke. She'd been polite and attentive, had made sure their glasses were always filled and had even brought Josh extra napkins for his rib dinner, but she hadn't made eye contact with any of the four guys she waited on.

"We're good," Tanner said quietly. Other than when he'd given her his dinner order, they were the only words he'd spoken to her—tonight or ever. But he hoped to draw her attention his way.

No dice.

"Separate checks, right?" she asked, tearing four slips from her order form. She studied each one before handing them out. Reaching across the table, she took Nate's empty plate, the V of her white T-shirt tugged down showing a flash of beige lace and the curve of her breast.

Tanner's gut—and, damn it, his groin—tightened. And the last thing he needed was his buddies giving him grief about getting a hard-on in the middle of the Ludlow Street Café. Jerking his gaze to the table, he gulped down the soda left in his cup, the melting ice cubes hitting his lips. He wished he could toss them in his pants.

"I'll be back in a few minutes to take those up for you," Jessica said.

He didn't look up until she walked away.

"Dude," Nate said, kicking Tanner's shin under the table causing his drink to slosh out of the cup and drip down his chin. "You're drooling."

Nate laughed at his own lame joke.

Tanner glared at his friend and basketball teammate. Sitting back in the booth, he wiped the back of his hand over the wetness on his chin.

Josh smirked as he counted out money. "If you want to tap that, you're going to have to do more than stare at her like a loser."

The back of Tanner's neck heated. "I don't even know her."

No one did. Jessica had moved to Mystic Point a few

months ago, and while she'd attended a few local parties, for the most part, she'd kept to herself.

"Sure you do," Josh said, shaking the remaining ice in his cup. "She's from Boston. She's the police chief's niece. She's hot. And, best of all, she's easy." Grinning, he shook an ice cube in his mouth then nodded at Nate. "She even gave Nate a pity screw."

Tanner's fingers twitched on his cup. The last thing he wanted to be reminded of was that his friend had hooked up with a drunken Jess. It made him feel... jealous. And possessive. Which was nuts since the girl wouldn't give him the time of day.

"There was no pity involved," Nate said, elbowing Josh hard enough to have him doubling over. "She fell for my charming personality, manly good looks and—" He stretched his arms overhead then brought them down, flexing his biceps. "My ripped bod."

Next to Tanner, Christian Myers dug his wallet out of his back pocket. "If you want to get to know her, ask her out. The worst she can say is no."

"Yeah, listen to Dr. Phil here," Josh said, chomping his ice. "If she shoots you down, you move on. No harm, no foul."

Tanner wished he'd never suggested they eat at the café. They should've hit Mickey D's instead. "I didn't say I wanted to ask her out."

"Keep denying it, brother," Nate said. "But the truth is written all over your face."

"Shut it," Tanner muttered.

"You need to relax." Josh, comfortable with his parents' money and his social standing as a member of one of the wealthier families in Mystic Point, sent Tanner a cocky grin. "Let me handle it. Excuse me?" he called to Jessica before Tanner could respond. "Waitress?"

Hands fisted on the table, Tanner leaned forward. "I will kill you."

Josh waved that away. "No need to thank me. That's what friends are for."

"All set?" Jessica asked when she reached their table.

"Actually, no," Josh said, giving her what Tanner recognized as the smarmy look he used when he thought he was being charming. "There's one more thing we need."

"Yeah? What's that?"

"We need you to go out with our friend here." Josh gestured to Tanner. "He thinks you're hot."

She glanced at Tanner dismissively. "Not interested."

"Come on. You have the chance to make this young man very happy." Josh trailed his fingers down the back of her hand and Tanner wanted to bash his friend's face in. "Think of it as your good deed for the day."

"You are a dead man," Tanner promised him, the words all the more threatening due to his low tone.

"Yeah, come on," Nate added. "We're heading out to Kane's Beach. Should be a good party. And since you don't drive, you could ride out with Tanner."

"You two are risking life and limb," Christian told them, not even looking up from his phone as he texted someone. "He'll kick both your asses."

That got Jessica to finally look at him with something other than pure disinterest. But the curiosity in her gaze only lasted a second. "Are you ready for me to take your checks up or not?" she asked Josh.

"Tell you what," Josh said softly, glancing around as if to make sure the other diners couldn't overhear. "You agree to show our friend a good time tonight and I'll throw in an extra fifty. Think of it as a different kind of tip."

Jessica went white and then her face flooded with

color. The rest happened in a blur. Tanner got halfway out of his seat, reaching across the table to wrap his hands around Josh's neck but Christian grabbed the collar of his shirt and yanked him back. At the same time, Jessica flicked her hand to the side, upending Nate's glass, spilling the remaining iced tea into Josh's lap.

"You bitch," Josh seethed as he leaped up.

"Oops," she said, her eyes glittering, her teeth bared in a fake smile. "Sorry." She swept up their cash and slips and sauntered away.

"I'm reporting her to the manager." Josh pressed paper napkins to the wet spot on his pants. "She did that on purpose. You all saw it."

"It was an accident," Tanner said.

Josh tossed the soaked napkins onto the table. "What?"

Tanner got to his feet, looked down at Josh, had the satisfaction of seeing the cockiness on his face be replaced by apprehension. "It was an accident," Tanner repeated softly. He sent Christian and then Nate pointed looks. "Right?"

Nate lifted a shoulder. "Sure. Don't be such a pussy, Josh."

"And you deserved it," Christian pointed out as he got out of the booth. "Just be glad Tan doesn't give you a beat down and let it be."

"Whatever," Josh grumbled as he left, hitting Tanner's shoulder as he passed him.

Tanner took a step after him but Christian raised a hand. "Ignore him," Christian said as Nate followed Josh out. "You going to the party?"

Tanner shook his head. "I have to work tomorrow."

Which meant getting up at 5:00 a.m. and spending the next ten to twelve hours sweating his ass off. Not that his buddies understood that. Half the time they got pissed at him for ditching them. Neither Josh nor Nate worked; both got their seemingly endless supply of cash from their parents. Christian logged a few hours at the video place but that was mostly nights.

"All right," Christian said, glancing at his buzzing phone. "Call me tomorrow. We'll hang, play the new *Call of Duty*."

"Yeah, whatever."

Christian walked out, texting as he went. Dude's girlfriend liked to keep close tabs on him.

Tanner waited a minute, then two, but Jessica didn't come back out from behind those swinging doors where she'd disappeared after taking Josh down a peg. The back of his neck got itchy. He hunched his shoulders and glanced around, saw Keira Seagren, a cute redhead in his grade who also worked there, watching him curiously. Feeling like an idiot, he lifted his hand in a half-assed wave and then walked out into the warm night.

Hands shoved into the pockets of his cargo shorts, he kept his head down and turned the corner to the parking lot behind the tall, blue building. The setting sun glowed brightly, stark against the darkness of the cloudless sky, reminding him of that scene in *Star Wars* where Luke steps outside to watch the two suns of his planet go down. The warmth of the day hung in the air, promising a hot, sticky night.

He rounded the back of a blue Camry and stopped, his mom's keys falling from his hand to land with a soft jingle on the concrete.

Jessica was there. Sitting on the top of a picnic table at the far end of the parking lot, her back to him, her head down, her light hair and white shirt like beacons in the growing darkness.

She turned to face him. He couldn't move, didn't

know what to do. Even with the distance between them, he could feel the heat from her glare. She didn't want to talk to him.

Figured she'd rather castrate him.

And damn Mr. Bauchman, his freshman year science teacher, for showing them that video of what castration entailed. He seriously could've lived his entire life without ever knowing its definition, let alone witnessed how it was done to bulls.

Her head held high, she turned away again. He quickly scooped up his keys. Eyes on the ground, he wove between two pickups to his mom's minivan. Unlocked and opened the door.

And made the mistake of glancing at her.

Before he could change his mind—or think better of it—he slammed the door shut and walked over to her.

She stiffened, her shoulders snapping back. "What?" she asked, the word practically dripping frost.

His mouth was dry. His palms damp. When he was a kid, his mom used to tell him that one magical day, he'd outgrow his shyness. It would thrill her if he suddenly started blabbering on about useless, stupid topics. If, even a few times, he struck up a conversation with strangers the way she did.

Why he should do that when he had no interest in doing so, he had no clue. But she still held out hope.

Because other people got nervous when he had nothing to say.

Which he didn't get. He liked the quiet. Liked listening. Watching. Taking it all in. Even his friends thought he was too shy or scared to talk to girls. Not true. He simply preferred to take his time and think about what he wanted to say first, that was all.

And right now, he wanted her to look at him. Had no problem waiting in silence until she did so.

She huffed out a breath, whirled around. Her eyes were blue, light blue like the midday sky over the water. And right now she was rolling them so far back, she probably caught a glimpse of her brain.

"Okay," she snapped, "the whole heavy-breathing, prank-phone-call thing is super freaky when you're doing it in person."

"You're not in trouble." He wasn't breathing heavily so he saw no reason to respond to that part of her comment. "I told Josh not to report you to your manager."

She looked at him as if she wanted to plant the thick heel of her shoe in his face. "My hero," she said, saying *hero* in a tone usually reserved for *slimy-Satan-loving-snake*.

He scratched his cheek. "I just thought you should know," he murmured, feeling like an idiot.

"Look, if you're hoping to get off tonight, you'll have to find some other girl." She sneered, her gaze raking over him in a way that made his balls shrink. "Or you could always take matters into your own hands. I'm sure you have plenty of practice with that."

He flushed so hard, sweat formed at the back of his neck, a drop of it sliding between his shoulder blades. She was pissed, obviously, and for good reason, but that didn't mean he had to take shit from her.

Even if she was beautiful.

"I'm sorry," he said quietly, "for what happened back there."

She studied him as is trying to decide if he meant it. But he only said things he meant. That was part of the reason he kept silent so often. He didn't see any point in spouting a bunch of bullshit. It was so much easier to stick with the truth.

"You're sorry your friend tried to pay me to have sex with you? Wasn't it your idea?"

"No," he told her, holding her gaze steadily. He would never treat a girl with such disrespect. But there was no point telling her that. Either she believed him or she didn't.

She frowned. But even with her brows pinched, her mouth an angry line, she was the prettiest thing he'd ever seen. She had these two, tiny braids at her temple that were pulled back with the rest of her hair, which was so pale, it was almost white. Her eyebrows were two shades darker than her hair and heavily arched. Her neck was long; her lips all shiny like she'd licked them or slicked them up with gloss.

The breeze picked up, ruffled a loose, pale strand of hair by her ear. His fingers itched to touch it. To see if it was as soft as it looked.

"I didn't tell Josh to talk to you for me, but I would like to ask you out." Her expression turned suspicious. Wow, what had happened to her to make her so cynical? And why did he want to find out instead of writing her and her bad attitude off? "Just a date," he continued. "We could go to the movies. Or out to eat."

Watching him as if he was a shark in the water and she was fifty yards from shore, she slid off the table. "I don't think so."

Humiliation and rejection settled in his stomach. He nodded. "Okay. Good night."

"Yeah," she said, as if trying to figure him out. "'Night."

He waited, watching the sway of her hips as she

walked away. And when she reached the employee entrance to the restaurant, he got what he wanted.

She looked back at him.

Grinning, he headed toward the minivan. And started planning how to win her over.

GRIFFIN OPENED THE door to the Ludlow Street Café and went inside, stopping at the end of a long line of people waiting to be seated. Feeling more than one curious gaze on him, he put on his fiercest scowl and scanned the large dining room. The place was packed. Noisy. And smelled good, really good, like grilled meat and French fries and apple pie.

He wondered if he'd been missing out on some great food by staying far away from the place.

Customers talked and laughed and ate while waitresses and a busboy wove around the tables delivering food or collecting dirty plates and silverware. It was a Tuesday, for Christ's sake. Didn't they all have anything better to do than go out for lunch?

He edged to the side, his eyes narrowing when he spotted her. Ignoring the waitress who was taking names at the head of the line, he crossed the restaurant.

"You must be pretty damn proud of yourself," he said softly, not letting his anger at her push him into raising his voice. He didn't lose control. That would make him too much like his father.

If the youngest Sullivan was surprised to find him in the café, towering over her, she didn't show it. "Hello, Griffin," she said, cheery as you please. She bit into a huge burger, chewed, swallowed, then sipped what looked like iced tea through a straw before asking, "Would you like to join me?"

He'd like to throttle her. Do whatever it took to scare

that welcoming smile off her pretty face. Put the fear of God in her so she left the past alone.

But it was too late. His father was in town. And it was all her fault.

His mother had called him not twenty minutes ago to tell him Dale had paid her a visit at the doctor's office where she worked. That he'd given her some line about being back in town to help the police find out what happened to Valerie Sullivan. Then he'd hit her up for money.

And she'd refused.

Griffin could only imagine how the scene had gone down. Dale wasn't a man to take being told no lightly. But his mom hadn't sounded afraid on the phone, or worse, hurt. She'd sounded determined. Able to stand up for herself.

Too bad she hadn't been that strong for the first twelve years of his life.

After he'd hung up with his mom, he'd driven straight to Nora's office only to be told by the receptionist that Nora had gone out to lunch. His first instinct had been to search for her here.

"What kind of game were you playing yesterday?" he asked, laying his palms on the table, leaned down to speak close to her ear. "Had you already found him when you walked into the garage? Did you have him hidden away somewhere while you waited for your chance to spring him on everyone?"

Realization dawned in her blue eyes followed by guilt. "I didn't—"

"Bullshit."

She flinched.

"Everything okay here, Nora?" a round waitress with

short, curly gray hair asked as she appeared by Griffin's side.

"Everything's fine, Sharon," Nora said as she set her food down, her gaze never leaving his. "Though when you get a minute, we could use some coffee."

Sharon glared at him as if she'd like to pour it over his head. Still, she left and came back a moment later with the coffeepot, poured two cups of it before leaving again.

"Is this about your father?" Nora asked when they were alone.

He straightened. "And here I thought playing dumb would be beneath someone of your superior intellect."

Her brows drew together. "No need to get sarcastic." She tipped her head from side to side. Exhaled heavily. "Could you sit down? I'm getting a stiff neck. Please," she added, looking all innocent and sincere in a crisp black shirt that accentuated the fairness of her skin, her hair pulled back into the same tidy hairstyle she'd had yesterday.

Desire—pure, basic and heated—stirred in his gut. *Not going to happen,* he assured himself and sat across from her.

She tore the paper off of a creamer, dumped it into the coffee closest to her. "I didn't find your father."

"No? So he, what…? Showed up in Mystic Point on his own?"

"As far as I know, yes."

Holy shit. Could she be telling the truth?

He sat up. "You told me you were going to hire a P.I. to track him down."

She opened a second creamer, added it to her coffee then picked up a third. "Dale showed up at my office yesterday afternoon before I even paid the retainer."

"He sought you out?" Her lips thin, she nodded. "Why?"

"He said he wanted to convey his condolences on my mother's death. But I think he was trying to play some sort of twisted psychological game with me. I reported his visit to Ross and Layne, but because Dale didn't make any overt threats, there's not much they can do." She stirred her coffee, round and round and round. "He wanted me to tell my father he'd stopped by to see me," she said in a rush.

That sounded like his old man. Manipulative bastard. "He wants to hurt you, or your dad."

"Probably. But I think it was more than that. It was like he was trying to get to me, to scare me. And I'll be damned if I'll let that happen," she said in that prissy tone of hers that had bugged the hell out of him yesterday. "So I'm not telling Dad—or anyone—about that last part."

"You told me," he pointed out.

She shrugged. "I trust you."

Feeling strangely unsettled, he pulled the other coffee cup toward him. Wrapped his hands around it. "You don't even know me."

Holding his gaze, she sipped her coffee. "I'm a good judge of character."

She wasn't. Couldn't be. She was too soft. Too naive. Especially if she thought she could hold her own against his father and whatever game Dale was playing with her.

Griffin wanted to tell her to keep her distance from his father. Warn her about the consequences of playing with fire. If you touched a flame, you were bound to get burned.

He wanted to protect her.

Damn it.

"You going to eat those?" he asked roughly then took a handful of her fries.

"Please," she said dryly, "help yourself."

He'd already shoved several into his mouth. Better than saying something he'd regret later.

She picked up her burger. Set it down again without taking a bite. "Can I ask you a personal question?"

Frowning, he washed the fries down with a gulp of coffee. "Hell, no."

"Did you ever imagine what it would be like," she continued, the fingers of her left hand rolling the wrapper from her straw into a tiny tube, "if your dad came back? I don't mean under the current circumstances, of course. But if he'd come back sooner. If he'd wanted to be a part of your life."

He almost didn't answer her, wouldn't have if she hadn't looked so earnest, so interested.

"The last time I was in the same room with my father he broke my left arm and three of my ribs. So, no," he said flatly, "I never imagined what it would be like if he came back. I already knew."

Her eyes softened and she reached across the table as if to touch his fingers, offer her support. Her compassion.

And the last thing he needed was her pity. He set his hands in his lap.

She flushed. Curled her fingers. "I'm sorry. That was a stupid question. It's just that…I used to think about it. My mom coming back. How different my life would've been with her in it."

He didn't care. Didn't *want* to care. "Different good or different bad?"

"I'm not sure." She shook her head as if ridding herself of any and all gloomy thoughts. Took a bite of her burger. "Anyway, all we can do is play the hand we're dealt, right? Make the most of it."

"Jesus, you're like a walking, talking ray of sunshine."

She batted her lashes. "Thank you."

"You would take that as a compliment." He stood and dug out his wallet. He needed to leave before she started spouting clichés about the golden rule and how things always worked out for the best and that, if he only believed hard enough, the cops would miraculously find irrefutable evidence of his father's guilt and put him away for life.

He laid enough money to cover his coffee and her lunch on the table. But he couldn't walk away. Not quite yet.

"My father's a dangerous man," he said. "A clever man. He returned to Mystic Point for a reason, and I doubt it has anything to do with admitting the truth about what happened between him and your mother. There's something here he wants, and he won't hesitate to take down anyone who stands between him and whatever that is. Do yourself a favor and stay out of his way."

CHAPTER FIVE

"Do you like it?" Erin Sullivan, Nora's cousin and lifelong best friend, asked excitedly as they sat at the kitchen table in Erin's parents' house Thursday evening.

Behind them, Aunt Astor snapped the ends off asparagus at the sink, a red chef's apron covering her black slacks and black-and-white designer top. Out on the patio, Uncle Ken used a long set of tongs to turn ears of corn on the grill while Erin's fiancé, Collin, pushed up his glasses, nodding at whatever advice or opinion his future father-in-law was imparting.

Uncle Ken did so love to share his wisdom.

Nora often had dinner there, had done so at least twice a week since she'd been old enough to walk. Tonight she, Erin and Astor were to go over arrangements for Erin and Collin's engagement party.

But first, she had to get through the next few minutes.

Working to keep her face grimace-free, she looked at the bridesmaid's dress on the laptop screen. "It's very... bright."

Bright. Yes. As in causing-mental-anguish-and-possibly-retinal-damage bright. A lemon-yellow bordering on fluorescent, it had an asymmetrical hemline and a double layer of ruffles across the angled bodice.

"I hadn't realized you were thinking of picking a one shoulder dress," Nora continued, her palms growing damp as she pictured herself stuffed in that dress at Erin's wedding next June. Dear Lord, she'd look like a rounder, heavier version of Pam Anderson. Minus the tattoos, toned arms and rock-star exes. "You always said that style reminded you of Disney's *Pocahontas*."

Erin tucked her chin-length, honey-blond hair behind her ear as she studied the screen. "I'm willing to make an exception in this case."

"Great," Nora managed weakly.

A few months apart in age, she and Erin had been practically inseparable since birth. They'd weathered the elementary school playground, middle school hormones and high school drama together. After graduation, they'd attended Boston University, sharing a dorm and then an apartment in the city until Erin got her degree and moved back to Mystic Point to accept a position as a kindergarten teacher.

Most days Nora didn't think anyone knew her as well as Erin.

Today wasn't one of those days.

"It's a lovely dress," she said, and hoped God didn't strike her down for such a blatant lie. She'd shell out five hundred bucks on the damned thing if it was what Erin wanted.

But she wouldn't be happy about it.

"Erin," Aunt Astor said, putting a fair amount of warning in her daughter's name.

"What?" Erin asked so sweetly, Nora's shoulders relaxed.

Her cousin was yanking her chain. Thank God.

"You suck," she said, smiling.

Erin laughed. "I can't believe you fell for it. Or that you thought I'd pick a dress that ugly for my wedding. That hurts."

"I thought maybe you'd taken a trip on the crazy train again."

"What have I done that's been so crazy?"

Nora tightened the back to the earring in her left ear. "Last week you wanted to rent fake British Royal Navy uniforms for your groomsmen to wear."

"The day before yesterday," Astor added, wiping her hands on her apron as she joined them at the table, "you told me you were going to call Westminster Abbey to see about flying the boys' choir over here to sing during the ceremony."

"But I didn't call them." Erin closed the laptop lid, her cheeks pink. "I was just brainstorming ideas."

"You need to stop watching William and Kate's wedding," Nora said. "Don't make us put you into some sort of twelve step program."

Erin sighed dreamily, her eyes glazing over as if she had the entire royal affair playing in her head. "But it was so…perfect."

"Yours will be just as perfect," Astor assured her, running a hand over Erin's hair. Though she'd recently celebrated her sixtieth birthday, Astor's skin still glowed, her face showing the barest of wrinkles thanks to a healthy lifestyle, minimal sun exposure and a heavy hand with a very expensive line of anti-aging products. "Just on a smaller, more personal scale. After all, your father and I had a very simple, yet elegant wedding and it was—"

"Written about in *Life* magazine," Erin and Nora said at the same time.

"Have I mentioned that before?"

"A few hundred times or so," Erin said.

"Is that all?" Astor asked in the precise accent that

made her sound like a Kennedy. "Well, remind me to regale you all once again with the story at dinner."

"Sorry I'll miss it," Anthony said as he came into the kitchen. "I'm going out with some friends."

"But I'm making that grilled salmon you like."

"Sorry, Ma." He stuck his head in the stainless steel refrigerator, straightened with a bottle of orange juice in his hand. "I've already made plans."

"Anthony Michael, does this look like a dorm room?" Astor asked as she squeezed juice from half a lemon into a bowl, her back to her son. "Or worse, a bachelor apartment?"

In the act of raising the bottle to his mouth, he slowly lowered his arm. "No, ma'am." He took a glass out of an upper cabinet. "How do you always know?"

She tossed the lemon into the sink, rinsed off her fingers and looked up at him. "I'm a mother."

"I can't wait until I'm a mother," Erin said. "I could use a few superpowers at work, including having eyes in the back of my head. Especially if this year's class has a kid that's half as bad as that Dakota Douglas I had last year."

Flipping through a book of wedding invitations, Nora nodded. "I won't have to spend hours poring over legal briefs. I'll be able to win all of my cases with a single, *Because I said so.*"

"The powers of motherhood are amazing," Astor agreed. "Unfortunately they don't often work on people who aren't your children."

"Yours worked on me," Nora pointed out.

Astor smiled indulgently. "That's because you're my other daughter."

Something in Nora warmed. How could it not? Astor's words were genuine, the sentiment as true as could be. Astor and Ken loved all three of their nieces but they held an extra fondness for her that went above and beyond what they felt toward Layne and Tori. Nora knew she held a special place in their hearts and in their lives. It was…nice. Comforting.

She adored her father, loved and appreciated her sisters for how they took care of her when she was little, but spending so much time at her aunt and uncle's house had taught her what it meant to be a part of a family. Being wanted by them had helped her get through her mother's abandonment.

But it had done little to soothe the sting of being left. Of knowing she and her sisters weren't enough to make her mother want to stay.

Anthony drained his drink, rinsed his glass and put it in the dishwasher then kissed his mother's cheek. "Bye. Don't wait up."

Astor held on to his arm. "Won't you at least eat first?"

"We'll probably have dinner at the club," he said of Mystic Point's country club. "Or maybe we'll try that new burger joint on Main Street."

"Are you sure?"

"Mom," Erin said. "He's sure. Let the boy go, now."

"All right. Be safe. If you're going to be drinking, be sure to designate a responsible driver."

"I'm not drinking tonight," he told her as if she was crazy to think a twenty-one-year-old college student would consume alcoholic beverages. "So don't worry." He turned to Nora. "I'll pick you up at seven-thirty tomorrow. Be ready." He saluted his father and Collin, then spun on his heel and walked out.

Astor watched the spot her son just vacated as if trying to use one of those maternal superpowers to bring him back again.

Erin put her arm around her mother's shoulders and squeezed. "Stop worrying so much about him. He's fine."

"I'm not so sure. I wish he would open up to us. Ever since it happened, he's barely spent any time at home. And when he is here, he's so distant."

It being the whole underage Jessica fiasco where Layne and Ross had caught him and the teenager in a compromising position in his parents' hot tub a few weeks back.

"He's probably embarrassed," Nora offered, reaching down to tug off her shoes. She wiggled her toes. "Jess really did a number on him."

"He shouldn't be embarrassed around us."

"Maybe not," Erin said as she took out a stack of white plates from the cupboard, "but we've all agreed to give him his space."

"Yes, we did." Astor looked, as always, perfectly put together and composed. Was it any wonder Nora wanted to be her when she grew up? "Although I was considering waterboarding him until he shared his feelings with us, I shall refrain."

Nora gathered Erin's things off the table including the binder of wedding ideas Erin hadn't been without since the day after Collin proposed two months ago. "Are we still on for the florist this weekend?" she asked.

"Ten o'clock Saturday morning. Why don't we have breakfast at the café before we go?" She looked at her mom and then Nora. "Eight-thirty?"

"We'd better make it seven," Astor said, taking a platter of salmon out of the fridge. "I told Tobey we'd meet him at the church at nine."

Erin set her fisted hands on her hips. "Mom, you didn't."

Astor scooped up the asparagus and added it to the pan. "Didn't what, dear?"

"You didn't hire Tobey Lacosta to sing at *my* wedding."

"I asked him to meet with us to discuss the possibility of you hiring him."

"I've already told you, I want a female soloist."

"That's only because you didn't attend Ashlee Sheffield's wedding. I swear when Tobey sang 'Ave Maria' there wasn't a dry eye in the entire church." She picked up the platter and crossed to the French doors. "What's the harm in giving him a chance?"

"No harm," Erin admitted, a pout clear in her voice. "But I don't like you making these decisions without even discussing it with me first."

"Of course not, dear."

Astor went out to the patio and shut the door behind her. Erin exhaled heavily, ruffling her bangs. "Just when I start to believe she isn't going to try to take over my wedding, she proves me wrong."

"Her finding a soloist doesn't quite qualify as taking over," Nora said, stretching to brush out a wrinkle on the white-and-green-checked tablecloth she'd spread out. "She's trying to help. She wants you to have the wedding of your dreams."

"Yes, but between her, Collin's mom and his stepmother, I have three of them to deal with. They all have opinions and suggestions…" She added air quotes. "Times like this I think Collin's right and we should elope."

"I hardly think you have grounds for elopement," Nora said, unable to keep the bite from her words. But really, when Erin went into this drama queen mode, the best way to get her out was to call her on it. "You're overreacting."

"I realize it might not sound like a big deal," she said in a patient tone Nora knew damn well she used on the five-year-olds in her classroom, "but I'd like to make the choices for my own wedding instead of having other people's wants shoved down my throat."

Nora opened the utensil drawer, took out forks and knifes and pointed them at her cousin. "You and Collin are lucky to have mothers who love you and want to be a part of the planning of your wedding. Your mom gets to help you pick out your dress and flowers and the food and music. She'll be there on the most important day of your life to watch you walk down the aisle." Nora slammed the drawer shut with more force than necessary, her voice shaking, her face hot. "Maybe you should be a little more grateful for what you do have instead of complaining about things that aren't a big deal."

The silence that followed her mini-tirade hung in the air, thick and heavy like fog over the water. She stared at the two-tiered, wrought-iron fruit basket on the island as if it alone could take away the lump in her throat. The resentment burning in her chest.

"I'm sorry," she forced out. "I'm…God, I'm jealous. And it sucks and I hate it because I love you and I want you have the wedding of your dreams. But your mother is here. She's always been here for you. You deserve to have everything you want, including your mother tearing up when she sees you walk down the aisle. I just… I want that, too," she admitted in a whisper. "And I'll never have it."

Erin, always one to be way too sympathetic, didn't

try to hold back her own tears as she hurried over to give Nora a hug. "Honey, I'm so sorry."

Nora returned the embrace for a moment before stepping back. But she squeezed Erin's hands. "Thank you, but you don't have to apologize. I don't want to do or say anything to ruin even a moment of us planning your beautiful wedding." She smiled, hoped her cousin didn't notice how her mouth trembled. "I'm just going to have to learn to deal with everything that's happened, the truth about my mom's disappearance and now Dale York being back in town."

As soon as Dale left her office Monday, Nora had called Layne and told her what had happened before spending the next forty-five minutes pacing like mad while she waited for the P.I. to arrive. She'd explained to Mr. Hepfer that his services were no longer needed, paid him generously for the time it had taken him to drive to Mystic Point, then met her sisters at Tori's house where they had tried to wrap their heads around this new development.

"You don't have to deal with it by yourself," Erin said. "You have Tori and Layne and Uncle Tim and you have me—" She nodded toward her parents and fiancé on the patio. "You have all of us. You'll always have us."

Nora nodded. "I know. And even though I may not act like it, I'm so grateful."

Even if, for the first time in her life, she wondered if settling for someone else's family would be enough for her.

FRIDAY MORNING, GRIFFIN walked up the short driveway, passing a brand-new Jeep on his way to Nora's tiny, saltbox house. It had white siding, blue shutters and a

cheery flower garden on both sides of the front stoop.
It was warm, bright and charming.

Like its owner.

He'd take cool, dark and sexy any day.

He knocked on the door. Up close he could see the
cuteness factor hid a few defects: peeling paint on the
shutters and the windowsills, aging siding. The roof
looked new as did the windows. But that still didn't
explain how someone with a junior lawyer license, or
whatever she had that gave her the right to spout off
about laws and justice, could afford a place this close
to the beach. Maybe her rich uncle helped her out. The
Sullivans liked to stick together.

He knocked again.

"I'll get it," a male voice called. "But if you're not
ready in five minutes, I'm leaving without you."

Griffin raised his eyebrows. So, Little Miss Sunshine
had male company.

The kid who answered the door had four inches on
him, though two of those inches seemed to be his mop
top hair. He came from money, Griffin thought, lots of
it if the preppy, designer clothes, casually tousled hair
and expensive watch were any indication.

"Nora home?" Griffin asked when the kid just stared
at him.

"Who is it?" Nora came up behind her boyfriend. She
had on a shiny red top tucked into a knee-length black
skirt that accentuated her small waist and the curve of
her hips. Her feet were bare, her hair once again in a
neat twist, a pair of red high heels hung from her finger by their straps.

"Griffin." She frowned and damn if he didn't rethink
the allure of sunny blondes after all. "Good morning."

He nodded. The kid glowered. Nora looked confused

and, if he wasn't mistaken, a bit sleepy. Must've been one hell of a night, he thought, oddly irritated.

"Your car's done," he said.

"And you came all the way over here to tell me that?" she asked, holding on to the kid with one hand while she struggled to put on a shoe. A tricky task given that snug skirt but you wouldn't hear him complain. Not when her movements caused the material to slide a few inches up her thighs.

The kid cleared his throat. Griffin slowly raised his gaze, sent him a smirk before facing Nora. "I brought it."

She blinked, froze, her hand still on the guy's arm. "You brought me my car." She made it sound like a question. "You brought it here."

"Did I stutter?" he asked mildly.

"No, it's just…that's a nice thing to do."

Now he grinned, slow and easy. "Angel, I'm all about being nice."

"And you're making jokes." She looked up at the kid. "It's a Friday-morning miracle. Go tell it on the mountain."

"Great," the kid said while Nora used him once again as a balancing board to slip her other shoe on. "Give her the keys and you can go."

Griffin didn't take his eyes off her. He liked how, with the heels and her being inside and up a step, she was eye to eye with him. "Cute kid. You adopt him?"

"Nah, he eats too much." The kid growled low in his throat. "What?" she asked. "You do. But he's right. You're cute. Adorable even."

His jaw worked and, if Griffin wasn't mistaken, when he spoke, his voice was a little deeper. "I'm also going to be late if we don't leave. Now."

"Well, go ahead. I have my car back so you're off the hook." She leaned up and kissed his cheek. "Thanks for playing chauffeur."

"No problem. But don't pay him until you double-check his work."

"Oh, Anthony," she said, exasperated and reproachful. "I know your mother taught you better manners than that."

Anthony jerked a shoulder. "I'm looking out for you," he muttered.

"I can look after myself." But she squeezed his hand.

"I'm starting to wonder about that," he said, sending a pointed glance at Griffin.

He loped down the sidewalk with all the confidence and swagger of someone who held the world in his hand. Who knew that if his grip slipped, Mommy and Daddy would do whatever it took, spend any amount of money, to fix all his problems for him.

"Had a sleepover last night, huh?" Griffin slouched against the door frame as Anthony backed out of the driveway. "And on a school night, too."

"I don't go to school."

"Maybe not, but your plaything doesn't look old enough to vote. If you wanted something young that would adore you, you could've adopted a puppy," Griffin said, not sure where the resentment in his stomach originated from.

"What are you... Oh. Oh." The second time she dragged it out so it was at least three syllables. Then she laughed. At him. Seemed to be a habit of hers. A bad one. "Anthony's my cousin. He's been taking me to work."

And that knot in his stomach loosened. "None of my business."

"No, it isn't," she said, way more freaking cheerfully than the situation called for. "But he'll get a kick out of you thinking he's some big stud who hooks up with older women."

"Glad I could make his day." He dug a folded invoice out of his front pocket. "Here's your bill."

She took it, read it. "Seems reasonable. Do you accept personal checks?"

"The kid was right," Griffin said because he didn't want her or anyone to think he took advantage of his customers. "You shouldn't pay unless you're sure you're satisfied with the work."

She studied him, her brows drawn together. He had the strangest urge to rub his thumb along that crease in her forehead. "I didn't want to offend you."

She was way too sweet. Too worried about other people's feelings. "I'm damn good at what I do. I don't mind someone checking my work."

Then she bestowed one of those warm smiles on him, making him feel as if he'd won the freaking lottery. "Okay, then."

She went down the walk to her car and studied the headlights. He pursed his lips as she bent, this way and that, her contortions doing some seriously interesting things to her skirt. Her shirt twisted tight against her breasts. And those shoes. Those damn shoes were putting ideas in his head better left for a woman who didn't look like an angel and want to dig up his past, want to take on his father.

"It looks great," she called as she sauntered in a hip-swaying stride back toward him, the rising sun haloing her hair. "Come on in, I'll get you a check."

"That's not nec—"

But she was already walking into the house, her

fresh, floral scent lingering. And he couldn't help but follow her. For his money, he assured himself as he stepped inside, shutting the door behind him. Not because he liked the way her ass looked in that skirt, how those heels made her legs look longer.

She wasn't in the same league as her sisters when it came to sex appeal but he could see why a man would be interested. Attracted. Yeah, he thought, watching her as she walked into the kitchen, he could definitely see the appeal.

And he viciously shoved his own interest and attraction aside.

He glanced around. Her house reminded him of where he and his parents had first lived when they moved to Mystic Point when he'd been nine. It had the same open floor plan—living room, dining room and kitchen all flowing into one another. There was no hallway, just two doors at the back of the living room—probably an extra bedroom and a bathroom—and a staircase in the front corner.

Of course their place had stained, matted carpet, holes in the drywall and mismatched, secondhand furniture instead of shiny wood floors and framed pictures, photographs and a white twig wreath decorating cream-colored walls. She had a deep green sofa facing the TV and two armchairs—one a flowery print, the other a burgundy that reminded him of her shirt. They were plush and feminine and enticing enough to make him want to take a seat.

"Can I get you a cup of coffee?" she called.

"I'm good." He wandered toward the staircase, checked out the framed photos on a skinny table underneath the window. He picked up a shot of Nora, wearing jeans and a green sweater, and a smiling boy with dark, floppy hair. Her arm was around the kid's shoulder and they were laughing, looking at each other instead of the camera. Behind them a Christmas tree twinkled merrily.

"That's my nephew, Brandon," she said, coming up behind him. "My gift to him was a trip to Boston for a Bruins game."

He set the picture down. He knew Tori had a kid, that she'd gotten pregnant during their senior year of high school, but it still came as a shock that Mystic Point's own living, breathing, walking, talking male fantasy was someone's mother. "You like hockey?"

"God, no. But I like my nephew." Her lips curved. His stomach pinched. "And I really like getting him better presents than Layne."

"You Sullivans take sibling rivalry to new heights."

"I prefer to think of it as a healthy competition. One that I usually come out on top of. I do, after all, know the way to a guy's heart. Food," she said, holding up a finger for each item listed. "Sports. Video games. Action movies—the more violent and unrealistic, the better."

"Angel," he murmured, "that list might be the way to your nephew's heart but you're nuts if you think it'll work on a grown man, one you're not related to." He shifted closer, scanned her face. "There's only one thing he'll want from you."

"Yes, well, I draw the line at pole dancing, making out with another woman or wearing anything made out of spandex."

His lips twitched. "You really do understand what men want."

She patted his hand. "You are, after all, but simple creatures."

Her skin was warm against his. Soft. Their eyes met and held while something elemental and intense arced between them. She swallowed, lowered her lids.

And shoved the check at him. "Here you go," she said breathlessly, her cheeks pink. He took it, careful not to touch her. "I appreciate you doing the work so quickly."

He folded the slip of paper, stuck it into his back pocket. "I'd say it's been nice doing business with you but I've never been much of a liar."

That grin was back, the one that made him feel like she was laughing at him. And that she wanted him to join in on the joke. "I can only imagine how much repeat business you get."

He shrugged. "Next time you feel like taking a crowbar to your Lexus, do me a favor and do some damage to the engine or even transmission. There's a bigger margin for me on those."

"I think my car bashing days are over, but I'll keep the advice in mind. Hey," she said when he crossed to the door, "if you drove my car here, how are you getting back to the garage?"

"I'm walking."

"It's at least five miles." She grabbed her purse from a small, round table, along with a laptop and briefcase. "I'll drop you off on my way to work."

"No payback for my making you hoof it to work in those heels the other day?"

"I've never been much into revenge," she said, mimicking his words. "Besides, I didn't walk to work. Anthony picked me up on the way…" Her mouth went slack. "Wait. Is that why you brought my car over here instead of waiting for me to pick it up? Because you felt guilty?"

"No," he growled, giving her the scowl that intimidated men twice her size. She wasn't fazed in the least. "I didn't want you at my garage again. I was worried you'd take that crowbar to my head this time."

"I thought you weren't much of a liar," she teased, opening the door. "I think it's sweet that you wanted to make amends."

Sweet. Him. Jesus Christ. He wanted to back her against that door, press his body to hers and show her exactly how far from sweet he really was. Wanted to shock her, to prove to her that he wasn't like the other men she knew. He wasn't polished and civilized with a veneer of politeness and charm.

He was real. He didn't sit back while someone poked at him. He pushed back.

"Well?" she asked, as she stepped onto the porch. "Are you coming or not?"

He didn't know and that was the problem. Didn't know if he was coming or going. Dealing with her made his head spin. Gave him a headache. He couldn't figure her out and that pissed him off.

Only one thing was certain. No one was to be trusted.

Not even curvy blondes with soft hands and warm smiles and a killer sense of humor.

"Yeah," he said after a moment. "I'm coming."

CHAPTER SIX

PULLING TO A stop at the sign at the intersection by her house, Nora turned up the air-conditioning. It wasn't that hot out yet but it was surprisingly warm in her car. Stuffy.

Maybe because the interior seemed to have shrunk, what with the silent man next to her.

He smelled good. Really good. Like a mixture of a subtle, spicy cologne and man.

She cracked her window, greedily inhaled the fresh air like a woman who'd spent the past five minutes with her head in a pillowcase.

God, get a grip. Griffin York was just a man. A sexy man, yes. She wasn't blind was she? But sexy or not he was also brooding and cynical and hauled that chip on his shoulder along with him everywhere he went, right next to the bad attitude he made sure everyone knew about.

"I'm not sure if you're aware of what's going on with your father…" Griffin continued to stare out the passenger side window. She had no idea what information he had, or if Dale had been to see his mother again. If his father had tried to contact him since he'd been in town. "Uh…anyway…Ross has interviewed him, twice, but so far he's sticking to his story."

She turned left onto Mechanic Street, tapped her fingers on the steering wheel to the Maroon Five song playing softly on the radio. "What story, you may ask?" she said, unable to stand his silence. "Well, let me tell you—"

"Not interested."

She gaped at him. "How can you say that?"

He had to be curious. No one could be that cold, that closed off. Could they?

He grabbed the dash. "Watch it," he said tightly.

She whipped her head around, saw she'd drifted into the wrong lane—and into the path of an approaching SUV. Unfazed, she yanked the wheel to the right, waved at the other driver, ignoring the way he laid on his horn.

Boy, she did not get Griffin. At all. But, if he didn't want to hear Dale's claim that he'd waited for Val half the night at the quarry but she'd never showed, that was his business. He could read about it in the newspaper. Or hear about it at Dale's trial. Because Ross was already trying to pick apart Dale's statement.

There were too many loose ends. Like why Dale had left his car at the quarry and what happened to her mother's vehicle. His answers didn't add up, and his vagueness about where he'd spent the past eighteen years only made him look more suspicious. Guilty. They could use both against him.

The truth would come out. She believed that. She had to.

"So," she said, racking her brain for a neutral topic of conversation, "how long have you owned the garage?"

"Five years."

"It must be interesting." She felt him look at her. "Taking things apart, putting them back together again. Learning how things work."

"It pays the bills."

"I can see you have a great passion for your business," she said dryly.

He shifted, thumped his fist against his knee a few times. "I enjoy my work," he finally said as if she'd tied a rope to his vocal chords and was pulling the words out of him. "And I'm good at it. But mostly, I was lucky. All I wanted was a part-time job so I'd have enough cash to buy cigarettes, beer and condoms."

"The holy trinity of teenage boys?"

His fast, appreciative grin was unexpected. And so appealing she was glad they were side by side so it hadn't hit her full force. "For me it was. But I didn't have much luck with the local businesses. There weren't many employment opportunities for a juvenile delinquent. By the time I walked into Eddie's I was sure he'd give me the same runaround everyone else had. Instead he hired me on the spot, told me I had a job there as long as I worked hard and stayed out of trouble."

"He gave you a chance," she said softly. Gave him an opportunity to be more than his reputation, more than Dale York's son, when no one else had done so.

Maybe it wasn't so surprising after all, him not wanting to talk about his dad.

"Yeah." Griffin shifted. "He taught me a trade and after he sold me the garage, he still came in every day, put in four hours of work. He told me he was bored but I think he wanted to make sure I didn't run the business he'd started into the ground."

Stopping at an intersection, she waved ahead a white truck. "I bet he's proud of how well the garage is doing."

Griffin lifted a shoulder. "He moved to Ohio about four years ago to be closer to his daughter and granddaughter."

"You must miss him."

"That's life. People come and they go. Best not to get too attached to them while they're around because eventually, everyone moves on."

And that was just about the saddest thing she'd ever heard.

"You're good at that," she said, glancing his way.

His glower deepened. "What?"

"Good at acting all scary and untouchable. My God, it must be exhausting, being so cynical and angry all the time. Must be lonely."

"I don't have time to be lonely," he grumbled. "Between customers and my half brother being at the shop all the time, I'm surrounded by people."

She refrained from diving into a dissertation about the differences of being alone and being lonely. "I didn't know your brother worked with you."

"Half brother."

"Which half are you claiming? The right half? Left? Top half?"

"Do you ever stop talking?" he asked grumpily.

"Rarely."

She had too much interest in other people. Everyone had a story and she enjoyed hearing their tales. Plus, she had a way with words, if she did say so herself. Of course, her family accused her of always twisting those words—hers and theirs—to ensure situations and conversations worked out to her advantage. But so what? Everyone had their special talents.

Besides, the quiet made her nervous. There were too many secrets in silence, so much left unsaid.

"Why the clarification about the status of your relationship with your brother?" she asked. "Seems like a sibling is a sibling to me."

"You would think that. You probably also believe in unicorns, fairies and campaign promises."

"Don't be ridiculous. I would never be so gullible as to believe a campaign promise."

She could've sworn she saw the corner of his mouth twitch. Maybe he wasn't as humorless as she'd thought.

"So, your brother. I take it he's younger than you? What's his name?"

"Tanner."

She waited but he didn't elaborate. "Has he been working for you long?"

"No."

"It's nice of you to hire him. I waited tables at the café under Tori one summer and let me tell you, it was hell. Pure. Hell. Working with family can be tricky."

Griffin slouched in his seat, all bad-boy attitude and sex appeal. "He doesn't work for me. I'm helping him restore a car and he's paying me back by putting in a few hours around the shop."

"Wow, that's—"

"Whatever you do, don't say I'm sweet again," he warned.

"I'm that predictable?"

"Pretty much."

That sucked. Guess she wasn't meant to be all mysterious and secretive and sexy like her sisters, who kept their thoughts inside their heads. Unless it came to her, of course, and the mistakes they deemed she'd made. Then they couldn't keep their mouths shut.

"What's Tanner like?"

"Why?" he asked, sounding suspicious.

"It's called having a conversation. But if it's too much for you, I'm more than happy to keep quiet."

"Promise?"

She pressed her lips together. He didn't want to talk to her, even about subjects that had nothing to do with his father, her mother or the past? Fine. She had better things to do than try to engage him in pleasant chitchat.

She was good with people, damn it. She slid a glance at Griffin. Usually. Then again, he probably hated everything that was right and decent in the world. Rainbows. Kittens. Pretty blondes.

She wouldn't take it personally.

But, okay, it bugged her. She was a very likable person. Cheerful and amusing and more than intelligent. Some would say charming. Utterly so.

Who was he not to notice?

"Do you want to know what I think?" she asked, her knuckles white from gripping the steering wheel so hard.

"Can I stop you?"

"I think you're sort of an ass. I mean, yes, initially I came to you with a request that didn't sit well with you. I wanted you to help me find the man suspected of killing my mother. How dare I? But really, you need someone to knock that chip off your shoulder." She flipped her head but the effect was lost because her hair was up. "I mean, who are you not to like me?"

"That what this is about?" he asked, sounding amused. Of course. The one time he's not growling and it's at her expense. "Your feelings are hurt because I'm not falling at your feet, giving you the adoration you think you're due?"

She blushed. Did he have to make her feel like such an insecure princess?

"Of course not," she said. "It's about you being so damn angry. I get that you had a tough life and I'm sorry for that—"

"You feeling bad for me, angel?" he asked softly.

His gravelly tone raked over her skin, causing goose-flesh to rise on her arms. Had something heated and heavy settling in her stomach. "It's not pity," she said, sounding a bit breathless. "It's understanding. Compassion."

"Exactly how compassionate are you feeling?"

Frowning, she glanced at him. "What?"

His mouth curved up but his eyes remained hooded. "I'm wondering what I can get out of you. What are you willing to do to show me how you…understand…what my life was like."

"Seriously? You're going to try to frighten me with some lame attempt at sexual intimidation?" She jerked the wheel hard, pulled into the parking lot of his garage with her tires squealing. She slammed on the brakes and he had to reach out and brace his hands against the dashboard. She wished she'd been going faster. "I realize that living with an abusive father was awful—"

"Don't go there."

"But that doesn't mean you have to be such an ass-hole."

"Such an ugly word from such a pretty mouth," he murmured.

She glared. "I have quite an extensive vocabulary. And I'm thinking of many, many adjectives to describe you. But let's part ways here before I lower myself any further. Thanks for fixing my car so quickly and for bringing it to me. Have a nice life."

But he didn't get out. She stared straight ahead at the large building, her heart racing. Finally, thankfully, he moved and the tension tightening her shoulders loos-ened.

Griffin climbed out of the car but before she could

peel out of there in all her pissed-off glory, he leaned back inside, one arm on the roof, the other holding the top of the door.

"What?" she snapped, unnerved to have all that intensity focused on her.

"Tanner's seventeen," Griffin said.

She blinked. "It doesn't mat—"

"He's a good kid. Bright. Quiet. Shy. He loves basketball, dreams of getting a scholarship to play at one of the big universities. He's good enough to make it, too. And the reason I call him my half brother," he said, his mouth a thin line, "is because I want to make sure no one thinks, even for a moment, that he came from Dale York." He tapped the top of her car. "Thanks for the ride."

Crap. Crap, crap, crappity, crap-crap.

Just when she thought she had Griffin figured out, that he was nothing more than an angry, bitter, scary, emotionally stunted man, he had to go and act like a real live human being. Had to make her wonder.

Damn him.

"ARE YOU STALKING me?"

At the sound of Jessica's voice, Tanner raised his head from where he was lining up sugar packets on the tabletop. He'd planned this, he reminded himself. Knew exactly how he wanted to play it. Cool. Confident.

But then he realized what she'd said.

"What?" he asked then winced. *Brilliant dialogue, dude.*

She set a hand on her hip. "I asked if you're some sort of deranged stalker. Because, in case you are, I think I should remind you that my uncle is the town's police chief."

He should probably smile to try to put her at ease but he'd never been one to force an emotion he didn't feel. "I'm not a stalker."

"Just deranged, then?"

His face heated. Shit. He cleared his throat, picked up a sugar packet. "No. I'm here… I wanted to…" But he met the blue of her eyes and his mind blanked, simply wiped clean like an eraser over a whiteboard.

"Get something to eat?" she prodded when he stared at her like a complete loser.

"Yeah." He straightened, rolled down the top of the sugar packet. Unrolled it. "I'm here to eat."

She looked at him as if his head was full of hot air and had sprung a leak. "So do you need a menu or what?"

"I'll have a dozen barbecue wings," he said, though he'd already eaten four slices of pizza with his folks. Then, realizing that wasn't much of an order he added, "And a loaded cheeseburger with fries."

She wrote it down, the glittery bracelet on her wrist catching the light. Her arms were super thin, her hands small and delicate. He rolled and unrolled the sugar packet. He bet he could hold both her wrists in one hand and touch his forefinger with this thumb. He bet her skin was soft. And warm.

The paper broke. Sugar flew across the table.

"Smooth," she said, her lips pursed at the mess.

Cringing, fighting the urge to hide under the table, he brushed the crystals into a pile.

"You want your food order put in now," she continued, tapping her pen against her pad, "or do you want to wait until your BFFs get here?"

"They're not coming." A fact he'd been glad about until now. He glanced around the room. It was crowded, with more people waiting to be seated. He'd stood in line twenty minutes—mostly because he'd wanted to be put in Jessica's section. But he was taking up an entire booth. He hoped that wasn't going to be an issue.

"They ditched you on a Friday night?"

"I ditched them." Sitting back, he brushed the sugar from his hands onto his jeans. "They're heading up to Gwen Silvestri's cabin for a kegger."

"You don't drink?" she asked, her tone skeptical, like he'd told her he had artificial lungs and no longer needed oxygen.

"No."

"Wow. A regular Boy Scout." She sounded less than impressed. "So you're going solo tonight and yet you waited in line until a booth opened up instead of taking a smaller table."

He bit the inside of his cheek. Guess he should've figured the lady working the door would've told her coworkers about him stubbornly refusing a table in a different area of the restaurant.

"I like it here," he said, holding her gaze.

She studied him intently. Then she nodded once as if coming to some monumental decision. "Good answer."

He opened his mouth, though he had no idea what he wanted to say, but Jessica's attention got caught by the hostess leading a group of three college-aged couples past the booth. They had money, that was easy enough to tell from their clothes and the way they carried themselves, as if they already had everything they wanted but asked for more anyway.

It was also easy because Mystic Point was a small town, and despite the guys in the group being four or five years older than him, Tanner recognized two of them—Brian Norris and Andy Cline—from when they were on the high school basketball team. Even as an eighth-grader, Tanner hadn't missed a home game.

But it was the third dude, the one Tanner didn't recognize, the tall one with curly hair and the gorgeous brunette clinging to his arm, that Jessica stared at. For a moment, her expression was completely open and Tanner couldn't miss the hurt on her face when the guy grinned at the brunette, the scorn as she took in the other girl's micro-mini, high heels and toned, tanned legs. The longing when she and the guy locked eyes.

And Tanner knew with a sudden, ferocious certainty, that he'd give anything to have her look at him like that.

The hostess tried to seat them at a table near Tanner's booth but the curly-haired guy gestured to a family of five who were getting up from another table. Smiling, he said something that had the hostess laughing and swatting at his arm before she led them over.

"You okay?" Tanner asked as Jessica stared at the table, her fingers curled around her order pad.

Her movements jerky, she brushed the back of her hand over her forehead. "I'm fine and dandy," she said, but she didn't meet his eyes. "I'll go put your order in."

As she walked toward the swinging doors at the back of the room, frizz-head's gaze tracked her.

The brunette drew the guy's attention back to her. Obviously Jessica and curly-hair knew each other. Hadn't he heard a rumor about her hooking up with some college kid? And that when he'd found out her real age, he'd dumped her?

He slouched in his seat, heard his mother's voice in his head telling him to please sit up straight and slid down even farther. If Jessica was used to college guys, if she preferred pretty boys with money and confidence who could take her places, buy her whatever she wanted and always said the right thing, he didn't have a chance in hell.

A moment later, Jess walked back to the table and set a glass of soda in front of him then held out a paper-wrapped straw. "Cherry cola, right?"

"Did I order this?"

Since he didn't take the straw, she tossed it onto the table. "I forgot to take your drink order. But I remembered you like Cherry Coke so…"

His jaw dropped and he quickly shut his mouth. She remembered? Maybe he had a shot after all. "I do. Thanks."

She turned to leave and without thinking it through or analyzing why he shouldn't, he blurted out the first thing that came to his mind. "What time are you done working?"

Regarding him steadily, as if trying to see inside his head, read his mind, she tipped her head to the side. The back of his neck prickled, his throat dry.

"Why?" she finally asked.

"I thought maybe we could do something after."

"You did, huh?" She edged closer. "Like what? Like you could do me?"

His heart pounded in his chest as if he'd just played two straight quarters of basketball. "Uh…actually." He had to stop. Clear his throat. Try to clear his mind of the vision her words had induced. "I thought we could catch a movie."

She sat across from him. He hurriedly shifted. His legs were long, his feet and hands big. He felt clumsy and awkward and was both of those things—except on the basketball court.

"Why do you want to go out with me?" she asked, leaning forward.

He mimicked her stance, realized that to an outside observer, they looked cozy. Intimate. "What?"

"It's a simple question."

Was this a test? If it was, he'd bomb it. Because to pass it meant he'd have to talk more, to be witty and charming and come up with some bullshit answer on the fly. He sucked at all of the above, at coming up with what people wanted to hear. He'd have to stick with the only thing he knew; the only way he knew how to be.

The truth.

"I think you're really pretty," he said slowly but instead of seeming flattered, she stiffened, her eyes flashing.

"That's all? You don't even know me. All you want is to get into my pants." Her voice was low and harsh but he could tell she wasn't just angry. She was offended. And hurt. "What did you think? That you and your friends can all pass me around like some blow-up doll?"

She got out of the booth and he found himself leaping to his feet. He bumped the table, caused his soda to rock back and forth, liquid splashing over the side. Somehow he managed to right the glass with one hand and take a hold of her wrist with the other.

"Sorry," he said, dropping her hand almost as quickly as he'd grabbed it. He stepped in front of her, blocking her escape. "You are pretty." She had to know that. Girls like her, beautiful girls, may pretend they didn't know their power, but they did. "But that's not the only reason I asked you out."

She crossed her arms. "Oh, do tell."

"You're…different."

"Different," she repeated flatly. "Because I didn't grow up here. Because my mom's in jail instead of being on the PTA."

He'd heard rumors about that, had hoped it wasn't true. No wonder Jess was so hard.

"Different because you didn't see me puke in the cafeteria when I was in the fourth grade. Different because you don't remember when I tripped down the stairs and broke my wrist in middle school because I was watching Lauren Morris walk up the stairs." He spoke slowly, weighing each word, choosing the ones he hoped would turn this whole conversation to his favor. "You don't know the stuff they say about my mom and her ex-husband or what people think about my brother. You're just…different."

She didn't give him an inch. Or an ounce of hope. "I have other customers to take care of," she said.

"Then I'll get out of your way," he muttered, stepping aside. "And I'll take my order to go."

Sitting down, he stared at the table while she walked away. He wanted to escape, but he'd placed an order and wouldn't skip out after doing so. Besides, he may be clumsy and shy and his parents may not be rich, but he wasn't a coward.

Getting his order to go wasn't about bravery, it was about pride. And he wanted to keep at least a shred of his.

So he waited. He tapped his foot. Drummed his fingers on the table. Wiped his damp palms down the front of his thighs then tore the paper from the straw and took a long drink of his soda.

Ten minutes later, Jessica came back and set a take-out box in front of him. "Need a refill?" she asked with a nod to his almost empty glass.

"No thanks," he said, digging into his back pocket for his wallet.

"My uncle's picking me up after work," she said, her

hands linked at her waist. "His girlfriend is making dinner so they want to do the whole family night thing." He stilled, watched those hands. Her fingers twisted and untwisted. Her nails were short and painted pink with bright blue dots. She huffed out a breath. "I don't work Wednesday night."

Now he lifted his gaze. Raised his eyebrows.

To his amazement, her cheeks turned pink. She glanced behind her at the table of college kids. Curly-hair was watching her, a frown on his too-good-looking face.

Jessica faced Tanner again. "Do you want to hang out Wednesday or not?"

"Why?"

"Because I think you're really pretty," she said, repeating his words.

Was she making fun of him? He wasn't sure, but he'd be damned if he'd stick around to find out. Tossing money onto the table, including enough to cover her tip, he picked up the food, stood and stepped toward the door.

"Wait," she called and, though it was idiotic to hope, to continue to want, he stopped. "You're honest, I'll give you that. And I'm trying to be more honest so maybe if we...hang out...some of that Boy Scout stuff you've got going on will rub off on me."

How did she make being a nice guy, a good guy, sound so freaking lame? "I'm not a Boy Scout."

"Close enough for me."

She once again glanced at the rich college dude.

Tanner's stomach cramped. "You trying to make that guy jealous?" he heard himself ask.

"Does it matter?"

"I'm not sure," he admitted.

"Why don't I give you my cell phone number?" she asked, taking a pen out of her pocket. "You can let me know when you decide."

But instead of writing her number on one of her order slips, she lifted his hand and yes, her skin was as soft, as warm as he'd imagined. Her head bent, she wrote on his palm. His fingers twitched at the sensation, of being close enough to breathe in the fruity scent of her perfume, to see the straight part in her pale hair.

"I've decided," he said gruffly. "It doesn't matter."

She raised her head. "Good. Call me tonight and we'll set something up."

Then she smiled, about knocking him on his ass.

No, he thought, it didn't matter. He wouldn't let it.

CHAPTER SEVEN

THE YACHT PUB had a nautical theme, framed photos of boats and their crews on the walls and warped, wide planks on the floor. A scarred, wooden bar ran the length of the long room with bottles of liquor lined up in front of a mirror behind it. Some industrious soul had hung white lights in the fish netting hanging above the small square space that passed for a dance floor. But what really set it apart from the places Nora usually frequented was the huge, stuffed swordfish on the wall above the cash register.

And the ruffled pink bra hanging from its long bill.

Standing inside the door, trying to get her eyes adjusted to the darkness, she wrinkled her nose at the scent of stale beer. Well, it certainly was…atmospheric. She rubbed at her suddenly chilled arms. Dimly lit, dank and mildly depressing.

No wonder that damn inner voice of hers was telling her to turn tail and run. Not to go through with what, not fifteen few minutes ago, had seemed like the greatest idea since that woman invented Spanx.

Stop in at the Yacht Pub and have a drink or two.

It was still a good idea, she assured herself, stepping aside as the door opened behind her and a middle-aged couple walked in. And, taking in the crowd, she wasn't the only who'd had it. Men in T-shirts, jeans and work boots sat at the bar, more people, of both sexes and all ages, crowded around tables and the booths lining the walls, a few played pool.

See? Great minds and all that.

She was a single woman out for a drink. No law against that. She had as much right to be there as anyone else. More so.

Lifting her head she crossed to an empty stool, sat down and laid her purse on the bar. Journey's "Faithfully" played on the jukebox, the song's mellow tune blaring over the sounds of laughter, conversations and sharp crack of pool balls.

Funny, but the last time she'd been here it'd seemed so much...bigger. Cleaner. More exotic and exciting. Then again, any bar would've been exotic and exciting to an eight-year-old.

The bartender, a petite bleached blonde in desperate need of a root touch-up, took Nora's order. As she waited for her drink, the back of her neck prickled with awareness. With unease. Someone was watching her. Slowly she scanned the room.

And locked eyes with the one, the only Griffin York.

The confidence that rarely left her stuttered then went splat at her feet.

He sat in a booth behind the pool table, a redhead—and really, there was no way that particular shade of red came from nature—hanging on him like barnacles on a ship. Even from across the room, she could feel the power of those green eyes, of that smirk.

He lifted his bottle of beer, tipped the head of it toward her in a mock salute.

She waved, making sure to grin widely at him, all warmth and friendliness. Mainly because she knew it would bug him.

It wasn't until she'd turned back to the bar that she let out a grimace. Griffin was here. Why?

She mentally rolled her eyes. Okay, it was easy enough to figure out why he was there. The Yacht Pub was a good place to go, she supposed, if you were a single man searching for…well…whatever someone like Griffin searched for.

Biting her lower lip, she checked out Griffin and the redhead again. Yeah, she could easily imagine what he searched for on a Saturday night. Alcohol. Sex. Though not necessarily in that order.

And, from the looks of things, he wouldn't have any problem with the sex part. At least not tonight and not with the redhead who was practically in his lap. None of her business, she thought firmly and averted her gaze. He could cozy up to whomever he wanted.

A man like Griffin, with his beautiful face, rough edges and sexy mouth, drew women to him like they were magnets and he was due north. Some probably deluded themselves into thinking he hid his true emotions behind his cynicism and sullen attitude. Believed they could change him, that they could heal the wounds of his past.

You feeling bad for me, angel?

She pressed her lips together. Yes, she felt bad for him, for the little boy who'd been hurt, abused by his own father. But she didn't confuse empathy with some deeper emotion. Wasn't foolish enough to fall for him just because he'd shown her glimpses of humor and sincerity.

"Here you go," the bartender said, setting a glass on a paper napkin and a bottle of beer next to it. "That's three dollars."

Nora reached into her purse. "Thanks." A memory tugged at her brain. "Aren't you Sarah Leon?"

"Use to be," she said, taking Nora's money. "It's Sarah Thurman now."

Nora held out her hand. "I thought it was you. I'm Nora Sullivan."

SARAH'S EYEBROWS ROSE, wrinkling her forehead. "Valerie's daughter?"

For a moment, Nora couldn't figure out what the other woman was asking. She was Tim's daughter. Layne and Tori's sister. Ken and Astor's niece. Erin's best friend.

She was Nora Sullivan and her mother had nothing to do with the person she'd made of herself.

Still, biological links couldn't be denied. "Yes," she said. "I'm one of Valerie's daughters."

"I haven't seen you since you were little."

"I was just thinking of how different it looks from the last time I was in here with my mom." Val had occasionally worked days and if Layne and Tori were busy with after school activities, Nora would hang out at the Yacht Pub, drinking Shirley Temples and coloring until one of them could come and get her.

Sarah nodded at an elderly man in a worn fisherman's cap who raised a finger for a drink. "I still can't believe Val's been dead all this time," she said, drawing a draft beer. "I covered for her that night. Maybe if I hadn't…"

"If you hadn't," Nora said gently, "she would've asked someone else."

After her mother's remains were found, Ross had taken statements from Nora and her family, along with Valerie's friends, coworkers…anyone and everyone who'd had contact with her during that time. Sarah had told him that Val had asked her to cover her shift at the bar the night she'd planned on leaving her family.

Nora sipped her beer while Sarah delivered the man's drink. "Did you ever see my mom with Dale York?" she asked when Sarah came back.

"All the time." She put away a bottle of what looked like rum then turned back, wiping her hands on a towel. "He'd hang out here, wait for her to finish her shift then they'd take off together." Her mouth pinched. "I hate to speak ill of the dead…"

"But?"

"But…I never understood why Val wanted to be with someone like Dale. Not when she had such a good man at home. Your dad, he was always so nice to all of us. He'd bring us burgers and fries or pizza at the end of the night, help clean up if she worked late. You ask me, he treated her like a queen."

He had. Nora and her sisters had witnessed how much Tim had adored Val. How he'd worshipped her. He'd loved her beyond himself, beyond reason.

And it hadn't been enough. She'd given up the all-encompassing love of a good man for someone dark and dangerous.

Her mother had been such a fool.

Nora wiped her thumb through a drop of spilled beer. "Did you ever happen to see Dale lose his temper?"

"Sure." Sarah took an order from the twentysomething waitress in faded jeans and a snug, pink T-shirt. Poured dark amber liquid into a glass. "Like I said, he'd hang around here until your mom got done and he often caused trouble, got into fights with other customers. I hate to say it but part of that blame was on your mom. She liked to flirt," she explained with a shrug as she used a hose to add soda to the drink. "And if a guy flirted back or got too friendly, York would start throwing punches."

Nora wondered how much strife her mother had caused here at the bar. Her coworkers must have resented her. She'd been so beautiful and so vain with that beauty, had needed to be the center of attention. To shine brighter than anyone else.

But she'd also been charming and funny and she'd had a laugh that no one could resist. Nora could still hear it to this day.

She sipped her beer in an effort to soothe her dry throat. "Did you ever see them fight? With each other, I mean. Did you ever see him hurt her?"

Shaking her head, Sarah started on the second drink. "Nothing like that. They argued, sure. Seemed everything they did was heated, amped up, you know? Like having a regular relationship wasn't exciting enough so they did everything they could to add big drama, big tension, to it."

Disappointed, Nora forced a small smile. "Okay. Well, thanks for your time."

"It's no secret that I wasn't exactly friendly with your mom," Sarah said, handing the drinks to the waitress, "but I was sorry to hear what had happened to her."

"Thank you."

Nora picked at the corner of the label on her bottle while Sarah moved down the bar to take more orders.

So much for hoping she could find someone to testify they'd seen Dale be violent toward her mother. Not that she wanted Val to have been hurt, but if she'd found someone who'd witnessed Dale being abusive, it could possibly turn the tide of the going-nowhere-fast investigation against him.

Often times, when one person came forward, it brought out others who'd been too scared to do so on their own. Memories were jogged and facts that had been long-forgotten—or hidden—were brought to light.

It'd been a shot in the dark but she'd had to try. Maybe she should hire Hepfer Investigations after all. Get them to trace Dale's movements after he left Mystic Point. In his statement to the police, he'd refused to divulge where he'd spent the past eighteen years, saying only that he'd done a lot of traveling.

An investigator could do some digging into that life, interview people Dale had come into contact with, those he'd befriended. Maybe they could find someone he'd confided in. Someone he'd mentioned the murder to. Confessed to. Maybe—

"Slumming?" a low, deep, familiar voice asked at her ear.

A shiver of awareness climbed her spine. Bracing herself, she swiveled and met Griffin's eyes. He was close, closer than he'd ever been to her. His hair was mussed, as if the redhead had run her fingers through it. Her stomach quivered. She wished she could smooth the dark, tousled locks, erase the other woman's touch. Wanted to trace her forefinger around the sharp line of his mouth, feel the roughness of the stubble covering his cheeks. Gently rub the dip in his chin.

She tucked her hands into her lap, twisted her fingers together. "Griffin. Hi." She somehow mustered up a smile. "How are you?"

"Always so polite," he murmured, easing back. But she didn't feel any less crowded, any safer. Especially when he skimmed that hot gaze of his over her face and then down to linger on the exposed skin of her upper chest before lazily climbing up her throat back to her eyes. "What are you doing here?"

Having a coronary if the racing of her heart was any indication. God, he was gorgeous. Sexy and potent and so incredibly bad for her. Like father like son.

And she refused to act like her mother.

"Having a drink," she said, lifting the bottle for a quick sip. Too quick of one it turned out because she inhaled wrong and coughed to clear her throat.

One side of his mouth kicked up in that pseudo grin of his. "Beer? I pictured you more of a rainbow drinker."

She licked a drop of beer from her lip. Her breath caught when he watched the movement, his eyes darkening. She cleared her throat. "You think I drink rainbows? What am I, a leprechaun?"

"Rainbow drinks," he said gruffly. "Ones that are pink or green or blue…"

"Colors of the rainbow. Clever. And while I'll admit I've had a colorful cocktail once in a while, I also like beer. How shocking. Oh," she added, her eyes wide, "and I watch football—professional and college—and love nothing more than having a hot dog—extra relish—at a Red Sox game. Alert the media."

"You are full of surprises." He didn't sound too happy about it. "The biggest one being that of all the places in Mystic Point where you could have a drink, you chose this bar."

He had her there. Usually when she went out, she hit a dance club with a group of friends, somewhere with bright, flashing, seizure-inducing lights and bass-heavy music so loud it shook the walls. There'd be sharply dressed men on the prowl. Women in short skirts and skyscraper heels dancing in groups, taking breaks between the good songs to do Jell-O shots or head to the restroom en masse.

But tonight she'd come to the Yacht Pub, with its neon beer signs, jukebox and jean-wearing clientele. Where her mother had worked. Where Val had met Dale.

Where she'd more than likely made plans to leave her husband. Her daughters.

"You're very interested in me all of a sudden," she said, sending him a flirtatious glance from beneath her eyelashes to cover the way her throat had gone tight with emotion. "It was only a matter of time before you fell for my charms. I mean, who could hold out against this—" she circled her finger around her face "—my sparkling personality and intelligence for long? But don't feel bad. Stronger men than you have tried and failed." She leaned forward and lowered her voice. "I'm sort of irresistible."

"That so?" he murmured. Their eyes locked and held and she realized immediately she'd made a tactical error, a big one, in getting that close to him. Her breath was trapped in her lungs, her pulse racing.

She tore her gaze from his and stared over his shoulder. Saw the redhead shooting her a *die-now-bitch!* glare.

"I think your date's getting lonely," she said, tipping her beer toward the back of the room.

He didn't even turn. "She's not my date."

"O-kay. Still, don't feel like you have to keep me company. I'm fine all on my own."

He glowered. "You shouldn't even be here."

"But I am here and I plan on staying," she said with what she considered remarkable patience. The man was getting on her last nerve. "And I'd rather drink my beer in relative peace, which is the polite way of saying I'd like to be alone. So go on." She made a shooing motion. "Go."

He glanced over her head, his eyes narrowing in a way that had nerves twisting in her belly. "No."

"What do you mean, no?"

"It means I'm staying right here." As if to prove it, he sat on the stool, lifted his hand to the bartender, raising two fingers.

"Why on earth would you do that when you've got Little Miss Hot Pants over there waiting for you?"

He grinned at her and those nerves spiked pleasantly. "Because, angel, I have a feeling being with you is going to be way more interesting."

GRIFFIN ENJOYED WATCHING the emotions play over Nora's face. Confusion. Anger.

And that damn curiosity he knew would get the better of her.

He'd unnerved her. Good. Why should he be the only one unsure of his footing?

"I don't like the sound of that," she said, edging closer to him again, her voice low and husky, her fresh scent wrapping around him. "You seem sort of…cheerful. It's freaking me out."

He ground his back teeth together. Cheerful. He was not and never had been cheerful. "Just getting ready to enjoy the fireworks," he said, flicking his gaze over her shoulder.

She frowned—adorably, of course. "What are you talking about?"

"Nora," her sister Tori said as she came up behind her. "What are you doing here?"

Nora briefly shut her eyes and mouthed what looked

to be "Why me?" before plastering on one of her smiles—this one strained around the edges—and facing her sister.

"Tori. Hi. That seems to be a popular question tonight," she said, sliding him a glance. "Wow, you look gorgeous," she continued, sounding nothing but sincere. "Love those shoes."

"Thank you," Tori said, but didn't return the compliment though Nora looked good, too. Damn good.

Her hair was down. But it wasn't straight, like her sisters', like he'd imagined. Instead it fell past her shoulders in soft waves. Her dark jeans hugged her hips and ass and the wide neck of her deep blue top showed the curve of her collarbone, the barest hint of cleavage.

She'd done something different to her face, too. Had added subtle, light color to her eyes, smudged a soft purple under her lower lashes making the blue of them stand out. And her mouth…he couldn't stop staring at her mouth. Not when her lips were all pouty and slick and red.

Come get me red.

Kiss me red.

"What are you doing here?" Tori demanded again, doing her best to raise the temperature in the bar in her tight, black jeans, skinny heels and low-cut purple top. Her eyes were smoky, her dark chin-length hair showing off the sharpness of her jaw. A devil to her angelic sister.

Who the hell would've ever guessed he'd prefer the angel?

"What's it look like I'm doing?" Nora asked, all radiance and light and good times. "I'm having a drink with my friend."

"Your friend?" Tori repeated, as if Nora had said she'd bellied up to the bar with a snake. She finally acknowledged him long enough to make eye contact. "Griffin."

"Tori," he said, mimicking her flat tone.

There was no love lost between them. He'd never had much use for her. She was more subtle in her dislike and mistrust of him than Layne, had never been blatantly antagonistic toward him. She kept her distance.

He'd prefer facing off against Layne again, as he'd done a few weeks ago several seats down. At least she was easy to read. Tori played a part, used her body, that perfect face, to get what she wanted. He didn't like to be manipulated. Even by a beautiful woman.

"Would you like to join us?" Nora asked, pleasantly.

Griffin about choked on his beer. She acted as if it was every day she hung out at the Yacht Pub tossing back a few brews with her good old buddy, Griffin York. He wasn't sure whether to be impressed by her casual attitude, or worried she really believed they were friends.

Either way, he couldn't resist going along with it. Was afraid if he wasn't careful, he'd have a hard time resisting *her*.

"Yeah," he said, patting the stool on his other side. "Join us."

"No," Tori said slowly, dragging the word out. "Thank you. But I would just love to talk with you," she said to Nora, jerking her head to the side so hard, Griffin wondered if she'd dislocated her pretty neck. "Privately."

Nora slid her empty bottle aside and picked up the beer Griffin had bought her. "I'm sure whatever you have to say can wait."

"And I'm sure that it can't," Tori snarled. She grabbed Nora's arm. Tugged. "Come on."

And for some reason, Griffin didn't like Tori, didn't like anyone touching Nora, making her do something she didn't want to do.

"You don't have to go anywhere with her," he said.

"This is a private matter," Tori said, leaning over the bar to glare at him. "A family matter."

He ignored her, held Nora's gaze. He wanted to tell her to stay, right there. To stay with him. He wanted her to blow off her sister. He wanted, he realized with a sense of growing horror, her to pick him.

Holy hell, he was losing his mind.

"I'll be right back," she said, as if it was a foregone conclusion he'd stick around waiting for her. As if he'd planned on spending the night hanging out with her, hearing her laugh, breathing in her scent. Being tempted by her.

She got to her feet on his side of the stool, her lush body brushing ever-so-subtly against his arm.

His mouth went bone-dry. Keeping his eyes straight ahead, he tipped up his beer. Drained half of it. No skin off his nose if she went with Tori, he thought, wiping the back of his hand across his mouth. Now that he'd lost his appetite for the redhead and slaked his thirst for a beer, he could head on home. Call it an early night. Nora had her sister, she didn't need him.

But he couldn't stop himself from searching them out. From searching Nora out.

They stood near the old tugboat wheel leaning against the wall. At the table next to them, three women he recognized from high school chatted amongst themselves, ignoring the sisters. He wondered if they were the reason Tori was there tonight.

Tori said something to Nora, her hands waving in the air before gesturing his way. Nora, her brow pinched, her mouth a serious line, nodded as if hooked by every word her sister said. But then she glanced his way and sent him a small, conspiratorial grin.

And his heart about stopped.

He rubbed his hand over the ache in his chest. She had a way of hitting a guy right between the eyes.

If there was one thing he knew other than how to fix cars, it was when someone was trouble. And Nora Sullivan with her warm smile, biting wit and ethereal beauty was nothing but. Thank God he'd given up trouble a long time ago.

Tori kept yakking and Nora's expression changed. Hardened. Hands on her hips, she laid into her sister like she was a Sunday schoolteacher and Tori had just uttered blasphemy. Her cheeks were flushed, her eyes blazing, her breasts rising and falling rapidly.

She was magnificent.

He needed to get the hell out of there before he started thinking unholy thoughts about a certain angel.

He finished his beer and got to his feet, refused to look back at the Sullivans as he walked past the bar. Before he could reach the door, though, it opened.

The man on the other side grinned. "Hello, son."

CHAPTER EIGHT

GRIFFIN'S BLOOD TURNED TO ICE, everything inside of him going brittle and tense, as if with the slightest touch he'd shatter, pieces shooting everywhere. The noise of the bar, the voices, the music, it all faded until the only sound he heard was his own pulse drumming in his ears. After all these years he and his father were face-to-face again.

Son of a bitch.

"What's the matter?" Dale asked, rocking back on his heels. "Nothing to say to your old man? No 'Hey, Dad'? Or 'Good to see you'?"

Griffin's hands curled. His muscles tensed. Dale looked the same, so much like he had all those years ago, it was as if they'd stepped back in time. His dark hair was threaded with gray and there were signs of age on his face and around his eyes and mouth, but his body was toned. Fit. He'd always prided himself on his looks, on the attention he got for them. Had worked hard to keep in shape, to make sure he was stronger than anyone else.

The past washed over Griffin, made him feel like the skinny, powerless kid he'd been. Trapped. Angry. Scared.

Goddamn it.

"Come on, now, boy," Dale said, all jovial charm when he wanted something. Except Griffin remembered how quickly that charm could change to fury. "Buy me a drink and we'll catch up. Do that whole father/son bonding thing." When Griffin remained silent, Dale's eyes narrowed slightly. "Or you could spot me a few bucks. We'll call it payback for all those years I took care of you."

If that didn't prove his father hadn't changed, nothing would. Dale always looked for the easy way out, the easy money. He'd always looked out for himself.

"No? Well, then, I guess I could always pay another visit to your mother." Dale's silky tone somehow gave his threat more impact. "She wasn't very reasonable when I talked to her the other day, but I'm sure I could persuade her to coming around to my way of thinking."

Griffin's chest tightened. His body shook as fury, hot and potent, raced through him. He wanted to shove Dale against the bar, press his elbow into his old man's throat and choke the life out of him. He could do it, Griffin realized. He could take on Dale and he could win. After all these years, he could finally protect his mother.

But Griffin had spent too many years solving his problems with violence, lashing out instead of walking away. He'd spent too many years acting like his father.

This time, he'd do the right thing.

Unable to look at Dale another second, to trust himself not to undo all his good intentions, Griffin brushed past his father.

"Don't you walk away from me, boy," Dale said, all false congeniality and humor gone. He seized Griffin's shoulder and whirled him around, curled his fingers into Griffin's shirt and shook him once, his face close enough that Griffin could smell the alcohol already on Dale's breath. See the rage in his eyes. "You think you're better than me because you run some dive garage? You always thought you were special, but look at you. You've always been worthless and you always will be."

Griffin knocked Dale's hand away, causing his old man to stumble back a step.

"Don't you ever talk to him like that."

Oh, shit. He turned as Nora, in all her huffed up glory, stalked toward them, her hair flying as she wound her way past tables of avid spectators. He'd been so focused on Dale, he hadn't realized so many people were watching them. That Nora had moved closer, close enough to overhear his father.

Standing off to the side, Tori watched her sister worriedly, her cell phone pressed to her ear.

Nora surged up to them as if riding a wave of scorn. Faced his father. "Griffin's twice the man you'll ever be."

Dale smiled, slow and easy, and slid his gaze over her, from the top of her hair to the tips of her toes. "You want to see what a real man's like, baby girl?" he asked in a slick tone that made Griffin's stomach cramp. He winked. "You come and see me."

"You bast—"

"Nora," Griffin said quietly.

She turned to him, her hair fanning out around her face, color staining her cheeks, her eyes flashing. She was like some bright, shining light, his very own avenging angel. She was beautiful.

Beautiful and fierce and smart and way too good to be coming to the rescue of the likes of someone like him.

"Leave it alone," he told her, holding her gaze. "It's not worth it."

He wasn't worth it.

"Come on," Tori said, taking a hold of Nora's arm. She watched Dale warily. "Let's get out of here."

"You have the look of your mother, don't you?" he asked Tori in an appreciative murmur as he blocked their escape, trapping her between him and a table. "I wonder if you do anything else like Val."

Both women blanched but Nora recovered first. "We're leaving," she told him. "Move."

"What's your hurry? Let me buy you two lovely ladies a drink. We can get to know each other."

Nora lifted her chin. "Go to hell." But her voice shook. Worse, under all that righteous anger, she looked scared.

His stomach churned. He wanted to yank her away from his father, wrap her in his arms and whisk her away. Keep her safe. Mostly he wanted to unleash a world of hurt on Dale. Knock his teeth down his throat.

He didn't move. He didn't look out for anyone other than himself. Not anymore. He didn't lose control. Wouldn't stoop to his old man's level. He couldn't. He was afraid that if he did, it would prove what everyone already believed, what he had always fears.

That he really was just like his father.

"You're way too pretty to be acting so ugly," Dale told Nora.

Then he reached out and trailed his fingers down her cheek.

NORA SHRANK BACK, her skin crawled. Time seemed to slow. She heard her own heavy breathing, felt the coldness of Dale's fingers on her cheek. Then the seconds sped up and her revulsion morphed into sudden, blinding fury. How dare he touch her?

Jerking back, she raised her arm to slap his hand

away. And was pushed aside when Griffin, with a low, vicious growl, leaped forward and punched Dale in the face.

Dale twisted away at the last second, probably saving himself a broken nose. Griffin's fist connected with Dale's cheek and he stumbled. Shook his head. And when he lifted his face, his grin promised retribution, brutality and a certain amount of glee at the possibility of the first two.

"Whoa," Tori said, snatching Nora by the back of her shirt when she moved to jump into the fray. "What do you think you're doing?"

"He needs me," she said, unable to take her eyes off the men. Dale smashed his fist into Griffin's face. She cringed.

"Don't even think about it," Tori warned harshly, wrapping the fabric of Nora's shirt around her fist. "You could get hurt."

"He's getting hurt," she cried, biting her lower lip as Dale landed another punch, this one to Griffin's midsection.

He was getting hurt because of her. For her.

"He should've thought of that before he started a fight." Tori tugged her to the side as a jostling, shouting crowd gathered around the grappling men.

Nora wanted to argue. Wanted to rail at her sister but she couldn't do anything but watch as Dale and Griffin tried to kill each other with their bare hands. Despite the age difference, they were evenly matched. Too evenly matched to Nora's way of thinking.

Punches were thrown, connected with flesh and bone. Grunts and swear words and the scent of blood filled the air. Men yelled encouragement, women screeched or hurried out the door. Sarah rushed out from behind the bar, a baseball bat in her hand, watched the battle as if waiting for the right time to get in there and start swinging.

Nora's palms grew damp, her head light. This wasn't anything like the fights she'd seen in movies and on TV. There were no witty one-liners, no acrobatics. It was dirty and physical and scarier than she would have ever imagined. Violent and all too real. She wanted to cover her ears, to turn away, but she couldn't. She forced herself to watch, her breath catching at every blow that landed on Griffin, her knees trembling.

Someone shoved their way through the crowd and Nora caught the familiar sight of a dark blue uniform.

Thank God, the cops were there.

And then Layne stepped into view, her gaze somehow zeroing in on her and Tori. Though it was the briefest of glances, Nora could easily read her sister's mind. It said: *you two are so going to feel the tip of my boot on your asses when I'm done here.*

"Let's get some lights on," Layne barked at Sarah as she and Officer Evan Campbell approached the fighters.

"You two," Layne yelled, "break it up."

When Layne's demand was met with Griffin landing a right jab to his father's chin, Evan attempted to subdue Dale by capturing his arms behind him. Dale responded with an elbow to the side of the younger officer's head, knocking him to the ground.

"Why isn't Layne doing something?" Nora asked worriedly. Great, she'd been reduced to the role of hysterical woman spectator. Soon she'd be wringing her hands and tearing out her hair.

"What do you suggest?" Tori asked, looking as calm as you please. As if this wasn't the first time men had

come to fisticuffs in her presence. Then again, it probably wasn't. "Take out her gun and shoot one of them?"

Nora glanced around frantically for a weapon—a
chair she could lift and swing or a bottle of wine—anything to stop the fight. To help Griffin.

Spying what she needed on the next table, she lunged
for it.

"That's our beer," one of the guys standing on a chair
watching the fight said as she picked up the pitcher.

"Next round is on me," she promised.

Then she whirled around and tossed the contents of
the pitcher at the fighters.

Too bad she did it as Layne joined the fray.

"You have got to be kidding me," Layne roared, holding her hands away from her beer soaked uniform top
as the men continued to fight.

Nora swung the empty pitcher behind her back. "I
was just trying to help."

"Well, don't." Layne reached for Dale but he roared
like a bear, throwing his hands up, knocking Layne
back two steps. "Damn it," she snapped, her hand going
to her gun belt. "Don't make me use this."

Dale lowered his head and barreled toward Layne.
Griffin, bloodied and bruised and dripping with beer,
stepped in front of her to intercept him.

Layne shoved Griffin aside, whipped out her Taser
and electrified Dale's ass.

He jerked. Convulsed. Then his eyes rolled back and
his knees gave way. He slumped to the floor, his body
seizing, his mouth hanging open.

"I have got to get one of those things," Tori said in
such awe, Nora couldn't tell if she was kidding or not.

Griffin, hair wet and clinging to the side of his neck,
beer dripping down the harsh lines of his face, swayed

then steadied himself by holding on to the back of a chair. His left eye was already turning an interesting shade of purple, the side of his lip was cut and he had a nasty gash on his forehead. He gingerly touched his fingertips to the laceration above his eye and flinched.

Wiping blood from his mouth with the back of his hand, he looked at Tori, then Layne, then Nora.

"God save me from the Sullivan women," he muttered.

GRIFFIN STEPPED OUT into the cool, misting rain. Tipped his face up to it, ignoring the sting as it hit his cuts.

"Is that really necessary?" Nora asked.

Layne, her fingers digging into Griffin's forearm, strode across the parking lot, dragging him with her. "Just following protocol."

"At least uncuff him," Nora said, scurrying after them as fast as her heels and those tight jeans would let her.

"Sorry," Layne said, sounding as if she really meant it. "But no can do." She opened the back of her patrol car. "I'm sure you remember the drill," she continued, "but watch your head. It's easier if you sit then swing your legs in."

Griffin sighed. The cut on his lip stung like a son of a bitch, his knuckles ached, his shoulders were stiff from his hands being cuffed behind his back. And now, he was about to ride in the back of a patrol car for the first time in almost fifteen years.

Sometimes life sucked.

Nothing new there, he thought, taking a seat.

Despite the rain and the fact that he and his old man were now confined to separate vehicles, most of the bar's patrons had gathered outside. The lights on the cop cars flashed, bouncing color against the aged siding of the bar. His father's rants about suing the Mystic Point Police Department for unlawful use of force rang in the night air.

"This is a travesty of justice," Nora insisted, looking all indignant and stubborn, her mouth set, her hair—that damn flowing hair—glistening with raindrops. "He needs medical treatment and you're treating him like a common criminal."

Layne kept the door open. He expected her to say he was a common criminal—like dear old dad—but she was playing this one pretty much by-the-book. Probably didn't want to give him any means to have the charges against him thrown out before she got him to the jail for processing.

"From all witness accounts, Griffin started the fight," she said, her tone reasonable and rational. The opposite of her emotionally charged younger sister. "What should I do? Give him a gold star?"

"He did not start that fight," Nora said. He half expected her to add a good foot stomp for effect. "Okay, yes, he started it, but Dale antagonized him."

He fidgeted. Felt like an idiot. Because his father hadn't goaded him into that fight. He could've walked away at any time without regrets. *Would* have walked way.

If Dale hadn't touched Nora.

"Unfortunately we can't go around punching everyone who aggravates us," Layne said, her stance one of confident law enforcer, her long legs braced, her hands loose at her sides. Rain dotted her uniform. Not that she could get much wetter, not after having a pitcher of beer tossed on her. They both smelled like a brewery and his shirt was sticking to his skin.

"Look," she continued, "he admitted he threw the first punch. Plus, there's a lot of damage to the bar, someone has to be held responsible for it."

"That's what I'm trying to tell you. Dale should be responsible."

"He will be. He'll be charged with resisting arrest and disorderly conduct."

Nora edged closer to her sister. "Can't you pull some strings and make this all go away? Please. For me?"

She was pleading with her sister. Proud, arrogant, justice first and foremost, Nora Sullivan was begging. For him.

"Sorry," Layne said quietly, "but you know I can't do that. Mr. York is coming with me."

"Mr. York would love it if you two weren't standing there discussing him," he said harshly, hating that Nora had set aside her principles, that she'd lower herself to ask her sister for such a huge favor for his sake. "Could we go, Officer Sullivan?"

"It's Assistant Chief Sullivan," she said through barely moving lips. "Why the rush? In a hurry to get to jail?"

"In a hurry to get this whole shitty night over with," he clarified.

Nora crossed her arms. "The least you could do is let him get medical treatment."

"We'll have someone check him out at the station."

"He doesn't look so bad to me," Tori said as she joined them in a hip-swaying walk that had half the men's tongues hanging out. She tipped her head to the side and studied him, then patted his shoulder once. "Don't worry, you're still all sorts of pretty and the ladies—and I use that term loosely—will fall all over themselves wanting to ease your aches and pains."

"Shut it, Tori," Nora snapped as she held her phone up to his face. She pressed a button and the flash went off.

Rearing back, he frowned, figured it looked damn intimidating given his current circumstances. "If that shows up on Facebook, I'm suing your ass for invasion of privacy."

She seemed taken aback. "You're on Facebook?"

"No. But it still better not end up there."

"I wanted to get a picture of your injuries," she said, checking the screen on her phone. Obviously satisfied, she tucked it into the front pocket of her jeans. "But at least it's good to see you didn't get that witty sense of humor beat out of you," she said with a shaky smile that broke his heart.

"I didn't get anything beat out of me," he said, each painful breath reminding him he was a liar. "I took it easy on the old man." Had been afraid if he'd let loose, he would've killed Dale.

He'd faced down Dale, and he while he wouldn't say he won the battle, for the first time in his life, he'd held his own against his father.

"If you'd taken it any easier," Tori put in helpfully, "you'd be in the hospital right now."

"Tori," Layne and Nora both said, their tones holding a warning.

She flipped her hair back. "I'm just saying what we're all thinking."

"What did we tell you about thinking?" Layne said.

Tori's eyes hardened but she batted her eyelashes. "Bite me."

"I'm in hell," Griffin murmured, shutting his eyes and leaning his head against the back of the seat. Every breath was painful; every word he spoke caused the cut on his mouth to reopen. Opening his eyes he glanced at the Sullivan sisters. "And you three are Satan's little helpers."

Tori's lips twitched but Layne shot him a professional cop glare, all dead-eyed and pissed-off. "You do remember the part about remaining silent, right?"

Nora ducked her head back into the car, blocking his view of her sisters. "Don't say anything to anyone. I'll meet you at the police station."

He struggled to a more upright position. "Wait… what?"

"Let me handle it," she said, patting his shoulder much the same way her sister had done.

His mind was fuzzy. He blamed her. Her and her fresh scent that seemed to wrap around him, egg him on to breathe it in. Breathe her in. Finally her meaning dawned on him. "You're not acting as my attorney."

"I know I'm not *acting* as it. I *am* your attorney."

"I didn't hire you." *I don't want you.*

Didn't want her involved in this mess. He cleaned up after himself.

She straightened, set her hands on her hips. "This isn't the time to be all stubborn and stoic and badass. In case you haven't noticed, you're handcuffed in the back of a police car. And you're not a kid anymore. These charges are more serious. You need an attorney and I'm here."

He scowled but it had no effect on her. "No."

"He's right," Layne said. "Let him call a lawyer once he gets to the station. You're a witness to the event in question anyway. And it's probably best if no other members of our family are involved—all things considered."

"Doesn't matter." Nora tossed her hair back reminding him of how Tori had done the same thing when she'd walked into the bar. "I'm not leaving him to face this alone."

"Yes," Layne said, edging closer to Nora. "You are."

"Ladies," he said, shutting his eyes. Damn, but his old man had hands like bricks. "No need to argue. There's enough of me to go around for both of you."

"We'll try to contain ourselves," Layne assured him before taking a hold of Nora's arm and pulling her aside. Not far enough as he clearly heard her say, "We *will* be having a nice, long discussion about this later."

"I can hardly wait," Nora said, not sounding the least bit intimidated, though he didn't doubt that was Layne's intention.

"Hey." Someone nudged his shoulder. Hard. "Did you faint?"

He pried his eyes open—well, one eye as the other was starting to swell shut. Through blurred vision, he made out Tori crouched by the car. "I couldn't be lucky enough to pass out."

Glancing behind her, she laid her hands on the edge of the seat and slanted toward him. Lowered her voice. "Thanks. For playing knight in shining armor in there."

He grinned then hissed out a breath when his lip split open ruining the effect he was going for. "That the best way you can think of to show your gratitude?"

Instead of getting offended as he expected, she studied him, her eyes shrewd. "Yeah, that's the best I can do. Especially when you and I both know the real reason you got your face pounded on. Who you were protecting in there."

He could deny it, but as he'd told Nora once, he'd never been much of a liar. Instead he shut his eyes. He felt Tori move away and then the door was closed. Layne got in, started the car and pulled away.

He kept his eyes shut. Didn't have to open them and look back to know Nora stood in the parking lot watching him get hauled off to jail like some lowlife. Like the kid he'd been long ago.

Like the man he'd always feared he'd turn into.

"Don't I rate the siren?" He couldn't stop himself from asking, though the thought of it blaring amped up his headache a notch.

"Only dangerous criminals get the full treatment, not idiots who get into bar fights," Layne said, taking a corner so fast, he slid into the door. "And the next time it happens, do yourself a favor and don't try to get between a police officer and one of the suspects."

Because she knew damn well he'd done that to protect her from Dale, he kept his tone mild when he said, "You're welcome, Officer Sullivan. Always pleased to assist Mystic Point's finest any way I can."

There wouldn't be a next time.

Being a knight in shining armor brought up way too many emotions he'd rather not deal with. Too many insecurities and fears and memories better left buried.

Plus, it hurt like hell.

"ARE YOU GOING through some late-stage teenage rebellion?" Tori asked as both squad cars' taillights disappeared around the corner. "Because I always told Layne she had it too easy with you. It wasn't normal for you to never get into trouble as a kid."

Nora dug into her purse for her keys. Where were they? "What are you talking about?"

"I'm talking about you and how I walked into a bar and saw you sitting there."

"It's a bar," Nora said, her fingers touching the cool, rough edge of her keys, "not a den of inequity. And in case you were wondering, it's not the first one I've been to. I mean, I did go to college."

"Yes, but you didn't go to bars like the Yacht Pub," Tori said, hot on Nora's heels as she made her way toward her car.

"You were there."

"Because Jenn wanted to see if her ex was there with his new girlfriend."

Nora pressed the unlock button on her keys. Her headlights blinked. "Jenn needs therapy. Or a restraining order against her for stalking."

"No argument there." Tori jumped in front of her, blocking the driver's side door. "But the point is I was there to support a friend while you were there with Griffin York."

Nora shook her keys. "I wasn't with Griffin. I was there. He was there. And we sat near each other."

Although that wasn't technically true. Griffin had come over to her. Had left the sexy redhead to talk to her.

Angel, I have a feeling being with you is going to be way more interesting.

He'd meant because of the drama of her sister showing up and finding her there. But her stomach had flipped at his words. At the look in his eyes. As if he wanted to spend time with her.

As if he wanted…her.

She was female enough to admit having that kind of attention from a man like Griffin, someone so darkly beautiful and sexy and intriguing was…well…it was flattering. Intoxicating.

Dangerous.

"It's been a rough time," Tori said, her expression softening, "what with the truth coming out about what happened to Mom. But that's no reason for you to act out—"

"Act out? What am I? Twelve?"

Tori waved her hands in the air as if wiping away Nora's words. "You were always such a good kid, so easygoing, so well behaved. You never rebelled as a teenager, never broke the rules or tested the boundaries." She grabbed Nora's hand. "It's only normal for you to be acting this way."

Nora narrowed her eyes. "Acting what way?" she asked slowly.

"Reckless. You've always been a bit rash, leaping first and asking questions later, but you've never been reckless before." She squeezed her hand. "Sweetie, this isn't like you."

Nora tugged free. "First of all," she said, surprised her voice was so even, so controlled when she felt as if she should have steam coming from her ears, "I'm not acting any way. I wanted to come to this bar so I did. As a single, responsible adult, I can do stuff like that. Or maybe you think the next time I want to leave the house to go somewhere other than work or a family function, I should call and ask your permission first?"

"That's not what I meant."

"Isn't it? You and Layne both still see me as an eight-year-old but I'm not. I'm a big girl now and can make my own decisions. And for you to insinuate otherwise is both condescending and insulting."

"We just don't want you to get hurt," Tori said as if that was enough reason, a good enough excuse to coddle her and treat her like a brainless idiot.

"My God, do you think I've lived in a bubble all

my life? Do you honestly think I've somehow skipped through life totally unscathed?" Her heart raced, her skin felt hot despite the cool rain. "Our mother cheated on our father. I spent most of my life thinking she didn't want us. I've been hurt before, Tori. I can handle it."

"Maybe you can. But do you really think you're capable of handling someone like Griffin? You saw him in there…you saw what he's capable of. He's as bad as his father."

Trembling with contained fury, Nora stepped forward. "What I saw was a man sticking up for me. Or would you prefer he stood there while Dale continued to try to intimidate us?"

"I'm not saying he didn't have good reason to step in—or that I'm not grateful he did, because I am. But you have to admit, there were other ways he could've handled the situation instead of throwing punches."

"Maybe, but that's not how it happened. And I'm certainly not going to hold his lapse in judgment against him when he has every good reason for wanting to lash out at the man who abused him and his mother. But that's not what you're holding against him, is it? You don't like him because he's Dale York's son."

"No, I don't like that he's the son of our mother's murderer. But more than that, I don't trust him. He obviously has issues—major ones—because of his past. You saw the look on his face during that fight. He was out of control, like a man possessed by his anger."

She shook her head even as the memory of the fight ran through her mind. Even as she wondered if her sister was right.

"Even if he wasn't Dale's son," Tori continued, "even if he wasn't unstable—"

"Oh, for the love of—"

"Even if he was some guy off the street with no problems and no links to our past, I wouldn't want him for you. He's a heartbreaker, honey. He'll use you up and then toss you aside when he gets tired of you and he won't care if you get hurt as long as he gets what he wants first."

"It's not like that between us—"

"Are you kidding or just blind? I saw how he looked at you. How he watched you."

Nora's scalp prickled. She felt breathless as if she'd run around the bar a dozen times. "Whatever happens, or doesn't happen, between me and Griffin is no one's business but ours. And now I'd like to go down to the police station and see if there's any way I can help him."

Tori's mouth thinned but she moved—grudgingly. But she held the door open as Nora got behind the wheel. "I don't want you to do something you're going to regret."

Nora jammed the key into the ignition, cranked it on. "You were right about me being a well-behaved kid. I like playing by the rules—"

"When it suits you."

She nodded once. "When it suits me. And while that may have made for drama-free teenage years, I'm not regressing into some wild child or reliving that childhood. But I'm starting to think that I've played it safe for far too long." She looked up and met her sister's eyes. "Maybe it's time to gather a few regrets."

CHAPTER NINE

HE'D BEEN RIGHT when he'd told the Sullivans he was in hell. And it didn't look as if he'd be getting out any time soon.

At least they'd taken the cuffs off him.

Uncuffed him, fingerprinted him, searched him for weapons, took his mug shot and were now tossing his ass in a holding cell. Things sure were looking rosy.

"Captain Sullivan's trying to find a judge to preside over your arraignment hearing tonight," the young cop who'd been elbowed by Dale said as he opened a cell door and motioned Griffin inside. "So don't bother getting comfortable because I doubt you'll be here long. Between us," he added conspiratorially, "I think she feels bad about having to bring you in."

"Great," Griffin said as the bars closed, locking him in the small cell. "Knowing I have Layne Sullivan's sympathy makes it all worth it."

The kid sent him a pitying look before walking away. Griffin leaned against the bars. His eye throbbed, his lip stung, his knuckles ached and now some snot-nosed cop felt bad for him.

The night wasn't over yet. In Griffin's experience that meant things were about to get worse. Somehow, someway. They always did.

Warily he eyed the lumpy cot against the far wall. He could catch a few hours of sleep, pretend he wasn't spending those hours as a guest at the local cop shop. Except every time he closed his eyes, he saw his dad touching Nora's cheek. Remembered how repulsed she'd looked. How scared.

In that moment, the past had risen up and swallowed him, taking him back to when he'd been a scared, helpless kid. He couldn't count the times he'd witnessed his father cornering his mother, putting fear into her eyes. How many times Dale had grabbed her, shook her, leaving his mark on her arms, her wrists. Pushed her, knocking her to the floor. Hit her, vicious, openpalmed slaps that left red welts. Punches that bruised her delicate skin. Kicks that broke bones. And though Griffin hadn't been big enough, strong enough, he'd done his best to help her. To save her.

He'd ended up as bruised as broken as she'd been.

His hands trembled, his stomach churned. He breathed through his mouth until the nausea passed. A reaction from adrenaline letdown, he assured himself. Nothing more. The past was over. He wouldn't let it affect him now.

He didn't regret stepping in at the bar but he couldn't afford to let things get any more mixed up. Couldn't let his emotions get tangled up inside of him. There had to be a clear line between the past and present.

He only wished he could put one firmly between who he was and who he'd come from.

The door down the hallway creaked followed by the unmistakable sound of high heels clicking against the floor. Griffin bristled, holding his breath. He slowly lifted his head, like an animal with the scent of something dangerous in its path.

She was here. Nora.

Damn it.

"Are you okay?" she asked as she reached him. The young cop who'd been trailing her stopped two cells down.

Nora's hair had dried and was all poofy, her makeup smudged, her shirt wrinkled and dotted with water spots. Still, she looked ready to kick some serious ass, to do whatever it took to right every wrong ever done.

She was seeing him behind bars, locked in a cage like some animal. Like someone who couldn't control himself. Someone like his old man.

He gripped the bars until his raw knuckles cracked and started bleeding again.

"What are you doing here?" he asked, more harshly than he'd intended but damn it, she shouldn't be here. Shouldn't be at the police station in the middle of the night worried about him or trying to save him.

"Where else would I be?" she asked, as if his question made no sense to someone of her superior intelligence. "They're charging you with Simple Assault though I tried to get them to reduce it to—"

"I don't want you here." Hadn't he already told her not to come? "Go away. Leave me alone."

She crossed her arms, her expression setting into stubborn lines. "I'm not leaving until you do."

"You're a smart girl," he said, and as he'd predicted, her lips flattened at his use of the word *girl*, "so you should be able to figure out when you're not wanted." He sent her a hard look. "Go save someone else, angel. I'm not interested in your help."

Stepping closer, she reached out as if to touch his fingers still wrapped around the bars. He lowered his arms. Hurt flashed in her eyes. She swallowed. "Griffin, you need me."

Because he was terrified she might be right, he

smirked. "You and that high opinion you have of yourself would like to think that, wouldn't you? But I don't. I don't need you."

He didn't need anyone.

To prove it, he went over to the cot and lay down on his side, his back to her.

The seconds ticked by. He felt her watching him, waiting for him to give in. Finally she exhaled heavily, the sound a cross between a sigh and a growl. "You can be such an ass," she said.

Her footsteps echoed as she walked away. He didn't sit up until he heard the door close.

Twenty minutes later, he'd counted the bars of the cell, the squares on the floor and the ceiling panels before the door opened again. Sitting on the cot with his back against the cold wall, both legs bent, he watched the young cop lead Dale to the holding cell across from him.

Griffin tipped his head back, hit the wall with a soft thud. He did it again. And again.

"You're not looking too good, boy," Dale called after the cop left. "Never did know how to keep your defenses up."

He stared straight ahead. His father had taught him all about defense. How to note any change, no matter how slight, in his father's behavior. How to duck one of his big fists coming at him, how to keep hidden when he went on one of his rampages.

Besides, Dale looked just as bad as Griffin did. He hoped he hurt twice as much.

"Those Sullivan women sure are something," his old man continued. "I'm not usually one to go for blondes, but that one could change my mind. Maybe once I get out of here I'll stop by. Pay the pretty little Sullivan daughter another visit."

Griffin's heart thudded heavily but before he could respond, footsteps sounded down the corridor again. A moment later, Layne reached him. Not so much as looking Dale's way, she unlocked Griffin's cell. "Your arraignment is in half an hour. It's your lucky night."

With his good eye, he looked from her to his old man to the bars on the cage. "Feels like it."

She motioned for him to turn around. When he did, she pulled his arms back and cuffed his hands again. "Let's go."

Griffin followed her for two steps but he couldn't do it. He couldn't walk away. Not when Dale was smirking at him, thinking he'd gotten the last word. That he still had a hold over him.

"Not a good idea," Layne murmured when Griffin walked over to his father's cell. But she didn't Taser him so he figured he had at least a minute to get his point across.

There, with the bars between them, Griffin met his father's eyes. "If you so much as think about going after my mother or Nora," he said, keeping his voice low, his gaze steady, "I will personally make sure you regret it."

"You might want to be careful how to talk to me," Dale said, his nose swollen, his face bruised. "I'm not going to be behind these bars forever."

"We can go again anytime you want, but you leave my family alone." Griffin stepped closer, close enough to see the unease in the old man's eyes, the uncertainty. And the growing anger. "As you noticed, I'm not a skinny kid anymore. And if you ever forget that, I'll be happy to remind you. Dad."

Dale's mouth twisted in his red face. "This isn't over, boy."

"Maybe not. But if you so much as breathe the same air as Mom or Nora, I will come after you and I won't hold back. Not again. I will end this. I'll end *you*."

"Time to go, York," Layne called. "Unless you'd rather spend the rest of your night here?"

He crossed to her. "What?" he growled when she kept shooting him glances.

"Just wondering what that was all about back there."

"Father/son chat."

"Uh-huh." At the locked metal door she stopped. "Am I going to have to rethink my opinion of you?"

"I wish you wouldn't," he said sincerely.

"Be that as it may," she said, unlocking the door and holding it open for him, "I'm starting to wonder if maybe you're not quite the asshole I always thought you were."

"Give it a few minutes." He brushed past her into the brightly lit hallway leading to the interior of the police station—and his freedom. "I'm sure your opinion of me will go back to normal."

SITTING IN HER car in the dark, Nora shivered. She turned up the heat, held her hands in front of the warm air blasting from the vents. She was cold. Damp. Tired.

And seriously pissed off at Griffin. More than that, worse than that, she was hurt.

God, how pathetic was that to admit? But there it was. She'd gone out on a limb for him, had argued with her sister over him and he'd pushed her away. Not that it had stopped her from representing him at his arraignment, but he hadn't looked at her the whole time, hadn't spoken to her. Hadn't thanked her.

Her fingers curled into her palms as she spotted him coming out of the local magistrate's office, his shoulders hunched against the rain, his head down. He looked like a loner. Solitary. A man with no one to count on, no one to turn to.

I don't want you here.

She straightened and flipped on her headlights, causing him to lift his head. She shifted the car into Drive. He may not want her help but he did need her. Whether he knew it or not.

Pulling to a stop beside him, she unlocked the door and rolled down the passenger side window. "Get in."

He hesitated, the action so slight, she might have missed it if she hadn't been watching carefully, then he stepped forward. "You don't give up easily, do you?" he asked, ducking his head to see inside the car.

"It's one of my more endearing traits." He opened his mouth and she held up a hand. "Why don't we just save the whole argument portion of this conversation? Either I give you a ride or you walk. In the rain."

She thought he'd refuse. Figured he'd let that damn stubborn streak of his push him into telling her he'd rather walk, five miles in the rain, instead of accepting help from her.

"When you put it like that," he said, opening the door, "how can I refuse?"

He must be in worse shape than she'd thought. Or he'd realized it was futile to argue with her. What she wouldn't give for her sisters to learn that lesson.

"Rockland Avenue, right?" she asked as he reclined the seat.

"My bike's at the bar."

"You're in no shape to drive a motorcycle. I'm taking you home."

Leaning his head back he shrugged and shut his eyes making it more than clear he didn't want to have any sort of conversation.

She pressed her lips together until they turned numb. Rude, ungrateful man.

She pulled out of the parking lot. Kept her gaze straight ahead. The windshield wipers swished softly, the rain pattered against the car. Underneath those sounds she heard the gentle exhalation of his breathing. After a mile, that breathing turned even, deepened, and she couldn't fight the urge to glance at him.

All she could make out was his silhouette, the strong line of his jaw, the outline of his broad shoulders and that dense, tousled hair. With every inhalation she breathed in his scent, all musky and pure male. Elemental. Enticing.

She slowed and crawled along Rockland Avenue, squinting at the dark houses until she finally spotted the one she was looking for. She pulled into the driveway and turned off the car.

Griffin stirred and sat up. "How'd you know which house was mine?" he asked, his voice gruff and suspicious.

She unbuckled and took her keys out. "I've taken up stalking you. Didn't you get that decapitated bunny I left on your front porch last night?" When he just stared at her she rolled her eyes. "I saw the tow truck," she said, nodding toward the truck parked in front of a two-stall garage, "and figured it out. I'm not just a pretty face, you know."

"The only thing more amazing than your skills of observation is your sense of humility."

"It has nothing to do with being humble," she said briskly despite her face warming. "It's honest. I'm

smart. I'm pretty. I also can't hold a note, have no sense
of rhythm and have very little aptitude for mechanical
things. I can barely run my microwave without an idiot's guide. It all balances out in the end."

While he seemed stunned silent by that bit of logic,
she got out of the car and hurried around to his side. She
opened the door and offered him her hand. He frowned
at it then, holding his right side, his other hand gripping the door for support, stood. His mouth thinned,
his face went white.

She stepped forward.

"I've got it," he growled.

Had she mentioned how stubborn he was?

She slammed the door shut, followed him up the
short walk. His steps were measured, careful, as if it
hurt to move. His house was dark, the shades drawn.
Other than the truck and the fact that he'd left a pair
of work boots next to the steps leading to a side door,
there were few signs anyone even lived here. No sort
of welcome anywhere. He may as well have put a big
sign that read Keep Out! Visitors WILL Be Shot on
the front lawn.

He slowly climbed the three steps, swaying when he
reached the top. She reached out to steady him but he
leaned forward, his shoulder hitting the wooden door
with a solid thump. Resting the back of his head against
the side of his house, he dug a key out of his front pocket
then, without lifting his head, turned toward the door.

She stood on her toes and peered over his shoulder
but couldn't see why it took him so long to open the
door. "I hope you have a first aid kit," she said, frowning. "Maybe we should have picked one up at the con-
venience store."

"I have what I need," he said over the soft click of

the lock turning. He opened the door and glanced at her. "And you're not coming in."

"Sure I am." To make it easier on both of them, she slipped past him to the center of the small kitchen, stopping by a round table. "Now, let's get you cleaned up and into your jammies."

He looked at her, then behind him, then at her again. "Anyone ever tell you you're a pain in the ass?"

"I have two older sisters. It was practically my nickname growing up." The room was too dark for her to get more than a vague impression of counters and appliances, the digital clock of his microwave glowing. She glanced behind her, saw a hallway.

Hoping her vision would soon become accustomed to the darkness, she felt her way out of the kitchen, heard him heave a sigh of frustration—or maybe resignation—behind her.

She came to what she assumed was the living room—at least she thought that huge lump was a sofa. Backtracking down the hall, she trailed her hands along the wall as she went. She opened a door on the right only to discover a coat closet. The next door was open. Stepping inside, she felt around until she found the light switch. Flipped it on to find a workout room, complete with free weights, a bench, treadmill and large, flat-screen TV hanging against the far wall.

"What the hell are you doing?"

She jumped and spun around with a squeak. She'd been so immersed in her search she hadn't realized he was right behind her. "Don't sneak up on me like that," she said, covering her racing heart with her hand.

"Sneak up on you? Lady, you're snooping around my house."

"I'm not snooping," she said, sounding prim and dismissive but really, he didn't have to make it seem as if she'd been rifling through his underwear drawer. "I'm looking for the bathroom."

She marched across the hall and flipped on the light in another room. Finally.

"Well?" she asked, sticking her head back into the hallway when he just stood there. He slouched against the wall all sexy and disheveled and brooding and dangerous. Good Lord, even with the cut lip and the black eye he was massively, potently sexy.

She set her hand on her cocked hip. "You want to get rid of me? Let me help you then I'll go on my merry way."

"How 'bout we skip the first part and get right to the second?"

"I can't just leave you here in the shape you're in. That'd be like...like...abandoning an injured puppy by the side of the road."

"A puppy?" he muttered, hanging his head. "Jesus."

"Would you please just come in here and let me help you?" she asked, searching his medicine cabinet.

He straightened and walked toward her, his gaze hooded, the uninjured side of his mouth curled up. "You going to tuck me into bed when you're through?" he asked, his voice husky and inviting as he drew close, so close she could see the pain lingering in his eyes, see how his mouth tightened with it.

Even when he was hurting, he kept it hidden. Maybe especially when he was hurting.

"Yes," she said dryly. "I find bloodied, bruised men irresistible. Take me, Viking God."

"Viking God?"

"Just a little fantasy I have going with the actor who played Thor." She set a bottle of pain reliever on the vanity next to the sink, considered the hydrogen peroxide but then dismissed it before pulling out a box of bandages. "Washcloths and clean towels?"

He came into the room far enough to open the door below the sink. She crouched, surprised to find folded piles of washcloths, hand towels and bath towels all lined up neat rows. Grabbing what she needed, she straightened, shut the medicine cabinet and caught sight of her reflection in the oval mirror.

And wished she hadn't.

Okay, so she'd looked better, she thought, fighting the urge to try to smooth her frizzy hair. A lot better. Using the heel of her hand, she rubbed at the streak of mascara running from the corner of her eye to her temple and deliberately turned from the scary image.

She opened the bottle of pain relievers and shook two out into her hand before holding them out to him. "Here."

He eyed the pills, took the bottle from the sink and shook a third into her palm before picking them up, his fingertips trailing across her skin. She rubbed her tingling hand against the front of her jeans as he bent, washed the medicine down with water from the tap.

When he straightened he seemed to have edged closer to her. A drop of water clung to his swollen lower lip and he wiped it away with the back of his hand.

The bathroom was small with the toilet between the sink and a bathtub that ran the entire length of the back wall. It was cramped and sparse and masculine with its brown walls and dark woodwork.

And way too intimate with him standing so close, his razor on the sink, his toothbrush in a glass holder, the scent of his aftershave lingering.

She wet the cloth with warm water then faced him,

her heels and his position—half-sitting against the edge of the counter—making them the same height. Biting her lip, she gently pressed the washcloth against the cut below his eye. In the harsh overhead light of the bathroom, he looked even worse than before. But he didn't flinch while she cleaned the cut and then gently wiped dried blood from his swollen lip.

He didn't move at all, just stared at the wall, his breathing steady and even.

How many times had he been hurt by his father before he'd learned not to make a sound, not to show anyone that he was in pain?

She rinsed the cloth, wrung out the excess water. "I know you're upset about what happened—"

"It was a fight. I've been in plenty of them."

"That wasn't just a fight and we both know it."

A muscle worked in his jaw. "Don't go there."

"I'm just saying if you want someone to talk—"

"I don't."

Her movements jerky, she reached up, brushed the hair on his forehead back so she could press the cloth against the cut there. She'd meant to keep her touch cool. Impersonal. But the strands were thick and soft and she combed her fingers through them once, twice, as she cleaned the blood from his skin. Held his hair back while she applied antiseptic ointment.

He didn't want her comfort, her sympathy. All she could do was clean his wounds. She couldn't heal his pain, couldn't change his past or the circumstances that had brought them here. Couldn't take away his anger, the bitterness he wore like a shield.

She couldn't fix him.

SHE WAS TRYING to kill him.

Griffin's fingers ached from gripping the edge of

the counter so tightly, his breath burned in his lungs. She was pressed against him, her breasts brushing his chest, her thigh rubbing his with every move she made. She was all lush curves and sweet smelling skin and soft hands.

Her fingers, combing through his hair, trembled. Lust settled low in his stomach, tightened his groin. She lowered her gaze to his, her eyes dark, her mouth no longer that glossy red, but bare. And damn her for it being even more tempting.

Her hands slid away from his hair, his face, to trail lightly across his shoulders, down his arms. She encircled his right wrist and tugged, holding the back of his hand up to study. His knuckles were scraped raw and swollen. Bruises were already forming around the base of his fingers.

And they hurt like hell.

Nora squeezed antibiotic ointment onto her finger then dabbed it on the cuts and scrapes, her touch gentle, her head bent over her work. "For someone who makes his living with his hands, I would think you'd be more careful not to injure them."

"Life's full of dangers," he said, his breath ruffling the top of her hair. "It's a risk just getting out of bed each day."

She lifted his other hand, repeated the process of tending to him. "Yes, what rotten luck that Dale's face just happened to get in the way of your fists."

When she finished and finally let go of him to put the cap back onto the ointment, he straightened, hissing in a breath when a sharp pain shot through his side.

She frowned. "Here," she said, reaching for the bottom of his shirt, "let me see…"

He crossed his arms, pressed his lips together against

the pain. "You're taking this playing doctor thing pretty seriously."

"I've always believed if you're going to do something, you should do it all the way." When she tugged on his hem, he held firm. She blinked innocently at him, her eyes lit with humor. "It'll be okay," she said so solemnly he didn't doubt she was messing with him. "I promise to be gentle."

He slowly lowered his arms, held his breath as she lifted his shirt and slid the material up past his rib cage. Her brow furrowed, she bent her head and studied his side, trailed her fingertips lightly over the ridges of his ribs. The muscles in his stomach contracted, sweat beaded along his hairline. Each touch was torture. And salvation.

"What's the diagnosis, Dr. Feelgood?" he asked, unable to hide the gruffness of his tone, the unsteadiness of his breathing.

"I have no idea." But she continued touching him, those featherlight touches that were driving him insane; her warm breath washing over his skin. "You've got a nasty bruise but I'm not sure if any ribs are cracked or broken."

"They're not."

"How do you know?" she asked, her voice strained. Wobbly.

He narrowed his good eye. What was going on with her? "I've had cracked ribs. Broken ribs. Twice. I know what it feels like." And while his side hurt, it wasn't near the pain that came with a more serious injury.

"I'm sorry," she said, her fingers splayed against his side, her thumb pressing against his hip point.

He wanted to grab her arms, shove her away from him. Was afraid if he did, he'd yank her close instead, beg her to touch him all over. "You're sorry? What the hell for?"

"He hurt you," she whispered. "I'm so sorry he hurt you."

Griffin's blood went cold. Because he knew she wasn't talking about the fight with Dale—or at least, not tonight's fight. She was talking about all the other times his father had hit him. Worse, she sniffed and looked up at him, her hair a tangled, golden mass around her face, her eyes glimmering with unshed tears.

No. Make that *hell, no.*

He inhaled sharply, ignored the pain in his side and swallowed back the bitterness rising in his throat.

She blinked and tears spilled over.

"Those for me?" he asked softly, edging closer, his knee bumping her inner thigh. He traced the billowy sleeve of her shirt. "What else are you offering?"

She rubbed away the moisture on her face. "What do you mean?"

He stepped closer, closer still, forcing her to back up, not stopping until she bumped into the wall. But she didn't seem frightened, more…curious. "I mean you're here to take care of me, right?" Laying the flat of his hand against the wall by her head, he leaned down, grinned as much as his split lip would allow. "I know exactly what would make me feel better."

CHAPTER TEN

"REALLY?" she asked, as if he'd just said he was thinking about repainting the bathroom. He wasn't sure if he was impressed he hadn't gotten a rise out of her—or disappointed she hadn't taken his bait. "And what would that be? A pity screw?"

"Aw, angel, I don't pity you."

"I was talking about things from my perspective."

Damn, but she was something, the way she went right for the jugular. There was no bullshit with Nora, no subterfuge. He could almost admire her for it. Almost.

But laying yourself bare that way only made it that much easier for others to take advantage of you. The sooner she learned that, the better off she'd be, he assured himself.

He leaned in even more, not stopping until there was only a breadth of space between them. Still she didn't shove at him, didn't freeze…just kept her eyes steady on his.

And he wondered if he wasn't making a mistake in pushing at her. If somehow, he'd be the one to end up learning a lesson.

He couldn't stop, though. Not with her scent muddling his thoughts, the warmth of her body beckoning him. He skated his gaze over her face and let it linger on her mouth for one long moment. "Come on, now. I promise to be gentle," he said, repeating her words in a rough purr.

She smiled, her face lighting up with its warmth.

His stomach tumbled to his shoes. His willpower waned. Want, unlike anything he'd ever experienced, the kind that brought a man to his knees, that left him open and vulnerable, slapped him.

"So, let me get this straight," she said, sounding very much like they were a courtroom and he was on the stand. "I'm supposed to believe that you want to sleep with me."

He felt edgy and wound up. Exposed, as if she could see right through him. He hated it.

Easing back, he sent her a hooded look. "What's so hard to believe? You're here—"

"Wow," she said dryly, "I'm surprised you ever have sex."

"You were all over me a few minutes ago."

"Yes, I can see how my cleaning your cuts could be misconstrued as a come-on."

"Look, if you're not interested, fine," he said, backing up until he was at the sink again. "Just thought I'd put it out there." Shrugging, he picked up the tube of ointment, turned it in his hands. "Can't blame a guy for trying."

She laughed tiredly. "No, I certainly can't. But I can—and do—blame you for that lame attempt at scaring me off when you should be thanking me."

"Thanking you?" he asked, deciding the best thing would be to skip right over the first part of what she'd said. "No one asked you to play Nurse Nancy."

"I'm not talking about that...or at least...not only that. I'm talking about how I got you out of spending the night in a cold, dark jail cell."

"They have this new thing at the jail. Electricity. Oh, and central heating. Besides, from what I heard, Layne was the one who found a judge willing to hold my arraignment tonight."

"Layne spoke with the judge after I asked Uncle Ken to pull a few strings for me." She pushed away from the wall, walked toward him slowly. "I stuck my neck out for you, went against my own family for you and you've been nothing but miserable."

Because that was exactly what he hadn't wanted. Her going to bat for him, asking favors for him. "What can I say? I get a little grumpy after I get the shit kicked out of me."

"No, that's not it," she said, her expression thoughtful. "We both know you gave as good as you got with your father. Just as we know why you threw that first punch. You did it," she continued in that unflappable tone he found both annoying and appealing, "for me."

He tossed the ointment onto the counter with enough force that it slid across the slick surface and landed on the floor. "You thinking I'm some sort of hero?" he asked flatly. "For all you know I was itching for a fight, just waiting for the day when I could get back at my old man and got lucky enough to get the opportunity tonight."

After all, that was what Dale would've done. Waited for his chance at revenge. Griffin looked just like his father, why should anyone think he didn't take after him in every way?

"No, that's not what happened." She sounded so certain...as if there was no doubt in her mind she was right. "You were protecting me. And I can't help but wonder if that's what you were doing back at the jail, too."

"Maybe I just didn't want you around."

"Or maybe," she said quietly as she crossed to him, "you were worried I'd run into your father again."

"Damn it," he snarled, his stomach tied in knots as he remembered how he'd felt when she'd stood up to Dale over him at the bar. How his father had looked at her. "You shouldn't be anywhere near him. Nothing about him should ever touch you."

"Nothing? Not even you?"

He stilled. "What?"

"You've never touched me. Not even when you were doing your best to convince me you wanted to swoop me up and into your bed."

"You've been nothing but a pain in my ass since you walked into my garage, you know that?" He sent her his best go-to-hell look. She just grinned, a sly grin that put him on edge. "I'm going to bed. If you're not going to join me, I'll walk you out."

Without waiting to see if she was following him, he went into the kitchen. He didn't turn on any lights, but he heard her approaching, the sound of her heels clicking loudly against the hardwood floor. He opened the door, gripping the doorknob with enough force to rip the damn thing off. He wanted her gone, needed her out of his house. She was pushy and stubborn and too damned perceptive.

When she reached him, she stopped and laid the flat of her hand lightly on his chest. He kept his eyes straight, gazing into the shadows of his kitchen over her head. His heart raced under her fingers.

"I'm sorry," she said as she rose onto her toes, "but I really feel like this is something I have to do."

He whipped his head down to look at her, unable to see more than the flash of her eyes, feel her moving ever closer to him. He shook his head once, a quick, decisive no. A warning. A plea.

She ignored them all. "Brace yourself," she said, her breath washing over him, "this might hurt."

And she brushed her lips against the uninjured side of his mouth.

He froze, unsure of his next move, his next breath. She kissed him again, her mouth clinging to his this time, her lips soft and warm and not at all hesitant. It did hurt, but some things were worth the pain. And having Nora's lips moving slowly, gently over his was one thing he'd gladly suffer any torment for.

Her kiss was sweet and he got lost in her, in her scent, the heat of her hand, the feel of her body against his. The tip of her tongue touched the corner of his mouth. He jerked back, his breathing uneven, his thoughts muddled.

She lowered back to her heels, her eyes steady on his as if it was every day she rocked some poor sap's world. "Good night, Griffin."

And she walked out the door leaving him alone in his dark house fighting the urge to call her back.

"Dude," Tanner breathed the next day when he arrived at the garage, "what happened to your face?"

"I ran into something," Griffin said.

Yeah, something like Dale's fists. Over and over again.

"Mom is going to freak."

Griffin would've pinched the bridge of his nose except his hands and face—hell, his entire body—hurt. Not enough to give him a good enough excuse to duck out on working on Tanner's car today. Just enough to remind him, with every move, every breath, that he'd been in a brutal, knock-down, drag-'em-out barroom brawl less than twelve hours ago.

Thank God for extra strength pain meds. The four he'd taken with his coffee an hour ago were finally kicking in.

"By the time she sees me," he said, "the worst of it will be healed." All he had to do was avoid her the next week. Maybe two.

Too bad word about the fight was probably already spreading throughout town. No doubt she'd find out and contact him by the end of the day.

"Uh…did I tell you Mom and Dad are going to stop by after church today?" Tanner asked as the sound of two car doors slamming reached them.

Griffin glanced outside…saw his mother and stepfather walking toward him in their Sunday best.

Shit.

He whirled around, pretended to be busy searching the shelves along the back wall for the box of parts that had come in Thursday.

"That's your car?" Carol Johnston asked incredulously as she and her husband came into the garage. "Roger, do you see what your son bought?"

"I see it," Roger said in his slow, laconic way.

"It needs a little work." This from Tanner.

"A little?" Carol asked and Griffin could easily imagine the raised-eyebrow look she was sending her younger son. "It's in pieces."

"It won't be," Tanner said and Griffin heard the shrug in his voice. Not much flustered the kid, that was for sure.

Carol sighed. "Griffin, are you sure you're going to be able to rebuild this…thing? I don't want your brother putting in good money after bad."

Feeling like a damned coward, he faced her, didn't feel ashamed in the least at the relief he felt that she was staring at the car instead of him. "I'm sure."

"Satisfied?" Roger asked as he bent and checked under the car's frame, heedless of his dress slacks and tie.

She smiled at Tanner. "It still seems like a risky investment. But if Griffin says—" She gave a soft, horrified gasp when she saw him. "You're hurt," she cried, hurrying toward him, her long, brown skirt swishing around her legs, her sensible pumps clicking loudly on the floor. "Oh, my God, oh, honey, look at you."

He knew it was bad, worse than last night. His eye was completely black and swollen shut, his mouth puffy and sore. Bruises, cuts and abrasions marked his face. He looked like he'd fallen face-first off a three-story building.

As she fluttered around him, gently brushing his hair back, tears in her eyes, guilt settled in his stomach, mixed with anger and resentment to churn there. Damn it, he didn't want or need her coddling him, didn't want her sympathy. It reminded him too much of the past, of how she used to have to clean him up, her hands unsteady, tears streaming down her face. She hadn't protected him.

Worse, it reminded him of the times, too many times, when their roles had been reversed, when she'd been the one bruised and beaten. He'd only been a kid but he'd had to take care of her. Had tried to protect her.

And he'd hated her for it. Hated her for not protecting herself, for not doing enough to get them out of their situation. Hated himself for being so angry with her still, for not being able to forgive her.

He caught her wrists, gently lowered her hands away from him and stepped back. "I'm fine."

"You're not," she insisted, her lower lip trembling, her hands fluttering in the space between them as if she was unsure of what to do with them. "What happened?"

"I fell," he said quietly. "Isn't that what I'm supposed to say?"

She blanched, her hands dropping uselessly to her sides. He rolled his shoulders back but the tension tightening his muscles remained. Regret turned in his gut, had a lump forming in his throat.

He wanted to apologize, to take it back but he couldn't. Not when she'd conditioned him to tell his teachers and the social workers that was what had happened whenever he had a new bruise. He fell. He ran into the door. He wrecked his bicycle.

All to protect that son of a bitch she'd married.

Roger came up behind Carol and laid his hands on her shoulders. When he looked at Griffin, there was no censure in his eyes, only sympathy. Understanding.

Griffin averted his gaze.

"Are you all right?" Roger asked.

"I'll live." He flicked his mother a glance. "I've had worse."

Worse like the night his father had come to the tiny apartment he and his mother had moved into after she'd finally left Dale. He'd tried to stand up for her that night, had tried to protect her and had ended up being beaten unconscious.

But before he'd slipped into oblivion, he'd heard his mother cry, heard her begging Dale to stop. Promising him anything, everything, to leave Griffin alone. She'd been helpless.

His mother stared at the floor, looking older than she had when she'd first arrived. "I'm sorry," she whispered.

"Yeah," he said, shoving his sore hands into the front pockets of his jeans, "me, too."

It was the best he could do.

"Are you in trouble?" Roger asked. "Because of the fight," he clarified when Griffin looked at him quizzically.

Griffin narrowed his eyes. "I didn't say I got into a fight."

"Word travels," Roger said, dropping his hands from Carol's shoulders and stepping up to stand next to her. "Adam Zurich came up to me after church, told me he was at the Yacht Pub last night and that you'd gotten yourself into a little scuffle. One that required the police to break it up."

"The police?" Carol asked, her eyes widening. "What happened?"

Tanner joined his parents, stood on his mother's other side. She slid her arm around his narrow waist. They were a good-looking family, despite Roger's shiny bald spot and his mother's extra twenty pounds. Roger was tall, tanned from working on the docks and usually smiling.

Completely different from her first husband. Then again, she didn't look much like the woman who'd been married to Dale York. After the divorce, she'd cut her long, brown hair pixie short and never grew it past chin length again. She had laugh lines around her eyes, creases around her mouth from years of smoking.

Tanner was the perfect blending of his parents. His father's build and hair color, his mother's eyes and nose. It was clear they belonged together. Belonged to each other. They were a unit. A family. One Griffin had never felt a part of, despite their best efforts to include him.

He'd never cared before, but now he couldn't help but wonder if he'd missed out on something.

Carol stared at him in concern, Tanner in curiosity. Another reason to keep his distance from any sort of relationship. No one to answer to.

"The cops just wanted to talk to me," he lied, leaving out the parts concerning handcuffs, his ride in the back of the squad car and the locked cell.

Leaving out the part about who he'd fought.

Roger studied him as if seeing past all his bullshit. "Adam also mentioned the name of the man you got into the fight with."

"Adam was just full of information," Griffin grumbled. He jerked his head at his mother. "Why didn't you tell her?"

"I thought you'd want to."

This visit suddenly made sense. His stepfather had known what went down last night and wanted to give Griffin the opportunity to come clean to his mother. To tell her before she heard it through Mystic Point's grapevine.

He was giving him the chance to do the right thing.

Roger really was one of the good guys. Quiet. Hardworking. Honest and honorable and he'd been more than fair to the rebellious teen he'd gotten saddled with when he married Carol.

He was everything Griffin's own father wasn't.

"Griffin," Carol asked, "who were you fighting with?"

He shifted. His mother didn't often use that reproachful tone with him. But when she did, it made him feel about ten years old.

"Dale."

She inhaled sharply. "Dale attacked you?"

"Not this time. This time I beat him to the punch. Literally."

"This is nothing to joke about," she snapped. "My God, you know what he's like. He could've killed you."

Yes, he knew very well what his old man was like. "I handled it."

"Why would you antagonize him that way?" she continued worriedly as if he hadn't spoken. "If you ran into him at that bar you should've ignored him. Walked away." Her eyes welled. "Why didn't you just walk away?"

"Why didn't you?" he asked softly. Why had it taken her so long to leave Dale?

Her mouth wobbled but she firmed it.

Roger stepped forward, laid his hand on Carol's lower back. "Adam also said two of the Sullivan girls were there and were involved."

"You got into a fight with your father over a woman?" Carol asked, her voice rising.

"It wasn't like that. Dale got grabby with Nora Sullivan so I stepped in."

That seemed to calm her though she looked less than completely pacified. "Which one is Nora?"

"The youngest."

She glanced at Tanner, who'd gotten bored with the conversation and was kneeling by the car, then took a hold of Griffin's arm and tugged him toward the door. "Are you and this...Sullivan woman...close?"

"No."

But they had been last night. They'd been real close when she'd kissed him. He hadn't been able to stop thinking about her since.

He wanted to call her. Had even picked his phone up before realizing he didn't know her number. And that was when he'd started thinking about what could happen if he stopped by her house, found himself thinking of excuses that wouldn't make him look like a complete idiot.

Except everything he thought of only proved he *was* an idiot.

"I barely know her," he told his mother.

"Just...promise me you'll do your best to stay away from Dale."

"I'm not going to hide from him." This was his town and he'd be damned if he'd let his old man take that away from him.

She twisted her simple gold wedding band. "I'm not asking you to. Hopefully he'll get whatever he came back for and leave before too long."

"Or maybe the cops will find enough evidence to arrest him for Valerie Sullivan's murder."

She smiled sadly. "From what I understand, that doesn't look like it's going to happen. But we can always keep praying it does."

Prayers had never done him much good. He'd stick with things he could control.

"Honey?" Roger called. "You ready?"

"Yes." Roger waved and headed out to the truck while Carol stepped forward as if to hug Griffin. He stiffened and she eased back but he didn't miss the hurt in her eyes. "Do you have everything you need for...?" She gestured to his face. "I could stop by your house, bring some antibiotic cream or—"

"I'm good. Thanks."

She cleared her throat and glanced at Roger who waited patiently. "Well...goodbye."

He nodded. Made it two steps before her voice stopped him.

"You could come over for dinner tonight," she said in a rush. "Roger's making his bacon cheeseburgers on the grill."

Every week his mother invited him to Sunday dinner and most weeks he found an excuse not to go. But today she seemed so fragile, so beaten down—not physically like she'd been by Dale—but emotionally. And Griffin was partly to blame.

"You making potato salad, too?" he asked.

"Of course," she said as if that was a given, which, he supposed it was. Any time they'd had burgers when he was growing up, she'd made potato salad. "And chocolate chip cookies for dessert."

Her voice didn't change but her expression was so hopeful, her eyes wary as if she was just waiting for him to say no. Her expectations, her hopes weighed down on him. Bound him, trapped him in the past and the present and the future she so desperately wanted.

She loved him. But she wanted more from him than he could give. His time and attention.

His forgiveness.

He couldn't just say no, not when looking at her made him feel like he'd been kicked in the throat. Not when he'd hurt her, deliberately and cruelly.

He couldn't give her what she really wanted, but he could give her this.

"Well, then," he said, "how can I resist? I'll be there at five."

WEDNESDAY MORNING, a sharp knock at her open office door had Nora raising her head from a particularly boring brief she was working on. Her eyebrows slowly crept up.

"Well, this is quite a surprise," she said. Griffin slouched in her doorway in his usual uniform of jeans and T-shirt. Today's shirt was white. She tipped her head to the side. "You know if you slicked your hair back and kept a pack of cigarettes rolled up in your sleeve, you could pass for Danny Zuko in *Grease*. John Travolta version."

Although not even John could pull off the smoldering, brooding look Griffin wore so well. Her heart sighed. The man was sexy even with those fading bruises coloring his face. Nothing she could do about that. It was his attitude that needed work. A lot of it.

"You need to bone up on your insults, angel," he said walking into her office. The sight of bad boy Griffin York sauntering in to see her was going to float the boats of the office gossips for at least the rest of the week. "I've found put-downs work best when the other person actually knows what you're talking about."

"If you don't know what I'm talking about," she said sweetly, "how do you know I was insulting you?"

That seemed to stump him but he just shrugged. "You have a minute?"

Did she have a minute after he was such an ass to her? After she'd kissed him—one hell of a kiss, too—and then spent over three days checking her phone for his call. One that never came.

"No." To prove how busy she was, she pulled the Lang folder in front of her, opened it and started reading.

He sat down in the one of the leather chairs in front of her desk. Drummed his fingers against the arm.

After five solid minutes of it, the damn tapping about

did her in. Sighing, she closed the folder, linked her hands and set them on her desk. "What can I do for you?" she asked, making sure her voice was super pleasant, that her smile was all sunshine and happy times.

It was either that or hit him over the head with her nameplate.

"Glad you found a few minutes to give me," he said, shifting forward. "I—"

Someone rapped on her door frame.

"Do you—" Russell Wixsom broke off when he saw Griffin. Flinched—probably at Griffin's bruises. They did sort of look painful. "Sorry. Didn't mean to interrupt."

"You're not," Nora assured him, ready to introduce the two men, but one glance at Griffin's glower changed her mind. "What's up?" she asked Russ.

He stepped into the room, smiled at her. "Just wondering if you have the Pecora file."

"I do…" She flipped through the files on her desk. "Here you go."

"Thanks," he said, taking it from her. He started to walk out, turned at the door. "Hey, a couple of us are going out for drinks after work. You interested?"

"Sure."

His grin widened. A fellow associate attorney, Russ was tall, blond and athletic. He was also smart and charming and he looked damn good in that expensive charcoal suit.

She wanted him to hurry up and leave so she could get back to looking at Griffin.

"I'll swing by around five-thirty," Russ said, "and we'll head out together."

He sent Griffin one more curious look, started to

shut the door but then seemed to change his mind and left it open.

"He's your type," Griffin said.

"Excuse me?"

"That guy. He fits in with the whole lawyerly thing you've got going on," he said, gesturing to her hair—pulled back in a neat bun—and her simple white button-down shirt.

"First of all, this *lawyerly thing* happens to be my job. Secondly, I don't have a type. But I'll take it as a compliment that you think a successful, handsome man would be a good match for me. Although I'm sure he only asked me to join them as a professional courtesy."

Griffin snorted, slid down in his seat, his legs straight, his shoulders hunched. "Don't let the polished veneer fool you. Under that suit is a man."

She blinked. Then laughed. "Thank you for that anatomy lesson. Please tell me that next you're going to draw me a diagram."

His expression darkened. "You with him?"

"Why, Griffin, are you asking if Russ and I are sleeping together?"

He straightened. Looked ready to chew up the leather chair and spit it out. "Never mind."

"Because I have to say, your interest in my sex life is very sudden. But before your head explodes, let me just say that I'm not sleeping with, dating, or even interested in Russ on a personal level." Well aware the door was still open she lowered her voice. "I wouldn't have kissed you if I was involved with another man." She leaned back. "Does that clear things up for you?"

"None of my business," he said, lifting a shoulder and looking as if he didn't care one way or the other.

But he did. Or he wouldn't have asked.

If that gave her a sense of pure female satisfaction, no one had to know but her.

"You're right," she said, proud her tone was so even, as if she hadn't spent way too much time the past few days remembering their kiss. Wondering why she couldn't stop thinking about someone so emotionally closed off. "It's not. Now, was there something specific you wanted from me? Or did you just stop by to share your wise and witty comments on my dating life?"

His mouth flattened. "Just wanted to see if we were square."

Pressing her fingertips against her temples she slowly shook her head. The man was giving her a headache. Thank God she was sitting behind her desk in her small, tidy office. It put her in the position of power. Of control.

Even if that power and control were all in her head.

"It must be the lack of caffeine so far today," she said, "but I'm afraid I'm not following you."

He shifted—in agitation? Frustration? Who knew? "You helped me out Saturday. At the police station and with the judge," he added, pulling something out of his back pocket, "and I wanted to take care of any business between us."

It was then she realized he'd pulled out a checkbook. She sat up straighter. Sounds from the outer offices filtered through the buzzing in her head, voices, the low clacking of fingers on keyboards, the occasional phone ringing.

She kept her smile firmly in place. "You came here to write me a check?"

"You acted as my lawyer," he pointed out, grabbing a pen from the wooden pencil holder Brandon had made her for her graduation from law school. Griffin started making out the check. "Despite the fact that I asked you not to, you still did."

"And now you want to pay me," she said, making sure it was clear in her mind.

He glanced up at her. "You're catching on."

Oh, she sure was. She stood and walked over and shut the door, leaned against it, crossing her arms so she didn't give in to the urge to wrap her hands around his stubborn neck and squeeze. "I may be catching on, but I'd like to make sure. You didn't come here to thank me for helping you out the other night. And you aren't here to apologize for being such a jerk at your house, nor did you come to see me because you felt something when we kissed."

His shoulders stiffened. "I'm here to pay you for the work you did for me."

She pushed away from the door. "Work you've made clear you didn't ask me to do," she said, wondering why it hurt so much that he thought so little of her. It shouldn't matter. He wasn't a friend, wasn't someone she ever had to see again. Best to move on and learn from her mistakes. And her first mistake was in thinking there was something more to Griffin than his hard exterior and snide attitude.

Lesson learned.

"Who should I make this out to?" he asked, as clueless as someone with a functioning brain could get.

And to think, she'd spent the past three days jumping every time her phone rang, stupidly hoping it was him. Maybe he wasn't the only idiot in the room.

"I don't care who you make it out to," she said, going behind her desk once again. She looked down her nose at him and smiled thinly. "But I'm sure you can guess where I want you to put it."

CHAPTER ELEVEN

GRIFFIN NARROWED HIS eyes. He didn't know what had set her off but he wasn't in the mood to play around.

Not after witnessing that slicked-up suit flirt with her. Couldn't she see that asshole wanted more than to have her join him and a few coworkers for a drink or two? How could she be so naive? So blind?

How could she even think about accepting some other guy's invitation after kissing him the way she had the other night?

Jealousy gnawed at his gut. Turned his vision a distinct shade of green.

"You did a job for me," he said gruffly, hoping if he ignored the unfamiliar emotions roiling through him, they'd eventually go away. "You should be paid."

"I did you a favor," she amended, looking all prim and proper behind her desk, not a hair out of place, her shirt demure with its tiny buttons and a ruffle at the collar. He wanted to muss her up, slide those buttons free and feel the softness of her skin. "Just like you did me a favor that night. As far as I can tell, we're even and I'd like to just forget the whole thing ever happened."

She was using her lawyerly voice, all reasonable and logical. It pissed him off.

He moved to the edge of the chair, his muscles tense. "Easy for you to say. I'm reminded every time I catch sight of my reflection. Every time I move too quickly."

Every night when he shut his eyes he relived the fight, the conversation with his father at the police station. Eventually exhaustion would overtake him. And that's when the real torture would begin.

She invaded his dreams. Night after night she came to him in his sleep. Touched him. Kissed him. Took him into her body, rose above him, her hips moving, her breasts swaying. Then she'd shake that glorious cloud of hair back and smile at him.

And he'd wake up gasping, his body hard and aching, his hands reaching for her.

"I'm so sorry," she said. "Maybe I should do something to help...ease...your pain and suffering."

His head snapped up. "What?"

"Really, it's the least I can do." She hauled her purse onto the desk and pulled out her wallet. "Is cash okay? I don't have my checkbook with me."

What the hell...? "What are you talking about?"

She widened her eyes. "You got hurt because of me. I should reimburse you."

He shoved to his feet, regretted it when his side pinched. "I don't want your goddamn money."

"No?"

"No," he ground out.

"But you acted as my bodyguard," she said, throwing his words back at him—which was a low thing to do. "I feel a certain amount of compensation is required." She held out three twenties. "Is this enough? I'm not sure what the going hourly rate is for bodyguards-slash-hired-fists these days."

He laid his hands on her desk, leaned forward. "Don't push me, angel."

"I'm terrified," she drawled, mirroring his stance.

"What's the problem? You wanted to pay me for something I did, why can't I pay you?"

"Because, damn it, I wasn't working. I was protecting you."

The words exploded out of him, hung in the air like fireworks, lit up for her inspection.

He exhaled through his teeth. Forced himself to straighten slowly and crossed his arms. He'd walked right into that. Followed her down the path without even considering where he'd end up.

Her expression turned smug. He shouldn't find it so sexy. "I knew you liked me."

Then she smiled at him. One of her real smiles, filled with warmth and humor that made him feel all heroic and right instead of how he usually felt. Angry. Toxic.

"Don't be letting that ego of yours grow," he warned but his voice wasn't as harsh as it could've been, "or there won't be any room left in here for us. I just didn't want to see you get hurt."

"Thank you. Now don't ruin this tender moment by offering to pay me again. If you wanted to see me or talk to me, you could've just called. I'd hoped you would."

Her sincerity knocked him on his ass. She shouldn't be so trusting. So honest. Didn't she know he could use those against her? She needed to learn how to guard her heart, her thoughts and feelings before she got hurt.

But he had wanted to check on her. For days he'd fought it, told himself that she didn't need his protection. She had her family, her sister the cop to make sure Dale didn't get to her, didn't hurt her. He'd even considered that Dale's interest in her could be based on something he'd seen in Griffin's eyes that night, something that had telegraphed his attraction for her to his father.

But in the end, he couldn't stay away. Not another day.

"Have you seen my old man since Saturday?" he asked.

"No," she said, frowning. "But Layne said Ross spoke with him again yesterday and he agreed to take a polygraph test. Which is surprising considering he's still making noises about filing a formal complaint against the MPPD for use of excessive force."

He would. "A polygraph's a waste of time."

"I agree. They're not reliable and aren't admissible in court, but I think Ross is using it more as an interrogation tool and not—"

"It doesn't matter. Because he'll pass it."

She stilled. "You think he's innocent?"

"I don't doubt he's capable of murder." It ate at Griffin, that he'd come from someone who was. He picked up her nameplate, turned it in his hand. "But guilty or not, he'll pass the test because he's a con man. A liar. He's good at it. He's even better at doing whatever he has to to get what he wants. And I think he wants you."

Her face went white. "What?"

"He sought you out. Found you when he arrived in town before he even went to the police station, and then at the bar he focused on you more than Tori." Griffin set the nameplate down with a thud remembering how Dale had zeroed in on Nora. How…self-satisfied he'd been when she'd confronted him. As if he couldn't have planned it better.

"I think he's trying to hurt my family through me." She raised her chin, a princess warrior. But her voice trembled. "I mean, what other reason could there be?"

"I don't know." He wished he did. "Just…be on your toes," he said, choosing his words carefully, because he couldn't be like her. Couldn't blurt out what he was thinking and let people see inside his head. Inside his heart. "My old man's sneaky."

He expected one of her wiseass comebacks, instead she slowly skirted the desk and closed the distance between them, her gaze intense. Searching. Compassionate.

"This is hard on you. Having your father back in Mystic Point. I knew it would be," she continued when he opened his mouth, "I mean, rationally I understood that, of course it would be…unpleasant…for you and your mother, but all I could think about, all I cared about was bringing him back here so we could get to the truth about what happened to my mother. I'm sorry," she whispered. "I'm so sorry I didn't consider what this must be like for you."

She was close. But not close enough. He shifted, trapping her between her desk and his body. "I don't want your apology," he said gruffly. "I don't need your pity."

"No?" she asked, her warm, coffee-scented breath floating across his chin, a challenge in the soft purr of her voice. "What do you want?"

He wanted her hands on him, pressing lightly against his chest like she had the other night. He wanted her mouth on his, warm and seeking. And she knew it. He could see the awareness in her eyes, just as he saw that she wouldn't be the one to make the first move. Not this time.

It was up to him.

NORA HELD HER breath, her eyes locked on Griffin's. She counted the heartbeats echoing in her ears. *One… two…* At three he leaned in, laid his hands on either side of her hips, capturing her without touching her.

She could've cried to have him so close and still not have him. Not fully.

Four...five...six... He ducked his head and hesitated, his mouth a hairbreadth from hers. Anticipation built. Made her dizzy. Or maybe that was because she'd yet to exhale. Either way, she'd slide to a puddle at his feet if he didn't kiss her and soon.

As if sensing her impatience, her greed for him, he smiled; a quick flash of that sexy, potent grin he was so stingy with. Her stomach tumbled happily.

He brushed his mouth against hers. The light rasp of his whiskers tickled her upper lip, her chin. His lips were warm, soft, as he settled into the kiss, deepened it until her thoughts grew hazy, her body lax. She skimmed her hands up his sides—careful of his injured ribs—across his chest to his shoulders. Linked her arms around his neck, arching into him, pressing against the hard planes of his body.

He growled, deep in the back of his throat, and swept his tongue into her mouth, his hands clamping on her hips, his fingers digging into the curve of her butt. She twined her fingers into his hair—

Someone rapped twice on the door. "Anyone here interested in going out—"

With a squeak, she broke the kiss and shoved at Griffin's chest.

He didn't move.

Stubborn man.

Mortified, frantic, she peeked around Griffin's broad shoulder and flinched to see her father standing in the doorway looking as if someone had just kicked him in the stomach.

She swallowed and shoved at Griffin until he gave

her enough room to slip out from between him and the desk.

"Daddy." Dear, sweet God, she was regressing. She hadn't called her father *Daddy* since she was a preteen. "Dad. This isn't—"

"You're not going to try to tell me this isn't what it looks like?" Tim asked in his low, familiar voice. "Are you, Nora Ann?"

First and middle name? That wasn't good. "No. This was exactly what it looked like. I was going to say this isn't Thursday." The day he and Celeste were due back from their trip to Maine.

"Astor called, asked if we could cut our trip short," he said, still staring at Griffin as if seeing a ghost.

"Oh. That's…" Inconvenient. Awkward. "Nice," she finished lamely. "Anyway, uh…hi." She hurried over and kissed his cheek. He held himself stiffly, his hand still on the door handle. "Hi."

"You already said that," Griffin pointed out as he slouched against her desk.

"What are you," she asked, her teeth grit in the facsimile of a smile, "the repetitive word police?" She linked her arm through her dad's and tugged him forward. "Should I even bother with introductions or—"

"No," Tim said, still not looking at her. "If you don't mind," he told Griffin, "I'd like to speak with my daughter. Alone."

Straightening, Griffin smirked, looking every inch what his reputation said he was. Trouble. "Sure." He swiped up his checkbook and met her eyes for a moment. "We were done anyway."

He walked out. She had no idea what he meant by that last comment, was getting tired of trying to figure him out. Tired of putting her whole self out there only to get bits and pieces of him in return.

"Is everything all right?" she blurted, hoping to head off what promised to be an uncomfortable conversation. "You said Aunt Astor called you. Is something wrong?"

"She's worried about Ken. Says he's been acting strange lately and she was hoping I could get to the bottom of whatever's bothering him before Erin's engagement party."

"I'd noticed Uncle Ken seemed a bit irritable lately. I figured he was working on a tough case. Did you speak with him yet?"

"I just came from his office. He's having a tough time with Erin's engagement. He's torn between being happy his daughter picked such a good guy, and wanting to lock her in a closet for the next fifty or so years." He nodded slowly. "I'm starting to think the closet theory has its merits."

She winced. Crap.

Tim shut the door. "What's going on between you and that York boy?" he asked quietly, his eyes—blue like hers—serious. A worn Red Sox cap covered his graying blond hair; his handsome face was lined by a life spent on the sea.

She sighed. "I wish I knew."

"When I heard you'd had him fix your car—"

"Wait," she said, holding up a hand. "You heard about that?"

He lifted his shoulders in a laconic shrug. "You have two sisters, an aunt and uncle who love you like their own and a town full of busybodies. Did you think I wouldn't find out about it?"

"What I think is that I should consider moving back to Boston."

"You don't mean that."

No, she didn't. Mystic Point was home. For good or bad. "So, how mad are you?" she asked, dreading the answer.

He studied her and she could almost see his mind working. She wished she'd inherited some of his patience and ability to weigh all the options, weigh his words instead of just spitting out whatever came into her head.

"I'm not angry," he finally said. "More like... shocked. Walking in here, seeing you with him..." He rubbed a hand over his face looking weary. Stricken. "He looks just like Dale."

"He's not his father," she said, wiping her damp palms down the front of her slacks. Then, because it had to be said, she added gently, "And I'm not Mom."

"No, you're not." He took his hat off, hit it against his jean-covered thigh. "God, but I loved her. So much." He ran his hand through his hair. It trembled. "I loved her too much."

"No," Nora said, appalled. She grabbed his hand and squeezed. "No. You loved her in the only way you knew how. Wholly. You gave her your heart. She was the one who made the mistake of not cherishing it."

Valerie was the one who'd chosen Dale over her family. Nora would never understand it.

"Before we found out the truth," she continued, "before we discovered what really happened to Mom, why she never came back or contacted us...did you forgive her?"

"I did," he said so simply, she had no choice but to believe him. "I had to. It was partly my fault she left."

"Dad, you can't blame yourself."

"I take my share of the responsibility for the failure

of my marriage. I did everything in my power to make her happy—and it took me years to realize this—but it was never enough. It never would've been enough. Your mother loved us the best she could but sometimes..." He put his hat back on, his eyes so sad, it broke her heart. "Sometimes, love isn't enough."

AT SEVEN, GRIFFIN sat on his couch drinking a beer, flipping through the channels on his TV. He should be at the garage. He had enough to do that he could go back there, work until he was exhausted. He'd come home an hour ago, planning on grabbing something to eat and then going back.

He bit into his ham and cheese sandwich, his shoulder muscles tight, his stomach in knots. Checked the time. Wondered what Nora and that prick attorney, with his expensive suit and conservative haircut, were doing right now. If she was smiling at him. Sharing one of her bright laughs with him.

Griffin threw the remote onto the coffee table. It slid across the glossy surface and landed on the floor. The back came off and the batteries flew out.

They'd probably gone someplace fancy and expensive. One of the restaurants on the water, he thought with a sneer, where they served tiny portions of food with names he couldn't even pronounce, let alone afford.

He slammed his head against the back of the couch. Stared at the ceiling. Son of a bitch.

Someone knocked on the door. He rolled his head to the side, considered ignoring whoever it was but they knocked again. His sandwich still in his hand, he stormed to the door and yanked it open.

"What?" he growled.

Tanner blinked. "Uh...hey, Griffin. This is Jessica

Taylor," he said, gesturing to the girl standing beside him on the porch. "Jess, this is my brother, Griffin."

Griffin nodded. She skimmed her gaze over his bruised face and then gave him a cross between a smile and a sneer, her pale hair giving her a ghostly appearance.

"You need something?" Griffin asked Tanner. The kid didn't usually come to Griffin's unless he was with their mom who had a bad habit of showing up unannounced. Griffin didn't want that habit to be passed down to her younger son.

Tanner cleared his throat then glanced at Jess. "Could you give us a second?"

She shrugged, took her phone out and started texting. Maybe she was mute. Christ knew when Griffin had been a teen he hadn't dated girls for their conversational skills.

Tanner stepped forward, forcing Griffin back into the house.

"I need a favor," the kid said in a low rush.

Griffin bit into his sandwich. "I'm not buying you any alcohol."

Tanner rolled his eyes. "Not that."

"I'm not giving you any condoms, either. If you're old enough to have sex, you should be old enough to buy your own protection."

The kid's face turned red and he glanced behind him but Jessica didn't seem to be paying them any attention. "Not that, either," Tanner said in his slow way. "Jess and I made plans tonight but her uncle and his girlfriend both got called in to work."

"So?"

"So we can't watch the movie we rented at her place

if no one else is there. And we can't watch it at my house because Mom and Dad are at a church meeting."

Griffin tossed the last bite of his dinner into his mouth. "Then do something else."

"There is nothing else. The movies playing at the theater downtown are lame and she wants to see this—" He held up a DVD from a local video rental place. "We need adult supervision."

"So why tell me?" And then it dawned on him. He about choked. "No."

Tanner just studied him in that nerve-wracking way he had that made him seem older than his years. "Why not?"

"Because I'm not a babysitter."

"You don't have to babysit us, you don't even have to talk to us—in fact, I'd rather you didn't. Just let us watch the movie here, we'll order pizza, we'll stay out of your hair. I promise."

"I'm not even going to be here," he said, already itching to get out of this uncomfortable conversation and back to his garage where no one would bother him. Where he could pretend he didn't care what Nora and the walking Ken doll were doing.

Damn that suit-wearing bastard. Griffin supposed it was too much to hope he wasn't anatomically correct.

"Please," Tanner said in a desperate tone Griffin had never heard from the kid before. "I'll owe you. I'll sweep the garage every day. I'll wash all the cars. I'll wash the tow truck. I'll—"

"Enough," Griffin said. "You're embarrassing yourself. Have some pride, man." The kid's face fell and Griffin felt like an ass. "You're willing to sacrifice yourself like that just to hang out with this girl one night?"

"Yes," Tanner said with such conviction, Griffin almost smiled. The kid had it bad for the little blonde, that was for sure.

He'd say he couldn't relate but he was afraid that would be nothing but one of those lies he claimed not to tell.

"You can hang out here," he said, not bothering to soften his grudging tone, "but don't bug me and don't expect this to become a regular thing. It's a one-time offer. The last thing I want is my place open to teenagers."

Tanner grinned. "Thanks, Griffin. Really. I owe you."

"I'll keep that in mind."

"Come on in, Jess," Tanner called.

"I have to call my uncle," she said, proving she did speak. She looked from Griffin to Tanner then at the living room. "Let him know where we're at."

"Sure," Tanner said, leading her inside as if he owned the damn place. "I'll get the movie set up."

And I'll just try to pretend I'm invisible, Griffin thought. *In my own damn house.*

He grabbed his empty bottle from the coffee table and went into the kitchen, opened the fridge for another beer but then thought about how that would look to two impressionable teens. Grinding his back teeth together, he set the beer back and picked up a soda instead.

Opening it, he glanced at the paperwork he'd brought home and set on the table earlier. Invoices and bills and orders he needed to make. At least he'd keep busy while two teenagers took over his house. And his TV.

"My uncle wants to talk to you," the girl, Jess, said, coming into the room. Without the sneer, she was cute with her pale hair and big blue eyes. "He wants to make sure it's really okay with you that we're here."

Griffin pinched the bridge of his nose. Seriously? He held out his hand and Jess gave him the phone. "Yeah?" he said.

"Mr. York. This is Chief Ross Taylor."

Covering the mouthpiece with his hand, Griffin tipped his head back and exhaled heavily through his teeth. Damn it. He'd known the name Taylor sounded familiar. "Your uncle is the police chief?" he asked her as Tanner joined them.

She nodded.

"Didn't I tell you that?" Tanner asked.

"No," Griffin snapped. "You didn't."

"Hello? York?" Taylor called through the phone.

Griffin jabbed a finger at Tanner. "You. Owe. Me. Big." He shut his eyes briefly then put the phone back to his ear. "Chief," he said. "What can I do for you?"

"You can make sure my niece isn't alone with your brother for any length of time over three minutes."

"Seems to me, quite a bit can be done in three minutes."

He could almost see the hard expression on the chief's face. He grinned.

"This is a bad idea," uptight Chief Taylor said.

"Probably," Griffin agreed, jerking his head toward the living room. Waited until both kids had taken his point and left the kitchen. "But let's let them do it anyway. They're here. I'm here. They'll watch a movie, maybe order some pizza and then you can pick her up. My brother is a good kid. You've met his parents… you've seen where he comes from. He's not going to try to take advantage of your niece."

"Fine," Taylor said, sounding as surprised as Griffin felt. "Let me talk to Jess again."

Griffin walked back into the living room and handed the girl the phone.

"Everything good?" Tanner asked, looking worried.

Good? He couldn't get his mind off a certain Sullivan and now he was stuck spending the next few hours with two teenagers.

"For you? Maybe. For me…not so much. But you can help make it up to me by ordering extra mushrooms and sausage on the pizza and being the hell out of here by eleven."

CHAPTER TWELVE

"Do you want something to drink?" Tanner asked Jess.

"I've got one," she said, lifting the can of soda he'd given her not twenty minutes ago.

"Oh. Right."

His face was hot. His stomach tight with nerves. It'd been easier when the movie had been playing. He hadn't had to worry about saying the wrong thing, about keeping her interest. Staring blindly at the credits rolling down the TV screen, he racked his brain, trying to come up with some witty comment. Some way to charm her into falling for him.

But he sucked at witty. Didn't know the first thing about being charming.

Out of the corner of his eye he saw her lift her right hand, brush her bangs to the side. Tonight her nails were painted a deep purple and she wore a scrolled, silver ring on her middle finger. He slid his left hand from his thigh onto the couch. Thought about oh-so-casually reaching over to touch that ring, maybe ask her where she got it. Tell her it was pretty. Then all he'd have to do is turn his hand over, link his fingers through hers.

He moved his hand back to his thigh. Rubbed his damp palm down the front of his shorts.

"You sure you don't want me to drive you home?" he blurted.

"In a hurry to get rid of me?" she asked, but he had

no clue if she was teasing or not. She wasn't like the other girls, all giggly and playful.

Leaning forward, he grabbed the remote from the table and clicked off the TV. When he sat back, he inched closer to her. "No. I just don't want you to be bored," he admitted, then mentally kicked his own ass. What kind of dork admits something like that?

She sent him one of those sidelong glances from under her lashes that girls excelled at. He wondered if they were taught it at birth. "If I get bored," she said, "I'll let you know."

No doubt about that. She didn't seem to have a problem expressing her opinion. "So do you want to watch TV or…"

His mind blanked. Or what? He had no idea. He wanted, badly, to inch over even more, to touch her hair. Those pale strands were such a unique color, he wanted to see if they were as soft as he imagined. And every once in a while when she moved, he'd catch of a whiff of her scent, something soft that reminded him of flowers and spice. Something different from the over-powering perfumes and hair spray the other girls he'd gone out with seemed to bathe in.

She leaned forward, set her can down, the movement causing her shirt to rise, exposing her lower back, the curve of her spine. "Do you have any cards?"

He jerked his gaze to hers. "Cards?"

"Yeah, you know, playing cards?"

He glanced behind them at the kitchen. Griffin hadn't come in to check on them, hadn't poked his head in offering to get food or drinks or asking if everything was okay like his mother did when he hung out with a girl at home. He didn't come right in and sit down, introduce himself and start asking Jess a bunch of questions about her family, her interests, what she wanted to do after high school.

He hadn't bugged them. Thank God.

"I'll go ask," he said, bumping her knee when he stood. He found Griffin at the kitchen table scowling at a paper in front of him.

"Playtime over?" Griffin asked, not even looking up from his work.

"I need a deck of cards," Tanner said, opening the drawer at the end of the counter only to discover a can opener and a spatula. He opened the next one—a roll of tin foil.

Griffin set the paper aside. "Get the hell out of my stuff."

"Why?" Tanner asked, yanking open a middle drawer. A hammer, two screwdrivers and a tape measure. "You hiding body pieces in one of these?"

"No. I'm not hiding cards, either. I don't have any."

Tanner gaped at him. "Everyone has cards. It's like a law or something."

"What can I say? I'm a rebel. Guess you'll have to find something else to do." He jabbed a finger at Tanner. "But keep it rated PG. Better make that rated G. If it wouldn't happen in one of those Disney cartoon movies, it better not happen in my house, hear me?"

"I hear you," Tanner muttered before going back into the living room.

Jess wasn't there.

His stomach dropped. He glanced around. She hadn't gone to the bathroom—he would've noticed if she'd walked past the kitchen. Her sandals were still on the floor in front of the couch, her phone on the coffee table.

He went out onto the porch and she glanced up at him from where she sat on the top step, her legs bent, her back against the porch post. "Sorry," he told her, "no cards."

She lifted a shoulder, went back to staring out at the street. "Mind if we sit out here for a while?"

"No, that's cool." The porch light illuminated her profile, highlighted her hair. He sat next to her, about jumped out of his skin when, a minute later, she tucked her bare feet under his thigh.

"Is that okay?" she asked, her big blue eyes on him. "My toes are freezing."

They were; he could feel them through the material of his shorts. "Yeah, that's..." He cleared his throat. "That's fine. You can wear my sweatshirt," he added, noticing how she rubbed her bare arms.

"Won't you be cold?"

"I've got another shirt on underneath this." It was short-sleeved but he'd get frostbite before he'd admit he was chilled, too.

He took off his sweatshirt, handed it to her and then quickly smoothed his hair while she pulled it over her head.

"Your hair's stuck on your earring. Here," he said, his voice rough. "I'll just..."

Holding his breath, he tugged the silky strands free as gently as possible then dropped his hand. Curled his fingers into his palm.

"Thanks." She rolled up the sleeves. "You really don't mind if I wear it?"

"Nah." It was worth cold hands and goose bumps to see her in his shirt. His last name was on the back along with the school's basketball logo, his first name scrolled on the chest above her heart. She tugged it over her bent legs making it seem like it was the only thing she wore. She looked adorable and sexy as hell.

His body stirred. *Oh, please, don't get a hard-on. Not now.*

"It looks good on you," he said. "Maybe you should try out for the girls' team. Get one with your name on it."

She snorted. "I don't think so. I've never played basketball. I've never played any sport."

"I could teach you." He stood and held out his hands. She stared up at him, then at his hands. After what felt like forever, she laid her hands in his. He pulled her to her feet, held on until they got to the bottom of the stairs.

He jogged to the garage, activating the motion sensor light on the corner of the building. Taking down the key from the top of the doorjamb, he unlocked the side door and grabbed a ball.

"Your brother doesn't own a deck of cards but he has a basketball and a basket?"

"I'm pretty sure the hoop was here when he moved in," he said of the backboard attached to the garage. But the net was new, and Griffin had installed the exterior lights a few years back. "He's always had a ball. I guess he comes out here and shoots around when he has time."

He bounced the ball to her. She jolted but caught it with both hands, held it out from her body as if it was a bomb instead of leather filled with air.

"Shoot it," he said.

She seemed so serious but then that jaded look came back to her eyes and she shrugged. Gave it a halfhearted attempt with both hands. But instead of going out, the ball went straight up.

He ran over, grabbed it before it landed, spun and did a layup, catching it as it fell through the hoop.

"Show off," she muttered but it lacked heat.

"Come on. I'll show you how to shoot." He stood next to her, licked his fingertips.

"Yuck. I am not licking my fingers. God, I'm not even sure I want to touch the ball again."

He elbowed her gently. "Don't be such a girly-girl." He took a jump shot and it swished in the basket. Moved to another spot, hit it again. Third spot, third all-net ball. He handed the ball to her. "Try again."

This time she mimicked him, angling her body and using her right hand to throw it up. The ball hit the underside of the front of the rim.

"Here," he said, rebounding for her. "We'll start with a free throw." He guided her to a spot directly in front of the basket. "A regular free throw would be back a few more feet but we'll start here until you get stronger. Stand with your feet hip-width apart, knees slightly bent. Bring the ball up, look underneath it. Shooting hand here," he said, his elbow bent at forty-five degrees, "free hand is your guide on the other side of the ball. Then you pick a spot on the rim, a dime-size spot and when you shoot, flick the ball." He demonstrated and the ball spun above his hands. He caught it. Did it again. "Inhale. And when you exhale, shoot."

He showed her and the ball swished into the net.

She tried. It came closer. He rebounded for her. "Good," he said. "But this time, try to hold the ball on your fingers. Don't let it rest on your palm."

She was so cute, standing there in his sweatshirt, her feet bare, her brows drawn together in concentration. "What's the story with you and your brother?" she asked as she shot short of the basket. "How come he's so much older than you?"

"My mom was married before. Griffin was fourteen when she and dad had me."

"He's like, super hot."

A weird feeling made his stomach turn. "He's old."

She shrugged. Shot and missed again, this one bouncing off the rim so he had to chase it. "I'm pretty sure hot outranks old every time."

His mouth tightened. "Whatever."

She laughed and then she smiled at him—a genuine smile that about knocked him on his ass and made him fumble his dribble.

"You're hot, too," she said. "Just more clean-cut and jockish."

He scratched the back of his neck feeling like he should apologize for being a good guy. What was up with girls and their fascination with bad boys? "The jock part fits," he said, turning and making another jump shot. "I'd like to play in college then professionally. But I'll get a degree to fall back on just in case I don't make it. Maybe in teaching."

"You want to be a teacher?" she asked, sounding interested instead of how other kids sounded—like teaching was for losers who wanted to make teenagers' lives miserable.

"Yeah. Maybe." He handed her the ball. "What about you?"

She seemed surprised. "What about me what?"

"What do you want to do after graduation?"

She kept her head down, traced the seams of the ball. "I don't know." She dribbled the ball, slapping at it with her palm instead of pushing it down. "I'd like to be a nurse," she blurted, her fair cheeks turning pink. "Pretty stupid, huh?"

"Why?"

Tucking the ball under her arm, she rolled her eyes. "Because my grades are pathetic, I'm only sixteen, I have a record and I haven't exactly been a perfect teen-ager."

"Who said you had to be perfect? Seems to me if you want something, it's okay to go after it."

"Maybe," she said, not sounding convinced. But her expression was determined as she squared off to the basket and shot. The ball hit the rim. And rolled into the net. "I did it," she breathed. Then she launched herself at him, throwing her arms around his neck. "I did it," she repeated, doing a little dance in place.

For a moment he froze, just stood there like an idiot while she was pressed against him but then he wrapped his arms around her. God, she smelled good and felt even better. Under his bulky sweatshirt he could feel the curve of her hips, of her breasts.

Laughing, her hair brushing his chin, she leaned back. "I'm glad you invited me over tonight."

"Me, too." Her hands were on his shoulders, his were at her waist. His pulse raced. He tugged her closer. "Jess, I—"

"This is going to sound stupid," she said softly, smiling at him in a way that made him feel like he'd just been selected first in the NBA draft, "but I almost backed out of tonight. I mean, after what happened with your friends that first night at the café, I thought you were just another guy who wanted in my pants. But Keira told me you weren't like that and I'm...well...I'm glad I listened to her. I had a lot of fun."

Her words washed over him like a cold shower. Shit. If he tried to kiss her now she'd never believe he wasn't just looking to get laid.

"I had fun, too," he said, stepping back and sticking his hands into his pockets. "Want to shoot some more?"

She picked up the ball and bounced it a few times,

looking, for the first time that he'd seen, truly happy. Okay, so nothing was going to happen tonight. He was patient. He could wait for her.

He'd wait as long as it took.

NORA PULLED TO a stop outside of Griffin's house and saw Chief Taylor's niece playing basketball with a tall, handsome teenage boy. More curious about Griffin's brother, about his life, than she should be, she shut off the ignition and got out of the car.

"What are you doing here?" Jess asked as Nora walked toward them.

She and Jess didn't know each other well, had no reason to when Jess had just been the girl who'd lied to and hurt Anthony. But now that Layne and Ross were an item, it looked as if their lives were going to be connected. Nora wasn't sure which one of them that annoyed more.

"Ross and Layne are still working so they asked me to take you home. Hi," she said to the boy as she held out her hand, "I'm Nora Sullivan."

"Tanner Johnston." His deep voice belied his baby face, but he was adorable. And he had his brother's eyes. "Nice to meet you."

"You, too." Nora glanced up at the house but the door was shut and she couldn't imagine Griffin staring at her from behind one of the windows. "You ready to go, Jess?"

"I need to get my shoes and stuff from inside."

"Do you want to come in?" Tanner asked.

And risk coming face-to-face with Griffin after he'd kissed her, sneered at her father and then left her office with that parting shot about them being done?

She'd rather strip bare, grease herself up with baby oil and roll around on the beach. In January.

"I'll just wait here."

Nora leaned back against her car as they went inside. A light breeze picked up, cooled her skin, filled her lungs. She shifted, mentally urging Jess to hurry up. She felt restless. Wired and antsy, her skin too tight, her shoes pinching her toes.

The front door opened and she straightened, her pulse quickening when Griffin walked toward her, all sexy and predatory with his broad shoulders and flat stomach, his jeans hanging low on his hips. But then he drew close enough for her to see his T-shirt was wrinkled, his feet bare, and he seemed human. Approachable instead of just hard and exciting and off-limits.

She forced a smile. "Griffin York playing chaperone. Who would've guessed?"

He glanced pointedly into the passenger window of her car. "Where's your date?"

"It wasn't a date," she said then bit the inside of her cheek. So much for not letting him bait her into an argument. "And I imagine he's at home."

Griffin's eyes, glittering green in the moonlight, met hers. "Didn't get to take you home? Didn't get to stay the night?"

"Obviously not. But if you're assuming there was no sex involved in my night, then you're not taking into consideration the possibility that Russell and I hooked up in the men's room at the restaurant before I left him there, weeping with gratitude."

"Sounds like you had a good time. And yet here you are. At my place."

He sounded smug, as if she'd come to see him. "I'm here because Layne asked me to pick up Jess."

If he thought that strange, he didn't show any sign of it. Then again, most people in town had heard about Layne and Ross being a couple. "She doesn't like you," Griffin said. "The kid."

Nora had assumed as much but hearing it caused a twinge, a small one. "What is she doing in there? Making an anti-Nora declaration?"

He lifted a shoulder. "It's obvious. You definitely rub her the wrong way."

"Well, perhaps the two of you could start a club."

"Maybe. But only if we can get T-shirts made up."

"With my face in a circle with a bold line going through it?" she asked sweetly.

"I was thinking of an X but a line would work. I'm guessing the reason she doesn't like you is because you don't like her."

"How can I dislike her? She's just a kid. One I barely know."

"Some people are just easier to read than others. You sure you're in the right business? I thought lawyers had to be able to sell a case. Your face gives you away."

Because she was afraid he was right, she worked on keeping her expression clear. "If only I'd had that insightful career advice before I wasted seven years on higher education. But seeing as how I did, and how I have student loans in the six figures, I'll just have to see this attorney thing through. Plus," she couldn't help but add, couldn't help goading him, "this way I get to keep seeing Russell every day."

"You didn't wear your hair down for your date with him," Griffin said.

Not quite what she'd thought his response would be. "I see we're on to the stating the obvious portion of our conversation. No, I didn't wear my hair down as I went out right after work. Which is obvious since I'm wearing the same clothes I had on this morning. And it wasn't a date. It was drinks with a group of coworkers."

He raised his eyebrows. "It's eleven. Must've been some heavy drinking going on."

"Okay, so the drinks led to dinner. We were hungry."

His eyes narrowed fractionally. "We?"

"Well, Russell and I were the only ones who stayed for dinner, but so what? Why shouldn't I spend time with him? And maybe you were right, maybe he is interested in me on a personal level, which he made clear," she stressed, "by telling me he finds me attractive and intelligent and enjoys being with me."

"Will you see him again? The next time you have drinks and dinner will you kiss him good-night? Will you let him take you home? Take you to bed?"

"Would you care if I did?" she asked softly.

Something hot and potent flashed in his eyes but was quickly banked. "None of my business."

"You're right. It's not." But it hurt, too much, that he didn't care enough about her to admit his feelings. Even if those feelings were anger that she'd been with another man tonight.

Her pride chafed, told her to walk away now, her head whispered that he wasn't for her. He was closed off and bitter and would never give her what she needed, what she wanted. Would never give her the unconditional love she deserved. But her heart, her heart begged her to stay. To give him another chance. That he was worth it.

She sighed. "I'm not interested in playing games," she said. "The way I see it, after I leave with Jess in tow, there's really no other reason for you and I to ever cross paths again unless it's by accident. So, if there's

something on your mind or if you're interested in seeing me again, you need to say so."

Their gazes locked. Nerves twisted in her stomach,
the silence roared in her ears.

The front door slammed shut and Jess came out the
house, Tanner following. "Here—" she reached for the
hem of the extra large sweatshirt she had on "—I'd better give this back."

"That's okay," he said, voice low and quiet. "You can
wear it home and I'll just get it back later."

"Okay. Thanks." Jess smiled at Tanner, looking like
a normal, sweet sixteen-year-old. Looking happy. "I'm
ready," she told Nora, her gaze growing curious as she
glanced between the two adults.

"Yeah," Nora whispered. "I'm ready, too."

Ready to leave, ready to give up on whatever crazy,
stupid idea she'd had about her and Griffin.

Her face flaming, she rounded the front bumper of
her car. God, she'd been such a fool. Putting herself out
there for him only to get nothing, *nothing* in return.

"You want to know what's on my mind?" Griffin
growled, stopping her before she could open the door.
"You want me to make it *clear* what I want from you?"

"I think we can all guess that," Jess piped up from
where she stood next to the car, the passenger-side door
open. "But, I, for one would still love to hear it. How
about you?" she asked Tanner, who stared at the scene
wide-eyed from down the sidewalk. He nodded.

Nora glared at her. "Why don't you wait in the car?"

"And miss this? Are you high?"

Before Nora could respond to that, Griffin stalked
over to her. Kept coming, forcing her to back up until
she was pressed against the car. "I've never, not once in

my life been jealous over a woman," he said, his eyes hooded. "Until today."

As declarations went, what it lacked in quantity, it more than made up for in quality. But it wasn't enough. Not quite. "And?" she asked.

His mouth flattened. "And I'm taking you to dinner. Tomorrow night. I'll pick you up at seven."

"You really think you're up for someone like him?" Jess called from behind her.

Nora ignored her. "I'm sorry," she said, shaking her head at him and his lame-ass invitation, "but are you ordering me to have dinner with you?"

"I'm asking," he said, as if grinding up the words before spitting them out.

"That's funny, because it didn't sound that way."

He edged closer, ducked his head to speak in her ear, his breath warm against her skin, his voice a low rumble that scraped along her nerve endings. "Have dinner with me tomorrow night."

Her mouth went dry. It wasn't perfect but it was the best she'd get from him. And it was enough for now. "Make it six-thirty," she said when he straightened. "I have an early day Friday."

Nodding, he raked his gaze over her slacks and blouse, her heels and updo. "Wear jeans." He went back toward the house, faced her at the edge of the sidewalk, his taller, younger brother behind him. "And, angel? If your hair is up in one of those fancy twists you seem to like so well, I'm taking it down myself."

"I actually don't take fashion advice from someone whose wardrobe consists of jeans and T-shirts so I'll be wearing my hair any damn way I please."

But the thought of him doing just that, of his fingers combing through her hair had her breathless and anxious and yes, damn it, aroused. And considering putting it up just to make sure he'd go through with his threat.

She raised her eyebrows at Jess from over the top of the car. "Are you getting in?"

"Yep. Just didn't want to miss anything."

They got in the car simultaneously. Pulling away from the curb, Nora couldn't resist checking her rear-view mirror. Smiled to see Griffin in front of the porch of his dark, lonely-looking house watching her.

"Didn't anyone ever teach you it's rude to stare?" Nora asked Jess, feeling the girl's eyes on her as they drove down the street.

Jess snorted. "My mom had other lessons to teach me."

Nora glanced at her. She knew from Layne that Jess's mom, Ross's sister, had a long history of drug abuse and was currently serving a sentence for possession. Hard not to feel for the girl when she'd had it so rough. But that didn't excuse what she'd done to Anthony.

"If you have something to say, say it."

"I'm just, like, surprised," Jess said. "I mean, that Griffin is hot. Smoking hot."

"Yes," Nora said dryly, turning left at the intersection, "how shocking that he'd be interested in me."

"I know, right? He's more Tori's type."

She strangled the steering wheel, forgot all about the sympathy she'd felt for Jess moments ago. "Well, be that as it may, he didn't ask Tori out, did he?"

He'd asked her.

CHAPTER THIRTEEN

"NO WAY," Nora said the next evening, crossing her arms and giving Griffin a mulish expression. "There is no way I'm getting on that thing."

Griffin squinted against the sunlight. They stood outside her house, him on the sidewalk in front of his Harley, her at the top of her porch stairs. She had on a flowy black tank top and dark jeans and, as he'd requested, her hair was down, falling to her shoulders like a golden cloud. "You afraid?" he asked, having a hard time believing the woman who'd faced him down in his own garage, beat the hell out of her car and confronted Dale York at the Yacht Pub was afraid of anything.

She lifted her chin. "How about smart enough not to get on a machine that can get up to great speeds. A machine that leaves nothing between me and whatever object we may encounter on our travels."

He lifted the helmet he'd bought for her earlier that day. A bright yellow one, the color reminding him of her. "You'll have a helmet on."

"Oh, well, in that case, why don't you just shoot my body out of a cannon?" She rolled her eyes. "A helmet," she muttered as if to herself in disgust.

His lips twitched and he slowly walked up the stairs. She stiffened but stood her ground. When he reached the step below her, they were eye to eye. Mouth to mouth. His hands tightened on the helmet.

"Come on, angel," he said softly in what he hoped was his best cajoling tone. "Come for a ride with me. It'll be fun."

She glanced behind him at the bike. Bit her lower lip. "I thought you were taking me out to dinner."

"I am."

"We can take my car—"

"Let me take you for a ride," he repeated smoothly, tucking the helmet under his arm so he could touch the loose strands of hair caressing her cheek. When she still hesitated, her eyes uncertain, he slid his hand around to cup the back of her head. "You'll be safe. Trust me."

She met his eyes, held his gaze for so long, his chest hurt. But then he realized that was because he wasn't breathing. He wanted, more than he cared to admit, for her to do just that. For her to count on him. With her safety. Her secrets.

Her heart.

But he didn't want to give her his heart in return.

And that made him a selfish son of a bitch. Like his old man. And, like his father, he wasn't willing to give up something he wanted. Even though he knew he didn't deserve it. Didn't deserve Nora.

She inhaled deeply, exhaled and her breath ruffled the hair at the top of his head. "Okay."

"You won't regret it," he promised more solemnly than the situation called for. But he wanted her to know she could trust him. And that even though he couldn't give her everything she deserved, he'd do his best not to hurt her.

He hoped.

NORA ALREADY REGRETTED it.

Her legs shook as she walked down the porch steps.

After her acquiescence about the motorcycle ride, Griffin had told her to change into a long-sleeve shirt—despite the warm weather. Now that she was dressed in what she deemed motorcycle-babe-worthy clothes—tight jeans, snug, long-sleeve shirt and her favorite black booties—she was at least externally prepared for this.

Inside, though, her heart raced. Her palms were damp and her stomach quivered.

Trust me.

She did. More than was wise considering they'd only known each other a short time and how closed off he was. He kept a part of himself separate. Protected. Spending more time with him when she wasn't sure he'd ever be able to fully open up to anyone was risky.

Her growing feelings for him despite her doubts scared her more than the two-wheeled death trap he wanted her to ride on.

But she couldn't refuse him, she thought as she approached him. He was beautiful, leaning against the bike, his arms crossed, his gaze hooded. And this time, he'd come to her. Had asked her out—though she'd had to push him into it.

She frowned. Maybe she'd had to give him a nudge in the right direction but he obviously wanted to spend time with her or he wouldn't be here. Wouldn't have brought her a ridiculously bright yellow helmet.

No, she couldn't refuse him. And that was just something she'd have to live with.

"Ready?" he asked when she reached him.

"Not really." But she took the helmet from his hands, shoved it onto her head. It was tighter than she'd imagined, seemed to close off all sound. "But let's do it anyway."

Grinning, he flipped the visor up. "What was that?"

"I said, let's do it anyway."

He straightened. "I'm blown away by your enthusiasm."

"You want enthusiasm?" she asked, as he swung onto the bike and put his own helmet on. "Try showing up for a date in a limo."

She had no idea what to do, how to even get on the damn thing so she stood there hoping maybe he'd forget the whole idea.

He lifted his visor and faced her. "You might want to come closer," he said, a note in his voice as close to teasing as she'd ever heard. She edged forward. "Now put your left hand on my left shoulder, step up on the foot peg with your left foot and swing your right leg over the seat."

"Foot peg?" she asked, looking at all the shiny and not so shiny pieces of the machine.

"Here," he said, kicking the back of his booted heel against a piece that stuck out from the bike.

She laid her hand on his shoulder, stepped up and swung her leg over.

"Good," he said, turning so she could hear him. "Now squeeze your knees against my hips. It'll help keep you more stable."

"I bet you say that to all the girls," she muttered, starting to sweat in her long sleeves and nerves.

He laughed.

And she knew no matter how terrifying the ride would be, no matter how her stomach churned or how many times her life flashed before her eyes it would all be worth it.

Because he laughed.

She slid her arms around his waist, pressed herself against his strong, solid back. Liked that she could feel his chest rising and falling with his breathing. That his heart beat steadily against her palm, the warmth of his skin seeping through his shirt. He started the bike, it rumbled underneath her, the seat vibrating between her thighs, and she tightened her hold on him.

"Ready?" he asked over his shoulder.

She wasn't. Didn't think she'd ever be. So she nodded and he slowly pulled away from the curb.

He kept to the speed limit but avoided the busiest roads as they made their way through town. Truth be told, she didn't see a lot of it as she kept her eyes squeezed shut. It wasn't until he went a little faster, when she smelled the ocean, felt the breeze cool that her eyes flew open in surprise.

They were outside of town now, driving down old Beach Road, a stretch of highway that paralleled the ocean. He handled the bike effortlessly and gradually she loosened her death grip on him. The wind, the road open before her, spinning past her in a blur should have terrified her—did terrify her. But it was also...freeing. Exhilarating.

And sexy as hell.

To her right, waves crashed along the rocky shore and she could've sworn she felt their cool mist along her hands, the back of her neck. The powerful machine rumbled beneath them, took corners with ease. By the time he pulled to a stop in front of run-down sandwich shop twenty minutes later, the muscles in her thighs ached from being so tense and she couldn't feel her butt.

It was great.

She dismounted and did a little ass-shaking jig on the sidewalk.

He cut the ignition, set the kickstand and got off the

bike. Took off his helmet, his hair all sexily mussed, a sharp grin on his face. "I take it you liked it?"

"Liked it?" she asked. "I loved it. It was… It felt… Wow."

Though that one word was grossly inadequate to describe the rush she'd gotten from being on the bike, the sense of pure freedom, he seemed to get it. He unhooked her helmet and tugged it off her head, his gaze darkening. "Yeah. It certainly is wow."

Her heart raced under his intense scrutiny. She didn't know what to do with him, how to handle him or her growing feelings for him. The more she was around him, the easier it was to convince herself that he could give her what she'd always dreamed of.

The kind of love her father had had for her mother.

She launched herself at him, not surprised at all when he caught her against him, his strong arm going around her waist.

"Thank you," she said, giving him a smacking kiss on the mouth. "That was awesome. When can I drive?"

"After you've taken the proper safety courses." His arm tightened around her for a moment, almost as if he was giving her a hug. "And you buy your own bike."

She pouted. "You mean you won't teach me how to drive your bike?"

"Nobody drives it but me."

She'd just have to figure out a way to convince him to let her be the first. She took a hold of his hand and tugged him up the walk toward the restaurant. "Come on. Let's eat."

Ten minutes later they were seated behind Beachy's Subs at one of the weathered, rough-hewn wooden tables overlooking the ocean. White-capped waves crashed against the rocky shore, shot water into the air. The breeze picked up the ends of her hair, blew them around her face. She brushed them back and peeled the lid off the foam bowl of clam chowder, then took the plastic spoon out of its wrapper.

She scooped up a bite, burning her tongue in the process. But it was so worth it. Humming appreciatively, she shoveled another spoonful into her mouth. "Can I have one of those?" she asked, helping herself to one of his onion rings. She bit into it as she reached for a packet of saltine crackers and caught him watching her.

"What?" she asked, wiping the back of her hand against her chin in case she had a drip she didn't know about.

"Just wondering if the rest of my food—and fingers—are safe."

"Oh, ha. Aren't you witty?" But she did slow down long enough to squirt ketchup over her pile of fries. "I'm hungry. I missed lunch. And this chowder is seriously excellent. Better than the café's." She jabbed her spoon in his direction. "If you tell my dad I said that, I'll deny it."

"Why would your dad care?"

"Celeste uses my great-grandmother Sullivan's recipe. Dad takes his family's chowder seriously."

Unwrapping his fully loaded steak sub, Griffin snorted. "Your secret's safe with me. I doubt your father and I will have much to say each other if we ever run into each other again." He bit into the sub, chewed and swallowed. "Not when he wants to rip my heart out and use it for fish bait."

"And after you were so charming and polite yesterday," she said dryly.

"If you'd wanted charming and polite, you would've stuck with the suit from your office. Instead you're breaking the rules by being with me. Maybe that's part of the reason you're here."

She shook her head. "God, that's pretty much what Tori accused me of that night at the Yacht Pub. That I'm going through some latent teenage rebellion."

His gaze on her was intense. Searching. "Are you?"

"Yes, Griffin. I'm using you to get back at my family for loving and taking care of me my entire life. For teaching me right from wrong and encouraging my goals and dreams. Those bastards."

"Maybe it's not them you're trying to get back at."

At his quiet words, everything inside of her stilled. Her appetite gone, she slowly set down her spoon. He thought she was lashing out in anger over her mother leaving. That couldn't be further from the truth. She didn't hate her mom, had never had the same issues over her abandonment that Layne and Tori did. Sure, Nora had grieved not having a mother like Aunt Astor, but mostly she'd pitied Valerie.

She'd had everything and had thrown it away.

"I'm not angry with my mother," she told Griffin. "Maybe I should be, maybe I should hate her but…" Nora shook her head, stared at the ocean. "I can't. She was just so…tragic…the way she was always searching for attention, for others to give her what she lacked inside. It didn't matter that she had a husband who loved her above everything else, that she had three healthy daughters, it wasn't enough. She wanted more. More money. More things. More time and attention. More excitement. I just find it incredibly sad."

Nora would do anything to have what Valerie had given up. To have a life in the town and with the people she loved, to have a home and a family of her own. To share that life with a man who loved her, beyond self, beyond reason.

"My old man was the same way," Griffin said, surprising her by offering information. "He never had enough and if he saw something he wanted, he took it. It didn't matter if it belonged to someone else."

"I'm sure my mother didn't put up much of a fight," she said "But no matter how…lacking…my mother was, she didn't deserve what Dale did to her. Didn't deserve to have him hurt her." Holding his gaze, she trailed her fingers across the back of his hand. "Neither did you."

GRIFFIN'S HAND TREMBLED so he slid it away from her touch. Hid it on his lap where she couldn't see his weakness. "The last time I saw my father—" Christ, he hated calling Dale that, hated how the word stuck in his throat, "The last time I saw Dale before he disappeared, Mom and I were living in this one-bedroom apartment over on Maplewood Ave. It was a dump," he said, staring over Nora's shoulder and seeing the past, "but Mom still had to work two jobs just to cover the rent. But it didn't matter how many hours she had to work or that I had to sleep on the floor or that we ate peanut butter sandwiches three meals a day because we were free from him. After all those years, we were finally free."

"Griffin," she said, drawing his eyes back to her sympathetic expression. "It's okay. You don't have to."

He did. He had to let her know what she was getting herself into by being with him. Had to warn her. "What's the matter?" he asked with a smirk. "Afraid of the truth?"

She looked so hurt, he wanted to take his words back but while he'd give her the truth, he drew the line at letting her see inside his head. His heart.

"No," she finally said, her soft words almost drowned out by the roaring ocean. "I'm not afraid of you."

Maybe not now, but she would be. She should be.

He rubbed his palms up and down his jeans, chose his words carefully. He had to get this right. Had to make her understand. "That night—this must've been three months before Dale left town for good, so I don't know if he and your mom were together yet—he showed up demanding money. Mom refused. Told him to get out of her house and not to come back."

Griffin had been torn between pride that she'd finally stood up to her husband and fear of what Dale would do. He'd been right to be scared.

"She refused and he hit her," Griffin said flatly, remembering the sound of his father's hand on his mother's face. How she'd cried out in pain. "He slapped her so hard she fell into the wall. Then he picked her up by her hair and hit her again. And again."

He took a long drink of his soda but it did little to soothe the rawness of his throat. "I tried to stop him," he continued, his voice sounding far away to his own ears. "I leaped on his back, kicking and screaming and punching but he flicked me off as if I was nothing." Had thrown Griffin off and into the door frame. He'd lain there dazed and hurt, the wind knocked out of him. Dale had loomed over him, violence and hatred on his face. "My mom screamed—I'd never heard her scream like that—and came at him like a woman possessed."

She'd scratched and clawed at Dale, her face contorted with rage and pain but she wasn't strong enough. Neither of them had been strong enough.

Griffin forced himself to meet Nora's eyes, steeled himself against the tears he saw there. "I couldn't do anything to stop him."

Nora's face was pale, her expression horrified. "Griffin…God…I'm so sorry."

"Don't," he snapped. "Don't you tell me you're sorry. You have no idea what it was like."

"You're right, I don't, but that doesn't mean I can't feel for that scared little boy. You were just a kid," she continued. "You can't blame yourself."

He shut his eyes because she saw too much. How could she understand him so well? Rising, he crossed to the edge of the picnic area, stared out at the ocean. A minute later, she joined him, her hip brushing his outer thigh.

"My father is a liar," he told her. "An abusive, violent bastard and a probable murderer." He glanced at her, kept his hands in his pockets. "That's what I come from. That's what runs through my blood."

That was why he shouldn't be near her. Why he had no right to touch her. To want her.

She stepped in front of him, her hair blowing wildly, a frown marring the smoothness of her forehead. "That's such bullshit."

He bristled. "What?"

"I said that's bullshit. You're you. You're not some…" She waved her hand in the air as if hoping the right word would land in her palm. "Clone of your father."

"Then how come every time I look in the mirror, I see his face?" he asked harshly. "Every day I'm reminded of what I come from, of who I really am."

"You may resemble Dale but you're nothing like him," she said firmly. "Nothing."

"How do you know? How could you possibly know?"

"Because I see you. You're honest and hardworking. You own a respectable business. You stand up for what you think is right." She laid her hand on his chest. His heart jumped. "You're a good man."

He wished he could be the man she saw, someone worthy of her. But he wasn't some freaking Prince Charming—he was flawed and carried the scars of his father's sins.

"What if the cops never get enough evidence to charge Dale with your mother's murder?" he asked. How would she be able to look at him if his father goes free?

"They'll find a way."

"I hope for your sake you're right, but when it comes to my old man I've learned not to underestimate him or what he can get away with."

"I have faith." She stepped closer, rose onto her toes and placed a warm kiss on the corner of his mouth. Fell back to her heels and smiled. "I have faith in you, too."

She shouldn't. He was a bad bet. He couldn't... wouldn't...give her what she deserved.

But he couldn't let her go, either.

ON THE RETURN ride to her house, with the ocean to one side of her, the setting sun to the other, Nora couldn't stop thinking about what Griffin had told her. She should be grateful—she *was* grateful—he'd shared a piece of himself, a small piece of his past and his pain. But she suspected he hadn't done it in order for them to grow closer. He hadn't wanted her sympathy or understanding.

It'd been a warning.

Don't try to understand me. Don't get too close to me. Don't fall for me.

As he slowed to take the corner to her street, she realized it was good advice. Smart advice—and she was nothing if not smart and more than capable of seeing when she was headed straight for disaster. For heartbreak.

He'd wanted to frighten her and it'd worked. She was afraid. Afraid it was too late. She was already falling for him.

He pulled the bike to a stop in front of her house and she dismounted, took off her helmet while he shut off the engine and swung off. After he set his helmet on the seat, he faced her, his gaze dark and watchful as he slowly dipped his head and took her mouth with his.

He kissed her softly, touched the tip of his tongue against hers. She'd expected heat and desire, but his lips moved over hers languidly, drugging her senses. Muddling her thoughts. Making her forget all the reasons she had to be careful around him. Why he was so dangerous to her.

Breaking the kiss, she shoved the helmet at him. "Thanks for dinner," she blurted breathlessly. "And for the bike ride."

Without breaking eye contact, he set the helmet aside. Stepped even closer, his knee bumping her thigh.

"I want to come in," he said, his voice husky and enticing. He reached up, rubbed the ends of her hair between his fingers, the backs of his knuckles brushing the top of her breast. "Invite me inside, Nora."

Yearning pooled low in her stomach, pushed her to submit to the inevitable.

Griffin in her bed.

Why shouldn't she give in, give them both what they wanted? She'd said herself he was a good man. Emotionally closed off, yes, but she had a better understanding of what he'd gone through. Why he felt the need to protect himself that way.

He was sexy and gorgeous and he wanted her.

It wasn't enough.

"I can't," she whispered.

"You can." He slipped his other hand under the hem of her shirt, his fingers warm and rough against her skin. "I want to touch you. All of you. I want to put my mouth here…" He touched his fingertips to her mouth, dragged the pad of his thumb against her lower lip. "And here…" Lowered his palm to her breast. "And here…" Slid his hand down her stomach, then lower, his touch featherlight between her legs. Desire slammed into her with enough force to steal her breath. "I want to watch your face as I make you come," he continued relentlessly in that same gravelly tone. "Let me."

Her knees were weak, her resolve waning. "I want to," she admitted. "I really, really want to." So much that she had to step back and put some distance between them. "But I…I need some time. And I need to know if you're willing to give me that."

If he cared enough about her to give her that.

He stared at her for so long, his expression hard, she was sure he'd say no. That he'd find someone else to scratch his itch instead of waiting around for her to make up her mind.

Then he nodded once, a quick jerk of his head. "You want time? Fine." Before she realized his intent, he yanked her to him and pressed a hard kiss against her mouth before setting her away from him again. "Just don't make me wait too long," he said before getting on his bike and riding away.

She watched his taillight disappear down the street, waited until she could no longer hear the low roar of the bike's engine. And tried to convince herself she'd made the right decision.

"That boy never did know when he wasn't wanted."

At the deep voice, Nora's scalp prickled, her hands went numb. She whirled around as Dale stepped out from around the corner of her house. He grinned at her. Winked.

"And now we're alone at last."

CHAPTER FOURTEEN

NORA GLANCED BEHIND her, but Griffin didn't come back—no matter how hard she wished for it. She had to face Dale on her own.

"What do you want?" she asked, proud her steady voice betrayed none of the nerves churning in her stomach.

He held up his hands, a gesture meant to make him seem harmless. It didn't. "I just want to talk to you. Let's go inside—"

"No."

Did he think she was an idiot? There was no way she'd let him inside her home where he could corner her. He'd hurt his wife and son, had killed her mother. It was much better, safer, to keep this meeting out in the open where her neighbors could hear her if she screamed. Where she had room to run.

"What do you want?" she repeated.

He grinned but his eyes on hers were flat and so cold, she shivered. "I have a proposition for you, a way for us to help each other."

She laughed harshly. "If you think I'd do anything to help you, you're crazy."

"If you don't do as I say or your family will be ripped apart. And it'll be all your fault."

Fear gripped her. Chilled her skin. "What are you talking about?"

He brushed a piece of lint off his sleeve. "I'm talking about the fact that I wasn't the first man your mother took as a lover. She cheated on your father, had a one-night stand." Dale's grin was smug. "She slept with her husband's brother."

A roaring filled her ears, drowned out the sounds of the night, of traffic and birds and her neighbor watering his lawn. Her knees threatened to buckle. She locked them, swallowed in an attempt to dislodge the lump in her throat. "You're lying."

He had to be. Yes, her mother had been unfaithful to her father—perhaps with more than one man—but Uncle Ken?

No, she thought firmly. Frantically. No! He'd never do that. He was good and honorable and honest. He loved his wife and brother. He'd never hurt them... never betray their trust that way.

Dale rocked back on his heels. "Denying it doesn't make it less true. I explained to your uncle that I'd take that truth public unless certain compensation was made to me, but so far he's been resistant to do the smart thing. Which is where you come in."

It was clear now. Dale hadn't come back to Mystic Point because of the investigation. He'd come back to blackmail Ken. Griffin had been right that day at the café when he'd said Dale had returned to town for a reason other than admitting the truth about her mother's death.

There's something here he wants and he won't hesitate to take down anyone who stands between him and whatever that is. Do yourself a favor and stay out of his way.

She wasn't in Dale's way, she thought dully. She was a means to an end.

"Ken hasn't agreed to my…offer," Dale continued, "because he thinks anything I say will be his word against mine. What he doesn't know is that I have proof of the affair. Living, breathing proof." He pulled a folded piece of paper from his pocket and held it out. "And it's standing right in front of me."

She shook her head slowly. "No. No." She hated that she sounded desperate and unsure. That he showed him any hint of weakness.

"Val didn't know for sure which brother you belonged to, not until you had your tonsils removed and she saw this." He shook the paper.

Nora stared at it, her heart screaming at her not to take it, to trust in the people she loved, to believe in her uncle. Her head told her Dale was nothing but a liar and a con man who'd resort to any means to get what he wanted.

But the faith she'd always had—that belief that everything would work out for the best—deserted her, leaving in its place the cold, harsh slap of reality. One she couldn't ignore.

Her hands trembling, she took the paper, unfolded it to reveal a copy of her medical records. She'd been five when she'd had a tonsillectomy so all she remembered were bits and pieces. The day of the surgery her mother had brought her balloons—a dozen brightly colored ones that filled the small hospital room—and then had gone to work. Nora's dad had been out to sea but when he'd returned a week later, he'd brought her a stuffed lion and had taken her out for ice cream though, by then, she could eat solid foods.

But her sisters had been there for her the entire time. Layne had spent the night at the hospital, sleeping in a chair next to Nora's bed. Tori had spent countless hours playing games and reading to her.

"This proves nothing," Nora said, hoping, praying, she was right.

"Maybe not, but it raised a very interesting question for your mother. You see, she knew her blood type was O, just as she knew her husband was type B. So when she saw there that you had type A blood, well…" He slid his hand into his pockets. "She realized that her… indiscretion with Ken had a lasting consequence."

Nora's thoughts tumbled, one after the other. She searched her memory, remembered what she'd learned in biology class. Bile rose in her throat, threatened to choke her.

Because any biological children of Val and Tim Sullivan would have either type O or type B blood.

Tim Sullivan wasn't her father.

She stumbled back a step. Her stomach cramped and she bent over, clutched her arms around herself. Oh, God. Oh, God, oh, God, oh, God. It wasn't true. It couldn't be. She couldn't catch her breath, her world spun and she collapsed, her knees hitting the concrete with a painful thud. "No."

"Now, this is what is going to happen," Dale said, squatting in front of her. "You are going to convince Ken to give me what I want. Once that happens, I'll take my money and your secret and leave town. You'll never hear from me again."

He'd disappear. Just like he did eighteen years ago. He'd never be punished for killing her mother. She raised her head, forced herself to meet his eyes. "And if I don't?" she asked hoarsely, her face stiff.

"Then everyone will find out the truth. The whole truth." He slapped his thighs and rose to his full height.

"I'm staying at the Wave Runner Motel. You have until noon Monday to get me my money." He walked up to her, stopping at her shoulder. "Don't take it so hard, baby girl. Either way you look at it, you're still a Sullivan."

AT ERIN AND Collin's engagement party Saturday evening, Nora chatted with friends and family, smiled in family photos, laughed along with the rest of the revelers. She loaded a plate with food, pushed it around with her fork in the hopes that no one would notice she hadn't eaten a bite. Carried a glass of wine around with her, sipping it whenever she felt her throat tighten, the tears threaten. She'd mingled and done her best to pretend as if nothing had changed.

As if her entire life hadn't changed.

But she couldn't let her guard down, couldn't let her act slip, not even for a moment. She was afraid if she did, she'd break down right there in the middle of the Seneca Country Club's restaurant. Half-listening to a conversation between a small group of women who taught with Erin, she lifted her glass to her lips. Froze to see her father and uncle standing off to the side by the bar.

They were so similar with their blond hair and tall, slim builds and blue eyes. Tim said something that had Ken laughing then clapping his younger brother on the shoulder before they joined the crowd again.

Nora's composure started to slip. She could feel it in the way her smile faded, in how her grip on the glass tightened. Excusing herself from the group, she wove her way through the crowd, her steps measured until she reached the dark hallway. Only then did she let the panic push her into a fast trot, her heels clipping against the tile floor.

Inside the ladies' room, she locked the door and exhaled, pressed the heels of her hands against the headache behind her temples.

She was exhausted. She hadn't slept in two nights, which was obvious, she thought as she caught sight of her reflection in the mirror above the sink. She had dark circles under her eyes that no amount of cover-up had been able to hide. Her complexion was waxy and stress lines bracketed her mouth.

After Dale had walked away from her two nights ago, she'd waited until Layne started her evening shift at the station then, using the spare key she'd given her, Nora let herself into Layne's house. When their father moved in with Celeste years ago, he left everything from his old life behind. Photo albums and scrapbooks, hand-drawn pictures from his daughters, old tax returns and a lifetime of papers from medical records to birth certificates.

Alone in the dusty, stuffy attic, surrounded by the memories of her childhood, she'd searched through at least half a dozen plastic totes before she'd found what she'd been dreading. A record from when her mother had gallbladder surgery and a card from one of the times her father had donated blood proved Dale was telling the truth.

She reapplied her lipstick then slowly lowered her hand as she studied the familiar lines of her face. Looking for something, any sign that she was still the same person she'd been before Dale had rocked her entire world.

That she was still Tim Sullivan's daughter.

The tube of lipstick fell from her fingers, slid into

the sink leaving a red smear. Her fingers trembled as she picked it up, put the lid back on and slid it into her clutch as someone tapped on the door.

Rolling her shoulders back, she unlocked the door, sent a smile at the middle-aged woman waiting in the hall then headed back to the party.

She turned the corner and stopped to see Griffin standing just inside the doorway, all rough edges and sex appeal in a pair of khakis and a blue, button-down shirt. He was here. He came.

She shut her eyes against the sudden relief that turned her legs to jelly, to the sting of tears behind her eyelids. She wanted to throw herself into his arms, press her face against his neck and weep. Wanted to hold on to him and never let go.

Hurrying toward him, she got stuck behind a large man holding a small infant and could only watch as Uncle Ken stormed up to Griffin.

"This is a private event," Uncle Ken said, his oh-so-polite tone unable to hide the thread of steel underneath it. "I'm afraid you'll have to leave."

"Must be you didn't get the memo," Griffin said, "but I was invited."

Uncle Ken bristled. "By whom?"

"Me," she said as she reached them. She slid between the two men facing off amidst the gaiety of free food and, even better, an open bar. "Griffin. Hi. Glad you could make it."

He inclined his head. "Angel."

Behind her, Uncle Ken stiffened even more. "What's going on here, Nora?"

"Griffin is my plus one. Is that a problem?"

Ken's eyebrows drew together at her harsh tone. "Of course not," he said, slowly. He leaned in close, touched her arm. "Honey, are you all right? Can I get you a soda?"

All right? She held back a hysterical laugh. No, she wasn't all right. She was miserable and heartbroken and so angry she wanted to slap him, to rail at him. How could he have done that? How could he have slept with his brother's wife?

How could he be her father?

"I'm fine," she said with difficulty, easing back so that his hand fell to his side. She pressed against Griffin's side. "I'm just fine."

Ken looked hurt and confused and she was torn, torn between guilt and resentment. Between the love she felt for him, had always felt for him, and her disappointment in him.

"Well, then, I'd better get back to the party," he said. "I hope you two enjoy yourselves." He sounded as if he could almost mean it. Almost. But she knew it was just as big of an act as hers because there was no way he wanted the son of the man who was blackmailing him at his daughter's engagement party. No way he wanted Nora around Griffin.

"We will," Nora assured him, as firmly as she'd told him she was fine, determined to make both statements true.

Behind them, a twentysomething couple entered the restaurant and Ken greeted them with a politician's smile. Nora tugged Griffin farther into the restaurant.

She led him to the table in the corner her family had claimed as their own. Tori's purse was on the table next to Celeste's camera bag. Her father had already taken off his suit jacket and it hung over the back of his vacant chair. Nora glanced around and saw her sisters having what looked like an animated—and quite humorous—

conversation with a woman they'd gone to school with. Her father and Celeste stood with their arms around each other's waists, Celeste's camera hanging from her neck. Erin and Collin stood by his grandparents' table while Astor and Ken worked the room like the social pros they were, handing out greetings and smiles, handshakes and welcomes with ease.

Everyone she loved would be hurt by the truth, their lives forever altered. She didn't think she could do that to them, couldn't hurt them that way.

But she was afraid she wasn't strong enough to hold this secret inside of her. It was already ripping her apart. She'd never be the same. Would never look at her life, her family the same.

"Can I get you a drink?" she asked Griffin, ignoring his scowl, how his expression seemed to get darker and darker the farther they made it into the restaurant. She had enough on her mind. "Or something to eat? They've set up a buffet in the back, the pot stickers are to die for." Nothing. He didn't even look at her, just kept glowering at the crowd, his hands shoved deep into the pockets of his khakis, his hair neat, his face clean-shaven. "I think they stuffed them with crack," she added.

His head swung up, his eyes narrowed. "What?"

"Just seeing if you're paying attention."

"I'll have a beer," he said, looking defensive as if he expected her to make some quip about his drink of choice.

"Okay," she said slowly, wondering if her calling and asking him to come there had been a mistake. "I'll be right back but feel free to mingle."

When she walked away she heard him mutter, "That'll be a cold day in hell."

Charming as always. She could be grateful that, at least, hadn't changed.

At the bar, she ordered his beer and herself a glass of Merlot and noticed Anthony hunched over a glass of whiskey in the corner. Thought about how, before she'd known the possibility that she wasn't just his cousin, but his sister, she would've gone over to him, nudged his shoulder. Now she kept her distance.

But then he tossed half his drink back and stared across the room.

Frowning, she followed his gaze. Her eyebrows rose at the sight of Jess leading Tanner over to her uncle and Layne. Nora couldn't stay away. She went up to Anthony and laid a hand on his arm. "You okay?" she asked quietly.

He raised his glass. "Never better." Then he drained it and held up his finger for the bartender to bring him another one.

Her drinks arrived and she bit her lower lip, glanced between her obviously miserable, quickly becoming inebriated cousin and her miserable, looked-ready-to-rip-out-the-throat-of-anyone-who-so-much-as-looked-at-him date.

And to think, she'd invited Griffin to get her mind off of her worries, to help her through a tough time.

Figuring she owed it to society at large to worry more about her date than Anthony, she picked up her drinks. "Take it easy on those," she told her young cousin softly.

He met her eyes and took a long gulp.

"Very mature," she told him. "But just remember this is your sister's night." She leaned closer so she could speak into his ear. "And if you do anything to spoil it, you will have to deal with me."

Glaring at her, he deliberately pushed his drink aside and then got to his feet and walked away.

At least that was one problem dealt with. She went back to her table. Griffin sat alone, his legs stretched out in front of him as he took in the room.

"Here you go," she said, handing him his beer as she sat next to him. She sipped her wine. A DJ played music in the other room where a small dance floor had been set up. The song selection was good and from what she'd heard, the food was even better. The place was packed as just about everyone Erin and Collin cared for was there to celebrate their engagement.

She only wished she could enjoy it.

"This what you're looking for?" Griffin asked, his voice startling her out of her thoughts.

She picked up a napkin from the table and blotted at the drop of wine that had spilled on her dress. "Excuse me?"

His gaze never wavered from hers. "This is an engagement party, right? To celebrate the perfect couple before they have the perfect wedding and live the perfect life? Isn't that what you want?"

She set her wineglass on the table, feeling as if there was more to his question "Not at the moment, no," she said slowly. But she couldn't deny she'd dreamed of having that perfect life with someone who loved her. "Right now I'd just be happy to get through this evening."

"This isn't exactly my scene," he said, sounding like a teenager.

She glanced around at her aunt and uncle's polished friends, the expensive decor and fancy dresses. "Yes, well, I don't think it's anyone's usual scene, at least, not for us normal folk."

"You look right here," he said gruffly. "In that dress
and those heels…your hair. You fit right in."

"Is that a compliment?" she asked, refusing to raise
her hand to her heat ironed hair or adjust the thin strap
of her sage colored dress. "Or an insult?"

"Can it be both?"

"No."

His lips twitched and for the first time since Dale had
told her about her mother and uncle's affair, the knot in
her stomach eased.

"You look good," Griffin said. "And you know it."

"Thank you so much for that heartfelt declaration,"
she said, telling herself it was stupid to feel disappointed. What did she want from him? A sonnet written
to her beauty, grace and charm? He liked her. Enjoyed
spending time with her. Hadn't he taken her on a fright-
ening—and yes, exhilarating—ride on his motorcycle?

She sipped her wine and noticed Griffin watching
her with interest and attraction and something close to
caution. She didn't care, couldn't worry about trying
to figure him out. She needed him tonight. Needed his
strong, steady presence to help her navigate the rough
seas threatening to drown her.

He was real, maybe the only real thing she had left
in her life. And she was going to hold on to him for as
long as she could.

TANNER FELT LIKE a complete dork.

His damn tie was crooked. He kept tugging at it,
trying to straighten it but it felt like it was strangling
him so he finally let his hand drop. The restaurant
was packed, so packed that he hadn't even realized his
brother was here until fifteen minutes ago when he'd
spotted Griffin sitting alone at the bar. When he'd gone

over to talk to him, it'd been clear Griffin hadn't wanted Tanner hanging around.

But he didn't know anyone else here except Jess and she was acting weird.

Weirder than usual, anyway.

For one thing, she kept smiling at him. And she touched him, like, all night long. His arm, his hand, his back. She'd even pulled him onto the dance floor when a slow song—one of those ones that sounded like it should be playing at someone's wedding—came on. Pressed up against him, her hips against his, her arms twined around his neck, her fingers playing with the hair at his nape.

He'd broken out into a sweat and was glad his mom had insisted he wear a suit coat to this thing.

Yeah, he thought, watching her from their table as she made her way back to him, a small plate of food in her hand, she was acting totally un-Jess-like.

And he thought he knew why.

"You should get up there," she said as she joined him, setting her food on the table. "They're almost out of those stuffed mushrooms you were inhaling."

"I'm not hungry." He winced to realize he sounded like a two-year-old. Cleared his throat. "The line must've been long."

She dragged a large shrimp through the cocktail sauce on her plate. "Not really."

"You were gone a long time."

"Aw, did you miss me?" she asked with a look from under her lashes that he couldn't help think seemed practiced. And contrived.

And a far cry from the way she'd looked at him the last few times they'd hung out—once at his house, twice at her uncle's. She hadn't touched him those times, either, hadn't flirted with him or hung on his every word like she'd done tonight.

"What's going on?" he asked quietly, ignoring the voice in his head telling him to quit being such a pussy and just enjoy whatever game she was playing. That maybe it would lead to him finally getting laid.

"An engagement party," she said, her silent duh implied.

He scooted his chair closer to her. "No. I mean what's going on with you? You're acting like..."

"Like...?"

He raised a shoulder. Glanced pointedly at the guy standing with a group of thirtysomethings. "Like the only reason you asked me to this party was so you could make that guy jealous."

She stiffened. "What guy?"

The same guy who'd been in the diner that day Jess finally agreed to hang out with Tanner. The same guy she kept looking at. The one who kept looking back.

"The one with the curly hair," he said, inclining his head.

She didn't follow his gaze, just bit into a shrimp. "Anthony and I went out a few times," she said after she chewed. "It ended."

"Yeah," Tanner said softly, watching her carefully, "but is it over?"

She smiled but it was so sad, it felt like he'd just taken an elbow to the gut. "Anthony says it is."

"Is that what you want?"

"Since when should it matter what I want?" she asked with a harsh laugh. "Look, I'm used to not getting everything I wish for. It's no big deal. He's just another guy."

Tanner wanted to believe that. Wanted to so badly, maybe more than he'd ever wanted anything.

"Besides," she said, sounding unlike herself again as she leaned toward him and trailed her fingers across his cheek, "I'm with you tonight."

She slid her hand behind his neck, gently pulled his face toward hers. His heart pounded. She was going to kiss him. Their first kiss, the event he'd been thinking about, hoping for over the past week was finally going to happen in a matter of moments, right there in front of a bunch of people he didn't know, his brother and very possibly her uncle.

Not to mention Anthony, the guy she wasn't even close to being over.

"Wait," he said, leaning back. Her hand fell from his neck and he immediately missed the feel of her warm fingers on her skin, could've kicked his own ass for stopping her. "I'm not doing this. Not like this, anyway."

Her eyes flashed, a hint of color entered her cheeks and she sat back, crossing her arms. "What is your problem?"

Really? Could she be that clueless? "My problem is I don't like being used."

She smirked. "Funny but that's not what you said the other day when I told you we could hang out. Now you've what? Changed your mind?"

He stood, looked from her to Anthony—who was watching them, his brows lowered, his hands stuffed in the pockets of his suit pants—and back to her again.

"Yeah," he said slowly, not sure if choosing his pride over a pretty girl was the smartest choice he'd ever made but unable to do otherwise. "I guess I have changed my mind." He held her gaze. "About a couple of things."

And he walked away.

CHAPTER FIFTEEN

"DUDE," Tanner said, walking up to Griffin as he shook his mom's car keys in his hand, "I'm taking off."

Griffin narrowed his eyes, looked behind the kid to the table where Jess sat by herself, a scowl on her face, her eyes shooting daggers at his brother's back. "You okay?"

"What do you care?" the kid asked.

Griffin sipped his beer. "I care if you wrap Mom's minivan around a tree because you're pissed off at some girl."

Tanner flushed. "Sorry," he said, man enough to look Griffin in the eye as he apologized. "I'm fine. I've just…had enough, you know?"

Yeah, Griffin thought as Tanner walked away, he did know. He'd had enough, too. Enough of being unable to take his eyes off Nora for more than a minute. Enough of sitting there feeling out of place, of having people send him curious, sidelong glances as if they knew he didn't belong there.

But he hadn't left yet, hadn't wanted to, not when watching Nora on the dance floor with her sisters kept him entranced. That damn dress of hers floated around her legs like fairies' wings. She wasn't the best dancer but there was no discounting how much he enjoyed watching her as she moved to the music, her hips swaying, her arms lifting above her head. Her smile, though not quite as bright as usual, still lit up the room.

He wanted to storm onto the dance floor, toss her over his shoulder and take her to his bed where she could smile at him, and only him. Where he could surround himself with her body, her sense of humor and her kindness and patience. Where he could take whatever she was willing to give.

But he was afraid whatever that was, it wouldn't be enough for him. Not nearly enough.

"Whew," she said, when she rejoined him, her hair sticking to the side of her neck, her face flushed, "it's hot in there."

In there being the room with the dance floor, the one that opened to the larger dining room. She sipped the ice water she'd switched to over two hours ago when her family had joined them at the table. The same time Griffin had gone to the bar for another beer and had decided to stay there instead of hanging out with a table full of Sullivans.

But she hadn't said a word, hadn't begged him to join her family. Had just made herself comfortable on the stool next to his, chattering away about this guest or that, pointing out some of the bigwigs her aunt's family knew who'd come in from Boston and Martha's Vineyard and Cape Cod, names he'd heard mentioned in the news or read about in the paper.

Christ, he really didn't belong here.

The song ended and another started, this one slower and melodic. Nora set her water down and sighed dreamily. "I love this song." She slid to her feet, smiled and held out her hand. "Come on. Dance with me."

He ground his back teeth together as he looked at her. "No."

She raised her eyebrows. "Why not?"

Because he couldn't be responsible for what he'd do if he touched her, if he held her in his arms, if she pressed those lush curves up against him. Because he was angry and embarrassed and resentful to be around these people with their perfect lives and their perfect pasts.

"Because I'm not interested in being a part of this dog and pony show you've got going on," he said.

Her smile strained, her movements jerky, she waved at an elderly woman who passed by them. "Excuse me?" she said through barely moving lips.

"No need to act all offended and pissed," he said mildly, finishing his beer. "We both know why you invited me here."

"Oh, believe me," she said way too sweetly for him to believe she meant it, "I'm not acting."

"You wanted me here to shock your family."

"Are we in some sort of teenage romantic comedy and no one told me?" she asked.

"You're the one who started this game. Don't blame me if things don't turn out the way you planned."

She stared at him as if contemplating how much effort it would take for her to break his neck and drag his lifeless body out back to the Dumpster. "Okay," she said softly as if talking to herself. "Okay, that's it. Come on."

"I told you, I don't want to dance."

When she looked at him, her eyes flashed but it was the hurt beneath that had him following her through the restaurant. To his surprise they didn't head toward the dance floor but wove their way toward the front of the building. He followed her, his eyes on her back, which was ramrod straight, her legs as they scissored quickly in those high heels, the way she held her head stiffly.

She flung open the door in a gesture he found both overly dramatic and endearing as hell. "Goodbye."

He stepped up close to her, making sure to keep on the inside of the building. "You kicking me out, angel?"

She tossed her head back, looking very much like Tori for a moment. "Damn right."

"What's the matter? Can't handle the truth?"

She glanced behind them then grabbed his hand and all but dragged him outside, around the front of the building to the side where the door to the kitchen had been left open. The sounds filled the night, competed with the ocean waves crashing onto shore.

"You want some truths?" she asked harshly, the moon glinting off her hair. "Here are a few. I didn't invite you to shock my family. If I'd wanted to do that, I would've shaved my head and joined an all vegan cult."

He shrugged, but couldn't shake the feeling he'd somehow made a misstep. Guess he'd just keep walking and see where he ended up. "Maybe you were trying to prove a point?"

"What point? That I'm an idiot who has terrible taste in the men I date?"

His breath hitched. "We're not dating."

"Not anymore," she muttered.

"Not ever."

Her eyes narrowed. "Is that what this is about? You don't want anyone to know you're with me?"

She made it sound stupid. It wasn't. It was for her own good. "I don't want people to get the wrong idea about us."

"And yet you agreed to come to this party tonight. You took me for a ride on your motorcycle. We had dinner together where any number of people saw us."

"I shouldn't have come here," he said. "I don't be-

long in a place like this with those people." *With you.*
"I should be down at the Yacht Pub having a couple of
beers not—" he waved his hand feeling inadequate and
stupid "—hanging out in some club with a bunch of ob-
noxious lawyers and teachers and doctors."

She tucked her silky hair behind her ear, but he noticed her hand was unsteady. "Well, that certainly clears
up a few things. So let me make a few things clear, too.
I invited you to my cousin's engagement party because
I wanted you here. I wanted you with me. I—" She
pressed her lips together, shook her head as if clearing out whatever she'd been about to say. "I thought
we'd have a nice evening, that maybe you could show
my family the side of you I see. Instead you sulked
and scowled and generally acted like some James Dean
wannabe, all petulant and moody, as if you were looking down on the rest of us."

Him? Looking down on a bunch of politicians and
millionaires? She had to be joking. "I told you," he insisted, wondering how this had gotten turned around
on him, "this just isn't my scene."

"Yes, you told me that. How stupid of me to think
that you'd be willing to set aside that chip on your shoulder for a few hours. Well, you're off the hook, Griffin.
So go. Leave," she said when he didn't move.

But to his horror, her voice cracked, her mouth wobbled. She blinked and tears slid from her eyes, trailed
down her cheeks.

Panicked, out of his element, he sneered. "Tears? I
thought better of you."

Those eyes flashed and she lifted her chin, wiped at
the wetness on her face. "That's not what this is about.
This is about you not wanting me to think better of you.
Well, congratulations. I no longer do." Hugging her

arms around herself she walked up to him until mere inches separated their bodies. "I needed you tonight," she whispered. "I needed you. I won't make that mistake again."

I NEEDED YOU tonight.

Three hours later, Nora's words echoed in Griffin's head as the night surrounded him, the moon shining brightly, stars blanketing the dark sky. He ran his fingers through his hair, tried to pace away the guilt gnawing at him. Up and down the sidewalk. Up and down.

Damn it, he shouldn't feel guilty. All he'd told her was the truth. He hadn't belonged at that party. She should've known that, should've seen it the moment he stepped into the country club in his casual clothes, the grease under his nails.

Instead she'd seemed so happy to see him, so relieved.

I needed you.

He stomped back the way he'd come. Shit.

A car's headlights cut through the dark night, illuminated him for a second before the car swung into the driveway. He stormed over, yanked open the door before she'd even shut off the engine.

"I don't want you to need me," he growled.

Nora gave him one of her cool, patronizing looks. "Yes," she said, climbing out of the car, forcing him to back up or getting one of her spiked heels through his foot. "You've made that perfectly clear."

She reached back inside for her purse, her dress floating around her thighs. Straightening, she slammed the door shut then walked past him as if he was invisible.

Leaping onto the porch, he caught up with her as she

dug her key out of her purse. "I'm not going to apologize," he told her.

Though an apology was stuck in his throat. One that told her how sorry he was he'd hurt her, that he hadn't meant to make her cry. That seeing her tears had torn him up inside and he'd do anything, say anything to get her to forgive him.

But letting the words out would give her power over him, would let her know that he cared. Made him worry that she'd use those words against him someday.

She didn't even glance at him, just unlocked the door. Before she could step inside, he laid his arm across the doorway, blocking her. "If you don't mind," she said, staring straight ahead, her voice all cold and prim, "I've had a really rotten couple of days and now I'd like to be alone."

That was wrong, he thought, his fingers tightening on the wood. Someone like Nora should never be alone. Especially now when she looked so lost, so scared. She needed someone to take care of her.

He went inside.

"Whoa, whoa," she called after him, following him into the kitchen. "Have you lost your mind?" she asked as he yanked open the freezer. "What are you doing?"

He grabbed a container of ice cream, slammed it on the counter. "Where are your spoons?"

"Get away from my ice cream," she snapped, reaching for the container.

He blocked her. "It's not for me." He opened a drawer, grabbed the first spoon he saw. "It's for you."

She froze, going so still he glanced over his shoulder at her to make sure she hadn't slipped into a coma. "What?"

He searched through her cupboards—her neatly organized cupboards filled with matching plates and serving trays—until he found a bowl. Using the spoon, he scooped out ice cream and slammed it down on the table.

"Sit," he ordered, feeling like an idiot. The back of his neck was hot and he was antsy and revved up. Out of control. He had no idea what to do, what to say.

All he knew was that he'd hurt her and he had to make it right.

NORA STARED AT Griffin. He stood with his feet apart, his arms crossed, his mouth turned down. He looked angry and out of place in her tiny kitchen with his dark clothes, his scowl.

"You want me to eat ice cream?" she asked. Her head pounded, her heart ached. She needed some space to sort through things, to figure out what to do next, but she couldn't do that with him there. "I'm having a hard time following your logic here."

"You're upset," he said as if through grit teeth. "Don't women eat ice cream when they're upset?"

Her hand fell to her side. "Griffin, why are you doing this?" she whispered, her throat clogging with tears. She blew out a shaky breath. "I'm not up for this. I don't want you here."

Wasn't strong enough to deal with her feelings for him, not tonight.

His expression grim, his lips pressed together, he nodded. "I know."

Then he pulled her into his arms.

Shock held her immobile for the length of two heartbeats but then she realized he wasn't trying to kiss her, wasn't trying to seduce her.

He was holding her.

His arms were wrapped around her waist, his hands splayed across her lower back. His cheek brushed hers, his skin smooth. He smelled of aftershave and the night air, felt solid and warm. She wanted to resist, knew she should. She couldn't keep deluding herself about him, couldn't keep convincing herself there was more to him than a gruff exterior, that he had more to give than the bare minimum.

Leaning back, she laid her hands against his chest ready to push him away.

He tightened his hold. "Don't," he said gruffly against her neck. "Let me. Just let me."

She shut her eyes, tried not to succumb to the feel of his arms around her, but he rubbed circles on her back, dragging the silk of her dress over her skin. Kissed her hair above her ear. Her temple. Her forehead. Then he tucked her head onto his shoulder.

Tears pricked behind her eyelids. She tried to swallow them, remembered his harsh words at the party when she'd cried. But it was all too much. Her uncle's affair with her mother. Dale walking around a free man. And Griffin—so confusing and irritating and wonderful.

A sob broke through her control. She wound her arms around Griffin's waist, fisted the back of his shirt in her hands and hid her face against the crook of his neck as she cried. He didn't murmur useless platitudes, didn't try to convince her that everything would be all right or talk her down.

He just held her close so she wouldn't fall off the ledge.

She cried until her throat was sore. Cried until her eyes burned, her nose ran.

And all the while, Griffin held her. Smoothed his hands up and down her back, over her hair.

Emotionally spent, physically exhausted, she finally raised her head. Sniffed then grimaced to see the evidence of her crying jag on his shoulder. She forced her fists open, released his shirt and stepped back.

She grabbed a paper towel and mopped her face, heard the sound of water running.

"Here," he said, holding a glass of water.

Looking anywhere but at him, she took it, drained it in a few swallows. "Thanks."

She felt his eyes on her as she wet a clean dish-cloth, kept her back to him as she pressed the cool cloth against her hot cheeks, her neck.

"Tell me," he said.

She faced him. She knew he wanted her to share what was wrong but she didn't know if she could. Saying it aloud made it all too real. Made it impossible for her to pretend it was all a horrible nightmare.

But he'd come there for her, had waited for her. He stood before her now patiently, his shirt damp from her tears.

"Dale was here," she said. "He was waiting for me the other night when you dropped me off after dinner."

Griffin's expression darkened, fury flashed in his eyes. "Did he hurt you?"

"He didn't touch me." But he had hurt her. Had enjoyed seeing her in pain. "You were right, he didn't come back to tell the truth about what happened to my mother. He's here to get money." She pushed away from the counter, crossed her arms. "He's blackmailing Uncle Ken. And he wants my help to do it."

"What could Dale possibly have on your uncle?"

She swallowed. "Me. He has me. Mom and Uncle

Ken had an affair, a one-night stand," she said, her voice raw. "I'm the result."

He flinched. "He could be lying. It'd be just like the old man to make something like this up."

"I thought that, too, hoped that was the case but... Tim Sullivan isn't my father. I have until Monday at noon to convince Ken to pay Dale. If I do, Dale's promised to leave town and never return."

"If you don't?"

"He'll expose the secret. Griffin, it'll tear my family apart."

"Your uncle doesn't know?"

She sank onto a chair, unhooked her shoes and slipped them off. "He knows Mom told Dale about the affair but he doesn't know about me. That he's my father."

Griffin crouched in front of her. "What are you going to do?"

"I'm going to ask Uncle Ken to pay." She'd decided at the party, watching her aunt and uncle slow dance, seeing her entire family together had made her realize she'd do anything to protect them from this secret. "I don't have any other choice." She just prayed Dale kept his end of the bargain and disappeared forever.

In a few days, this would all be over. They could all put the past behind them.

Griffin surged up. "I should go."

She blinked. Frowned. "What? Why?"

"You don't need me here." He held himself rigidly, his hands fisted at his sides. "How could you want me here after what my father did to your mother? What he's doing to you?"

"Damn it, Griffin, you're not your father. And I refuse to let you take responsibility for his actions. Or maybe you think all children should shoulder that responsibility? Maybe it's all my fault my mother and uncle had an affair."

"Don't be stupid," he snapped.

Her eyes about popped out of her head, her blood heated. "Me?" She jumped up, poked him in the chest. "Listen, buddy, there's only one stupid person in this room and it sure as hell isn't me."

He grabbed her finger, held it against his chest. "Don't poke me," he warned, his tone dark and dangerous.

"Or what?" she asked, tired of being cautious, of playing it safe.

He hesitated, his fingers tightening on her hand, his eyes heating.

"Looks like you don't have to wait anymore," she told him, then she rose onto her toes and crushed her mouth to his. She poured her heart and soul into the kiss, hoped he understood she was willing to give him anything he desired. Everything she was.

He set her back, held her at arm's length, a muscle working in his jaw. "I don't want to take advantage of you."

Any remaining resistance she'd held against him crumbled. He was so good inside, even if he couldn't see it. But she saw. Surely she could do this. She could be with him tonight, could give him her body, and possibly her heart, without expecting anything in return.

Without falling even more in love with him.

"How about I take advantage of you then?" she asked. She kissed him again, pressed against him until his body lost its rigidity, until he kissed her back, long and deep and hard.

Taking his hand, she led him to her bedroom. She

crossed to the bedside table and turned on the lamp. He didn't come closer, just stood in the doorway watching her as if worried this was some sort of trick, that what he wanted was right beyond his reach and would remain there.

So she went to him, brushed her mouth against his, placed small, openmouthed kisses along his jaw, his neck. She licked the line of his throat, tasted the salt of his skin, then pushed aside the collar of his shirt and gently bit on the corded muscle at the base of his neck.

He groaned and stabbed his hands into her hair, held her head still as he kissed her ferociously. Unable to stop touching him, she slid her hands across his shoulders, down his arms to his wrists and back up again but it wasn't enough. She needed to feel his skin, needed his warmth and strength.

Working her hands between their bodies, she freed the buttons on his shirt, yanked the tail of it from his pants then shoved it down his arms. She leaned back. She wanted to see him. Wanted to remember this moment, this night, forever.

He was perfect. Dusky skin, a sprinkling of dark hair across his wide chest, flat abs. She smoothed her palms over his chest, across his beaded nipples. He kissed her again, trapping her hands between them. Her fingers curled, scratched his skin and he deepened the kiss, his hands gliding underneath her dress to trail up the back of her thighs.

Spinning her around, he edged her forward until she stood before her large dresser, their reflection in the mirror. He tugged down the zipper at her back, pushed the straps off her shoulders. She slipped her arms free and dragged the dress past her hips. It pooled at her feet and she kicked it aside as Griffin reached around and unhooked the front of her bra.

She watched their reflection as his big hands pulled the cups aside exposing her breasts. Her nipples tightened. Her breath caught. He hooked his forefingers under the straps and slowly drew them down her arms.

"Angel," he said huskily, reverently, his body big and warm at her back, "you are so beautiful."

Her eyes on his in the mirror, she lifted his hands to her breasts. "I'm not an angel."

"Nora," he breathed, cupping her. "Beautiful, sweet Nora."

He rubbed his thumbs across her nipples, gently pinched and pulled until she bucked against him. He slid his hands across her rib cage, over her belly to her panties, pulled them down. She stepped out of them as he gathered her hair in his hand, latched his mouth onto the side of her neck and suckled gently.

She gasped, pressed back into him. He rolled his hips, his khakis rough against her skin, his erection nestled at the base of her spine. His hand went to the dense curls between her thighs, his fingers warm…his touch sure.

Pressure built. Her body heated. He laid the flat of his other hand on her stomach, held her against him. The sight of them in the mirror, his expression so fierce, his hands on her undid her. Her breathing quickened, her pelvic muscles contracted.

Looking into his eyes, she flew over the edge into pleasure.

GRIFFIN HAD NEVER seen anything so beautiful. Nora leaned back, her head against his shoulder but her eyes stayed on his in the mirror and he watched them darken as her body convulsed with her orgasm.

She was bowed back, her back arched, her hair brushing his chin, her ass pressing his arousal, her lips parted on a soundless gasp.

When she came down, he stroked her hair, laid his mouth on the side of her neck, the salty taste of her skin on his lips. He gripped her hips and gently turned her around, pressed a soft kiss to her still open mouth. She was so lovely, so perfect. She deserved for him to be gentle. To take care of her.

But her hands went to his pants, began unfastening them.

"You in a hurry?" he asked on a half-laugh as she fumbled with his belt, yanked his zipper down.

She kissed him, a hard, possessive kiss that about knocked him off his feet. "Yes."

And she shoved his pants and briefs down his legs then made a sound of exasperation to realize he still had his boots on.

Before he could move, she knelt in front of him and untied his boots, tugged at them until he toed them off. Then she pulled off his pants.

And the sight of her kneeling by his feet, her hair a golden cloud, her skin still flushed from her orgasm about did him in.

She trailed her fingernails lightly up the back of his calves. He shuddered.

"The bed," he managed to say through grit teeth.

She just shook her head and continued that slow torture. Across each knee, up the front of his thighs around to his ass and back down again. The next time she went up, she used her fingertips, her touch featherlight, up his inner thighs before tracing the underside of his penis. It jumped.

Sweat broke out along his forehead. He fisted his hands at his sides while she touched the length of him. Tipped his head back on a groan when she circled the head then wrapped her soft, warm hand around the base and kissed the head.

He yanked her to her feet, kissed her voraciously.

"Bed," he said again when he came up for air.

Her arms linked around his neck, her beaded nipples brushing against his chest, she leaned back and shook her head. "I like it right here."

She reached back and opened the top right drawer, took out a box of condoms and shook out a package.

His head was spinning, his body throbbing. He couldn't wrap his mind around what she was saying, what she was doing. But then she slowly rolled the condom on him and turned back to the dresser, her hands on the glossy top.

She smiled at him in the mirror.

Any and all thoughts of taking his time, of showing her what she meant to him, of treasuring her, flew out of his head. She wanted him. Here. Now. And he couldn't hold back.

Watching her reflection, he rubbed the tip of his erection against her opening. So slick. So hot. She bit her lower lip. Then he entered her slowly, never taking his eyes from her face, from the pleasure in her expression.

He held her hips, adjusted her better against him and stroked in and out. In and out. Her eyes went glassy and unfocused. Her mouth opened on a soundless cry. His pulse thundered in his ears. His movements quickened. He felt her tighten around him.

"Griffin," she gasped, her gaze holding his. "I see you. Only you."

He knew what she meant. He'd told her when he looked in the mirror he saw his father.

She saw only him.

It was that thought, knowing it was true, that sent him tumbling over the edge, taking her with him.

CHAPTER SIXTEEN

"I'LL GO with you," Griffin said the next morning while Nora made scrambled eggs.

She glanced over her shoulder at him, her stomach flipping pleasantly. They'd made love twice more, once in the shower—where brooding Griffin York had gently washed her hair—and again an hour ago when he woke her with kisses, his big body pressing her into the mattress, his arousal nudging her heat.

Now he stood at her counter making toast, his feet bare, his shirt open, his hair mussed. He was all scowly and so sexy she wanted to push him onto a chair, straddle him and do it all—every position they'd tried, every touch they'd shared—over again.

But not until she'd had something to eat. She wasn't a robot after all.

"Where are we going?" she asked, turning the burner off and sprinkling salt and pepper into the pan.

The toast popped up. "When you talk to your uncle tomorrow."

She stilled but then forced herself to go through the motions of plating the eggs, getting forks from the drawer. "Thank you," she said. He couldn't know how much it meant to her that he offered. "I would love to have you with me…"

He looked up from buttering the toast, his eyebrows drawn together. "But?"

"But…I think…given the nature of what Uncle Ken and I have to discuss, it would better if I went alone."

"Are you sure?"

She nodded, squeezed his arm. "Could you… Do you think maybe you could maybe meet me after, though?" She tried to smile, to lighten her tone. "I promise not to cry on your shoulder."

"I don't mind if you do," he told her so solemnly, so sweetly, her throat clogged.

She cleared it. "Thank you," she said, setting the plates on the table before pouring orange juice into two glasses.

He sat and dug into his eggs, grabbed a piece of toast from the pile he'd made. She could easily imagine him, in her kitchen, making breakfast with her day after day. Could picture him in her bed at night. Could see him in her life, with her, forever.

"What?" he asked around a mouthful.

"Hmm?"

"You're staring at me. And you're smiling."

She scooped up a bite of eggs. "I'm only staring because you're so damn pretty. And the smile is just one of those biological responses to happiness." She chewed. Swallowed. "You should try it some time."

His lips turned up, his gaze heated. "If you keep doing that trick you did last night in the shower, I'll never stop grinning."

"Yeah," she said smugly, knowing exactly which trick he meant, "that's a good move. Although—" She dropped her voice, slid her hand up his thigh. "I'm not sure I've perfected it yet. Maybe I need more practice."

He covered her hand with his. "You kill me," he said softly, his gaze serious. "In the very best possible way."

Her heart tumbled, then fell when he lifted her hand and pressed a warm kiss to her palm.

Someone pounded on the front door. Nora frowned and glanced at the microwave clock. 8:11.

"Hold that thought," she told him, getting to her feet.

When she reached the front door, she opened it to find Layne and Ross Taylor. "Well," Nora said, taking in their dark blue uniforms, the identical grim expressions on their faces, "this can't be good."

"You're not answering your phone," Layne said as she pushed past Nora and walked into the living room. Ross at least waited until Nora stepped back, gestured for him to enter.

"No," Nora said, shutting the door, "I'm not." She couldn't even remember where she'd left her cell phone after getting home last night and she'd never bothered getting a landline. "I've been busy."

"So I see," Layne said flatly as Griffin entered the room.

"I'm pretty sure everything we did last night was still legal in the state of Massachusetts," he said, causing Layne's eyes to narrow dangerously. "No need to arrest us."

"What's going on?" Nora asked before Layne could think of one of her pithy responses. "Is everything all right?"

"Actually we were hoping to find Mr. York here," Ross said with a nod toward Griffin. The chief was all competence and control with his steady blue eyes and Boston accent. "I'm sorry to have to inform you that your father has passed away."

A chill gripped Nora. Had her hugging her arms around herself. She looked to Griffin but he seemed as shocked as she was so she turned back to Layne. "What? What did he just say?"

"He's dead," Layne said, sounding like a cop, emotionless and removed, but her eyes told another story. "Dale York is dead."

THE BASTARD DIED in his sleep.

Griffin grabbed a beer from his refrigerator, twisted the cap off and drank deeply. Wiped the back of his hand across his mouth. Sudden, severe cardiac arrest according to the coroner who performed the autopsy. He hadn't suffered.

He should've suffered. For what he'd done to Nora, for what he'd done to Griffin and his mother. Christ, he'd taken Valerie Sullivan's life. For that alone, he should've spent the rest of his miserable life in prison. Instead he'd never be punished, never be found guilty.

The truth would never come out.

He took another drink. Maybe that was for the best. At least this way, Nora wouldn't have to worry about the secret of her mother's affair with her uncle coming to light.

He blew out a shaky breath. He'd left her yesterday. Had just…walked out after Chief Taylor and Layne told them a hotel maid had found Dale's body early that morning. He hadn't been able to face her, not when he'd had too many emotions roiling through him. So he'd pretended not to see the hurt in her eyes, how stricken she'd seemed when he left without a word.

He'd spent the rest of the day on his bike, drove up the coast until night had overtaken the day, then he'd gone even farther until he'd had to stop, to spend the night at some dive motel. After catching a few hours of restless sleep, he'd turned back to Mystic Point.

He'd wanted to call her. Had even rode past her house, stared at the windows like some damn stalker, hoping and wishing for things he could never have. But it was better to be alone. Safer.

He lifted the bottle back to his mouth. The sound of the front door opening had him turning, his shoulders tensing.

But it wasn't Nora walking into his house as if she owned the place. It was his mother.

He never should've given her a key.

She shut her eyes in relief when she saw him, her hand over her heart. "You're here. Thank God. I was so worried—"

"What are you doing here?" he asked, cursing himself when she flinched.

Like she used to when his father raised his voice. Raised his hand.

But then she straightened her shoulders. "I'm here because you haven't returned any of my phone calls. Because you're not at work." Her tone softened and she stepped closer. "I'm here because I was worried."

"Well, as you can see, I'm fine." He lifted his beer, drained it and got out another one. "Just fine."

She frowned. "Do you think that's going to help?"

"It can't hurt."

Nothing could hurt him. He wouldn't let it.

"Why don't you come over for dinner?" she asked gently.

"I'm not hungry."

"Griffin," she said, approaching him like she would a wounded, wild animal, "honey, I don't think you should be alone. Come with me. Come home."

Resentment built, tightening his chest with pressure. With bitterness. "You never gave me a home."

But she'd given one to Tanner. Had married a good man, had raised her second son in a house without violence and anger and fear.

"I did my best," Carol said, her eyes stark.

"You stayed with him," he said, the words ripping from his throat. "You stayed with that bastard for all those years."

His words seemed suspended in the air between them. Ugly. Accusing. His stomach churned. He'd only said the truth, he assured himself, but he couldn't help but wonder if he'd gone too far.

Too bad he had no idea how to take his words back. How to fix it.

His mom blanched and she swallowed visibly. "The first time Dale hit me," she said softly, "was shortly after we were married. I was shocked. I'd never been hit before, never had anyone hurt me. Up until then he'd been so…wonderful. So charming. When he apologized, I forgave him. When he told me it'd never happen again, I believed him. How could I not? He seemed so sincere. So truly sorry." Her fingers were white on the strap of her purse. "I loved him. Had vowed to love him for the rest of my life."

"It doesn't matter," Griffin said, not wanting to hear this, not wanting to see how much Dale had damaged her. How much pain Griffin's words had caused her.

She just shook her head. "But then it happened again. And again. And I started to wonder what I was doing wrong. Why I kept making the same mistakes, the ones that pushed him to hurt me." Tears glimmered in her eyes but her voice was strong. "I started to believe it when he said I was ugly and stupid and worthless. That no one would ever love me but him. That he'd kill me if I ever left him, if I ever went against him."

Griffin's stomach burned. He lifted an unsteady hand to reach for her. She stepped back and he let his arm drop. Knew that the least he could do was hear her out. She deserved that much from him. That much and so much more.

"All I could think about was getting through the day without setting him off," she continued relentlessly. "I learned how to gauge his every mood and I hid my bruises the best I could and, yes, I taught you how to live in fear because that was the life I knew. That was the only life I felt I deserved. But then you got old enough, big enough to try to protect me, and he hurt you, too. And I'm sorry for that, Griffin. I'm so, so sorry. I can't change the past, I can't undo the mistakes I've made or give you the childhood you deserved. And for that, you'll never forgive me, will you?" she asked, her voice shaking. "I've tried so hard to make it up to you but it's never enough. It'll never be enough for you."

He didn't answer. Couldn't. All he could do was stand silent while she walked away, shutting the door quietly behind her.

Griffin was afraid she was right. Afraid he couldn't forgive her. That he didn't know how. Wasn't capable of it.

And what kind of man did that make him?

AN HOUR AND another beer later, someone knocked on the kitchen door. Griffin ignored it, not even looking up from where he sat at the table, his legs out straight, his shoulders hunched. They knocked again. By the third time, the knock had changed to a pounding and, from the sounds of it, a few kicks for good measure.

Grabbing the bottle, he stormed over and yanked open the door.

Nora, holding two plastic bags and looking beautiful and untouchable, smiled at him.

Goddamn it.

He slouched in the doorway. Took a drink. "Something I can do for you, angel?"

She raised an eyebrow, looking at him in that way that made him feel like she could see inside his head. Didn't he deserve to have some thoughts of his own? He didn't want to share every damn piece of himself.

"Nope," she said, ducking under his arm and into the house.

He stood frozen staring out at the side of his garage. What the hell had just happened?

He slammed the door shut. "I don't remember inviting you in," he said as Nora stood in his dingy kitchen looking as out of place as a nun in a strip club with her dark jeans and a short-sleeve top that barely skimmed the waistband of her pants. Her hair spilled down her back, those damn diamonds at her ears.

"If I waited for you to invite me in," she said in that calm way of hers that only made him feel more out of control, more like he wanted to shake that calmness out of her, shock it out of her, "I'd still be outside."

"Look," he said as she unloaded take-out boxes onto the small table, "I'm not in the mood for company."

"Oh, but you hide it so well beneath your polite veneer."

That was the problem. He wasn't polite. Wasn't polished. Didn't care to be.

He frowned at the delicious smells coming from the container. "What is all of this?"

"It's food."

"You cooked me dinner?"

She smiled. "I don't cook," she said as if that was the

most ridiculous thing she'd ever heard. "I picked it up
from the café." She glanced around, though he had no
idea what she'd be looking for. "Why don't you open a
bottle of wine and I'll set the table."

"I don't have any wine." Who the hell did she think
he was…that pretty-boy suit from the office? "I don't
like wine."

She opened a cupboard. Shut it. "I do. Merlot is my
favorite but I also like other reds."

"What the hell are you looking for?" he asked, telling himself he didn't care what kind of wine she liked.

"Where are your… Never mind," she said, taking
down two mismatched plates. "Found them."

"Why are you doing this?" he asked, crossing his
arms. "Why are you here?"

She met his eyes. "Because I thought you could use
a friend."

Because his son of a bitch father had died, leaving
more questions than answers.

But he didn't have friends. It was easier, safer, to go it
alone. Always. He didn't trust anyone with his thoughts
or feelings and he knew that's what a friend, what any
kind of relationship entailed. And he wasn't about to
give away a piece of himself like that. Ever.

He edged toward her, backing her up until she was
against the counter. She wasn't wearing heels, so he
towered over her. But she didn't seem afraid. Just tipped
her head back and met his eyes. Watching. Waiting.

"Is that what we are?" he asked, cornering her between the edge of the counter and his body. Kept moving closer until he felt the heat from her body. He
trapped her between his arms, his hands on the counter. He didn't trust himself to touch her. Not today.

Maybe not ever again.

"Do you kiss your friends the way you kissed me the other night?" he asked lowly, his groin tightening at the memory. "Touch them the way you touched me? Do you do the things you did to me to all your *friends?*" He bumped his hips against hers, let her feel what she did to him, what he wanted from her. "You think I want your friendship?"

"I don't know, Griffin. Why don't you tell me?"

"I already got what I wanted from you." He smirked, kept his gaze hooded. "But if you're up for another go, I'm willing."

She looked at him with understanding. With sympathy. It killed him. "You don't have to act this way," she said softly. "All tough and cynical and bitter. Not with me." She laid her palms on his chest. His heart skipped a beat. "It's okay if you're upset or scared or angry. You can talk to me. You can tell me."

He forced a harsh laugh, his gut twisting when her hands slid away, when hurt flashed in her eyes. "Christ, you really have no clue what I'm about, do you?"

Her throat worked as she swallowed. "Maybe not. But I do know one thing. You're scared to death of me. You don't have to be." She cupped his cheek, her hand soft and warm, her fingers unsteady. "I won't hurt you, Griffin."

Her strength, her honesty was too much for him to handle. Too hard for him to resist. But she was right. He was scared of her. Scared of his feelings for her.

She met his eyes and for a moment, he got sucked in. Sucked in by her openness, by how trusting and so freaking optimistic she was. She wasn't for him, damn it. He only went after things he knew he could get, he knew he deserved. He never wished or hoped for more because doing so ended one way. With disappointment.

But he wanted her. For the first time in his life, he coveted something out of his reach.

He was too afraid to take the chance of going after it. Too afraid of what it would feel like if he didn't get it. If he didn't get her.

Better to end this now before someone got hurt.

He wrapped his fingers around her delicate wrist, pulled her hand away from his face and stepped back. "Thanks for dinner," he said, keeping his voice cool, "but like I said, I'm not in the mood for company."

She nodded slowly. "I see. So you'd rather be alone."

"Now you're catching on."

"Oh, I'm pretty good at catching on," she said hotly as she stormed over to him. Slammed her hands on her hips. "You're trying to hurt me. My question is, why?"

She sounded so upset, looked so confused, he fidgeted, had to fight the urge to take her into his arms. "There you go," he said, stuffing his hands in his pockets, "making everything about you."

Her eyes widened and she tossed her hands into the air. "Yes, how egotistical of me to think the man I'm involved with is pushing me out of his life."

"We're not involved," he said quickly. "And you're not in my life." He lifted a shoulder, ignored the sense of panic climbing his spine, coating his mouth. The feeling that something precious was slipping right through his fingers. Something he'd never get back again. "We slept together. It didn't mean anything."

NORA COULDN'T BREATHE. It felt like she'd been kicked in the chest. She was shaking. With rage, she assured herself. Not because of his cruel words. Not because she was close to begging him not to do this, not to end what was between them. What could be.

"You don't want it to mean anything," she said, unable to stop her pain from leaking into her voice.

She didn't mean anything to him.

And she wanted to be special, wanted to mean the world, at least to one person.

It hurt…God, it hurt so much she was surprised she was still upright, still able to meet his gaze. Everything about this, about him, was wrong. His eyes, those green eyes that had looked at her with so much heat when they'd made love, so much longing, were now flat and cold.

"Either way," he said, leaning back against the table, "the end result's the same."

Her face was numb. The scent from the burgers and fries she'd brought made her ill. She held her hand under her nose, worked to keep the contents of her stomach from rising.

"You're right," she whispered. "The end result is the same."

She crossed to the door, her legs like rubber, her heart aching. She stopped as fury leaked through the pain. Pain he'd had no right to cause.

"I was such an idiot," she told him, staring at the door. "Such a fool. I convinced myself there was more to you than that cloak of bitterness you wear, that chip of resentment on your shoulder. My God, I was honestly going to settle." The fact angered her. Humiliated and shamed her. "I was going to settle for whatever scraps of emotion you tossed my way, whatever amount of caring I could pry out of you."

She opened the door then faced him, wanted to see him, one last time. Wanted him to know what he'd done to her. Wanted him to know she'd survive him. She'd be stronger. Smarter.

She'd protect herself better.

"I deserve better," she said, her fingers tight on the door handle, the cool night air beckoning. "I deserve so much better than you."

CHAPTER SEVENTEEN

"MOM GOT THE FLOWERS you sent yesterday," Tanner told Griffin as they worked on the car Sunday afternoon.

Griffin tipped up a bottle of water, drank deeply then put the cap back on. "Yeah?"

"Yeah. She cried. I think they were happy tears," he added quickly when Griffin's mouth thinned. "At least, that's what she told me."

Although Tanner hadn't believed her at first. Not when she'd cried so hard—much harder than when she'd gotten all teary-eyed that Mother's Day a few years back when he and his dad had bought her that fancy rosebush she'd always wanted.

He had no idea what the flowers were for, either. Their mom's birthday wasn't until February and all the card said was *It's Enough. Griffin.*

But Tanner had noticed she'd tucked the card onto her dresser mirror along with his and Griffin's school pictures.

"She wanted me to invite you to dinner tonight," he continued.

"What's she cooking?" Griffin asked, tossing the empty bottle into the trash.

"Some sort of chicken."

"Sounds good. Tell her I'll be there." He nodded toward the door. "Looks like you've got company."

Tanner turned.

And saw Jessica walking across the parking lot toward them.

Shit.

He wanted to toss his wrench down and walk away. He didn't want to talk to her. Didn't even want to see her.

Even though he'd thought about her constantly since he'd left her at the party a week ago.

But if he walked, she'd think she had some sort of hold over him. That he couldn't handle sharing the same air as her. That he still liked her.

Then she was there, standing in the doorway, her shorts showing off her tanned legs, her tank top revealing her sunburned shoulders. She seemed unsure. Nervous.

Good.

God, but she was pretty.

He squeezed the wrench. She'd used him. And he'd let her. But no more.

"Hey, Tanner," she said.

He nodded and felt Griffin give him a sidelong look. Whatever.

Griffin wiped his hand on the rag he carried in his back pocket. "How's it going, Jess?"

"Fine." She cleared her throat. "Thanks."

Silence. Heavy-duty, totally uncomfortable silence.

Griffin elbowed Tanner in the side. Hard. Tanner scowled at him. Griffin raised his eyebrows, tipped his head toward Jess.

Tanner gave one quick shake of his head.

No. He didn't want to talk to her.

"I think I hear my mom calling me," Griffin said, walking toward the doorway. "Coming, Mom."

He went outside and around the side of the building.

So much for the bond between brothers.

Tanner went back to work, felt Jess come up behind him.

"So, this is your car?" she asked, close enough now that he could smell her perfume.

He nodded.

She walked around it and try as he might, he couldn't help but watch her. Her brows were drawn together, her hair down and stick straight. She trailed her fingers along the driver's-side door and he noticed she'd painted her nails a glossy blue.

When she was done circling his car, she stopped next to him. He stared at the spot where the engine would go—once Griffin ordered it. "It's a piece of shit," she said.

Tanner stiffened and faced her. "It's a work in progress."

She pursed her lips, her eyebrows raised. "O-kay. If you say so."

He tightened the bolt, wrenched it too hard and hit his knuckle. "What do you want?"

"God, can't a person drop by and say hello?"

"No."

She huffed out a breath. "Look, there's no need to be a jerk. I'm...I'm sorry, okay? So let's just pretend the party never happened and we can go back to how it was before."

He stilled, slowly straightened and faced her. "How what was before?"

"Me and you." She chewed on her thumbnail, the act in opposition to her hip-cocked stance. "We can hang out and stuff again."

"You want to hang out with me?" he asked, wanting to make sure he was following her.

She dropped her hand. "Well, yeah. I mean...I...I had fun when we were together. Didn't you?" she asked, sounding so unsure and nervous he almost forgot his resolve not to let her get to him.

Almost.

"Yeah, I had fun."

She smiled, relieved. "Great. So—"

"But it's not enough. Not if you're going to use me to try to get to some other guy."

"I said I was sorry about that," she pointed out, not sounding very sorry to him. No, she sounded more pissed off that he wasn't falling at her feet forgiving her. "I was just... It was a mistake and I..." She pressed her lips together. "I'm sorry if I hurt your feelings."

Humiliation washed over him. If this was anything close to what love was like, he didn't want anything to do with it. "You didn't," he said, hoping she believed him. "I just don't like being used."

She nodded, stepped closer to him. "Okay. I mean, that's fair. And I promise it won't ever happen again."

He studied her. She seemed sincere enough but who knew what went on in the minds of girls? They were unpredictable and never did or said what you expected them to. Never reacted how they should and always kept guys guessing.

He'd give up on them but it seemed a little early in his life to quit on something so promising.

"You want me to forget it?" he asked, knowing he probably sounded like an idiot, repeating what she said but he couldn't help it.

"Yeah." She licked her lips. "And we can, you know, go back to being friends."

And there it was, that kick in the balls, the one he'd

known—damn it, he'd known—was coming. The one he'd tried to convince himself wouldn't hurt.

"No," he said, his lips barely moving.

Because he couldn't stand there and look into her blue eyes one more minute, because it killed him to be so close to her and not touch her how he wanted, not to give away his feelings, he turned on his heel and stalked to the other side of the garage. Stared blindly at the tools lined up neatly there.

"Why not?" she asked, hurrying after him.

He turned and gave the wrench a sidelong toss. It crashed into an oil pan with a clang. "Damn it, you really don't get it, do you?"

She took a step back as if he was one wrong word from going completely psycho on her. "Get what?"

That she was trying to push him into the Friend Zone, the place where a guy's hopes went to die.

Once you were in the Zone, you never got out.

"That I don't want to be your friend," he said, his voice rising despite his best efforts to be all cool and controlled. He stormed over to her, took a hold of her by the upper arms, noted that her eyes widened, her throat worked as she swallowed. But she didn't struggle. Didn't push at him or yell or kick him.

He wished she would.

"I don't want to be your friend," he repeated, softer this time, loosening his hold on her so he wouldn't hurt her.

"What do you want?" she whispered, her eyes searching his.

His heart pounded. "I want this."

And he kissed her.

Her curves were soft against his body, her lips warm and she tasted like mint and soda. It was a banner day—

one for the record books, really. Because after a stunned moment she kissed him back, her hands hesitantly going to his shoulders, her fingers digging into his skin.

When he leaned back, he could see interest, attraction and uncertainty in her eyes. It was the last that had him letting her go and stepping back. That told him he had to let her make the next move.

Even if that move was to step away from him.

"That's what I want," he said, shoving his hands into his pockets where they couldn't get him into any trouble. "If you want that, too, you know where to find me."

He bent and swiped up his wrench and went back to work on his car. After a moment feeling her staring at him, he heard her walk away, her flip-flops clapping against the cement floor.

He hung his head, wanted to bang it against the car frame a few dozen or so times. He'd blown it. But maybe that was for the best. Maybe they weren't meant to be.

This Zen shit sucked.

He rolled his shoulders back, prepared to forget she'd ever been there, that he'd ever touched her, that his mouth still tingled from the feel of her lips. His cell phone vibrated. Pulling it from his front pocket, his stomach dropped to see he had a text from Jess. His palms sweating, his heart racing, he opened it.

Want to go to the movies tonight? My treat.

He glanced around, even jogged to the doors and checked up and down the street but she wasn't anywhere to be found. But she'd texted him. Was asking him out after she'd come over to the garage to apologize. She knew he wanted more than friendship and she wanted to go out with him.

Grinning he read her message again, took a deep breath and answered.

Yes.

"WE'RE CLOSED," GRIFFIN told Layne flatly. What the hell was it with people just showing up on a Sunday afternoon? First Jess had come and done some sort of a number on Tanner, one that had, admittedly, gotten the kid out of the funk he'd been in for the past week.

But now he wouldn't stop smiling and the constant singing along with the iPod was driving Griffin nuts. Kid couldn't hold a note.

Layne smirked at him, tossed her long fall of hair over her shoulder. "Sure looks like you're open to me."

"Looks can be deceiving. Take off," he told Tanner who was pretending not to watch Griffin and Layne. "We'll finish this up tomorrow."

Tanner shrugged. "Yeah, okay. I'll just clean up."

The kid was always good about putting stuff back where he found it and he kept the garage spotless. "That's okay," Griffin said, having a feeling he didn't want his little brother witnessing whatever had prompted Layne's visit. "I've got it."

"You sure?" Tanner asked, shooting a worried glance at Layne.

"Tan. I've got this."

Though it was kind of nice to have someone worried about him, have someone watching his back. Even if it was a seventeen-year-old.

"You're coming to dinner, though, right?" Tanner asked.

"I said I was, didn't I?" Hadn't counted on how relieved he'd been when Tanner had relayed their mom's message. That she wanted him to come. That she understood what the flowers, what the card meant. That he forgave her. "Now beat it."

He waited until Tanner had climbed into the minivan before facing Layne. "What can I do for you, Officer?"

She raised her eyebrows in an innocent gesture that wouldn't fool a blind man. "Me? Not a thing." And she didn't correct him of her title or rank or whatever the hell cops went by. Oh, yeah. Something was definitely up. "I was in the neighborhood and thought I'd drop by. See how you were holding up." She strolled inside his garage, forcing him to follow her. "I heard you paid to have your father's remains cremated."

"Someone had to." And he hadn't wanted the state stuck with paying the bill. "You didn't get what you wanted." Layne raised her eyebrows. "Dale never paid for your mother's death."

"It would've been tough getting a conviction," she said, "but I would've loved to have seen him go to trial. Maybe this was fate's way of taking care of things for us."

Griffin didn't believe in fate. You made your own luck. "Still, I'm…" He stopped, rolled his head side-to-side. Forced the words out. "I'm sorry your family didn't get the justice you deserve."

"I almost believe you mean that."

"I don't give a rat's ass what you believe," he told her mildly. But he had meant what he said. More than wanting justice for them, he wanted Nora to find some semblance of peace with the past.

Even though he worried he'd never find that peace for himself.

"Anything else?" he asked, wanting to ask how Nora was, if she'd mentioned him. He kept his mouth shut.

"No, that about covers it," she said with way too much cheer. She glanced at her watch. "I'm running late so I'll just get going. I told Nora I'd meet her at the café."

He stiffened at the mention of her name. "Then you'd better get going."

"I'd better." Layne watched him carefully in that cop way of hers she had. "It's my turn to try to talk her out of leaving Mystic Point."

Everything inside him seemed to still, went cold. "What?"

"Oh, that's right. You two haven't been…hanging out lately so you probably don't know…"

"Don't know what?"

"She's moving to Boston. I'm not sure why, but a few days ago she told us all she was offered a job at some prestigious law firm there. And that she's accepting it."

"Good for her," he managed to say, feeling as if someone had cut off his air supply.

"I guess. I'm not crazy about her not being here all the time but…" Layne said giving a what-can-you-do gesture. "She has to do what's best for her and her career."

And with a wave she strutted herself out of his garage.

He stared at her back. It didn't matter what Nora did, where she went. Didn't matter if she was in Mystic Point or Boston. He wasn't for her.

He had to let her go.

"I JUST DON'T understand why you want to move back to Boston," Layne said as Keira delivered their lunches. "I thought you wanted to work at Uncle Kenny's firm. That you wanted to live in Mystic Point."

"Things change," Nora said. And she'd been through

too many of them to continue to stay here. It was too painful. There were too many things she couldn't have. Too many secrets.

Layne took the cucumber slices off her grilled chicken salad and set them aside. "Is this sudden need to escape the only town you've ever wanted to live in because of Griffin?"

Her mouth thin, Nora stabbed her fork into her fried haddock. Griffin. Just hearing his name made her blood boil. Her heart hurt. Damn him. "This has nothing to do with him. I just…I realized that it's time to give up on some dreams. Time to change those dreams," she amended.

"Maybe," Layne said, looking over Nora's shoulder toward the door. "Or maybe it's time to realize everything you want is right here."

"What the hell do you think you're doing?"

Her eyes wide, Nora slowly lowered the forkful of coleslaw she'd been about to bite. She looked from Layne—who was way too casual as she sipped her iced tea—up to Griffin's furious face. Couldn't think, not when he was glowering at her, all but vibrating with annoyance.

"Eating lunch?" she asked, not sure what he was asking, why he was there.

He laid his hands on the edge of the table, leaned forward until his face was inches from hers. "You're not doing it," he snarled.

"That lunch *is* awfully heavy on saturated fats," Layne said, spearing a piece of lettuce.

Nora scowled. "I like saturated fats." She looked up at Griffin, refrained from rubbing her bowl of coleslaw into his face. Mostly because that would be a waste of excellent coleslaw. "What are you, the diet police?"

"Damn it, Nora," he said, smacking his hand against the table. "You're not leaving."

"And that's my cue," Layne murmured. She stood, took a step then reached back for her salad. "Play nicely."

"Did you think I'd feel guilty if you moved to Boston," Griffin asked. "If you left your family and the life you wanted because of me?"

Nora glanced around, noticed a few of the other diners were watching them curiously. "What are you talking about?" she asked lowly.

"I'm talking about you running back to Boston to avoid me."

She narrowed her eyes, jabbed her fork in his direction and wasn't sure whether to be relieved or disappointed he straightened in time to avoid the tines puncturing his skin. "Did you really think I'm leaving town because I'm what…? Too overwrought about you not wanting to be with me that I couldn't face life here without you? Oh, or I know, maybe you thought I was so heartbroken that the thought of us running into each other at the grocery store would send me into some suicidal frenzy? And you think *I* have a big ego?"

He flushed. Stabbed a hand through his hair. "Yes. No. I just…I don't want you to give up the life you've always wanted because of me. I don't want you giving anything up for me."

"Believe me, I'm not." Not completely. But a girl was entitled to a few secrets, right? Especially from the man who broke her heart.

Pointedly ignoring his presence, she picked up her roll, had it halfway to her mouth when he grabbed her wrist and yanked her from the booth. People were watching, staring, so she didn't haul off and kick him like he deserved. Just smiled as she jogged to keep up with his long, angry strides as he tugged her through the restaurant and out the front door.

Outside, he didn't even slow, continued around the corner and to the edge of the parking lot. "Tell me why you're leaving," he demanded.

She yanked free of him. "You have lost your mind." She stepped to the left. He blocked her. To the right. Same thing. "Seriously?" she ground out.

"Tell. Me."

"I can't stay here," she blurted, holding her blowing hair away from her face. "It's too hard. Being around my sisters, my father…working with Uncle Ken, helping Aunt Astor and Erin plan the wedding…knowing the truth…" She shook her head slowly. "It's too much."

"You didn't tell Ken?"

"I couldn't. With Dale dead I didn't see any reason to. Not when it'll only hurt so many people." She inhaled a ragged breath. "So now that your conscience is clear and you don't have to worry about little ol' me, you can go back to your cave—I mean, your garage—and finish living your life all by yourself. Because there's no way in hell I'd let you, or the fact that I stupidly let myself fall in love with you, run me out of town."

I STUPIDLY LET myself fall in love with you.

No. She didn't mean it.

But this was Nora. She didn't lie. Didn't play games. She was open and honest and giving and trusting. She was everything he didn't deserve and everything he wanted.

"You can't leave," he said, pretending not to hear the desperation in his tone. "If you do, Dale wins. Is that what you want?"

"No one won. My mother is dead. Dale is dead. And I'm…God, I don't even know what I am. *Who* I am."

"You're Nora Sullivan. You're Tim Sullivan's daughter. Layne and Tori's sister. You are who you've always been and you're strong enough to deal with this. Smart enough to know that it's what's inside you that makes you the person you are, not who your parents are." Taking a chance, he stepped closer, grateful when she didn't move away. "Brave enough to face this, to accept it and to choose to be the same person you were before you found out."

Her eyes welled and she averted her gaze, staring over his shoulder at the back of the building.

"I miss you," he said quietly, too far gone to worry about his pride or the fact that she was justified in wanting to kick his teeth in. She couldn't leave.

"Good," she said so fervently it was all he had not to drag her against him and kiss the hell out of her.

"Could you look at me? Please?" She did but seemed reluctant. His stomach twisted with nerves. "I was wrong," he said slowly.

She raised her eyebrows when he remained silent. "That's it? That's all you've got?"

"What else do you want from me?"

"I want you to show some emotion. I want you to be honest with me."

He'd admitted he was wrong, told her he'd missed her. What did she need? Blood? How much more was he expected to give? He had to keep some things to himself or he'd have nothing left.

"I want to be with you," he said.

"Why?"

He tugged on his ear, felt as if the ground was shifting beneath his feet. "Because."

"Why, Griffin? Is it because of the sex? Because we both know you can get that from any number of women in town."

"I...I care about you."

She shook her head sadly as if he was completely clueless. "Not good enough. Don't you get it? I want it all. I want the man I'm with to give me the love I deserve. A grand, all-encompassing, passionate love. The kind that's forever. The kind that my father had for my mother. Except, unlike her I'll appreciate that love. More importantly, I'll return it. So if you're not able to tell me why you want to be with me, if you aren't willing to put it all on the line and let me into your life fully, then there's nothing else to talk about."

She sounded final, her words felt like some sort of death knell. He didn't know what to do or say, how to convince her. Wasn't sure he could open himself up to her, expose himself to that kind of risk.

But the thought of a life without Nora was even more terrifying.

He took her hands in his, held on when she stiffened. "You make me want things," he said, choosing his words carefully, afraid he'd mess it up anyway. Her fingers twitched in his. "Things I've never let myself want before. A future. A home. A family of my own. Someone to share my life with. I want to share my life with you, Nora, because you're the best of everything. You have strength and kindness. Humor and intelligence. And you have my heart." He lifted her hand, placed a kiss on her palm. "Right here. Don't give it back. Please."

Her breath caught, her eyes glimmered with tears as she searched his face. He kept his expression open, let her see everything. How much he loved her, how much he needed her. His hopes and his fears.

Finally, giving him a shaky, beautiful smile, she cupped his face with both hands. "I won't give it back," she said, her voice thick with tears. "I'll cherish it. And I'll give you mine in return."

He kissed her, his angel, his love, and knew he'd finally found his salvation.

* * * * *

You can find more information on upcoming Harlequin® titles, free excerpts and more at www.Harlequin.com.

HSRCNM0812

REQUEST YOUR FREE BOOKS!
2 FREE NOVELS PLUS 2 FREE GIFTS!

Harlequin®

Super Romance®

Exciting, emotional, unexpected!

HSR11

HARLEQUIN®

SYTYCW

SO YOU THINK YOU CAN WRITE

Harlequin and Mills & Boon are joining forces in a global search for new authors.

In September 2012 we're launching our biggest contest yet—with the prize of being published by the world's leader in romance fiction!

Look for more information on our website, **www.soyouthinkyoucanwrite.com**

So you think you can write? Show us!

*Welcome to the Texas Hill Country! In the third book
in Tanya Michaels's series* HILL COUNTRY HEROES,
*a desperate mother is in hiding with her little girl.
The last thing she needs is her nosy Texas Ranger
neighbor getting friendly....*

Alex raised her gaze, starting to say something, but then she froze like a possum in oncoming headlights.

"Mrs. Hunt? Everything okay?"

She eyed the encircled silver star pinned to his denim button-down shirt. He'd been working this morning and hadn't bothered to remove the badge. "Interesting symbol," she said slowly.

"Represents the Texas Rangers."

"L-like the baseball team?"

"No, ma'am. Like the law enforcement agency." Maybe that would make her feel safer about her temporary new surroundings. He jerked his thumb toward his house. "You have a bona fide lawman living right next door."

Beneath the freckles, her face went whiter than his hat. "Really? That's…" She gave herself a quick shake. "Come on, Belle. Inside now. Before, um, before that mud stains."

"Okay." Belle hung her head but rallied long enough to add, "Bye-bye, Mister Zane. I hope I get to pet Dolly again soon."

From Alex's behavior, Zane had a suspicion they wouldn't be getting together for neighborly potluck dinners anytime in the near future. Instead of commenting on the kid's likelihood of seeing Dolly again, he waved. "Bye, Belle. Stay fabulous."

She beamed. "I will!"

Then mother and daughter disappeared into the house, the front door banging shut behind them.

"Is there something about me," he asked Dolly, "that makes females want to slam doors?"

The only response he got from the dog was an impatient tug on her leash. "Right. I promised you a walk." They started again down the sidewalk, but he found himself periodically glancing over his shoulder and pondering his new neighbors. Cute kid, but she seemed like a handful. And Alex Hunt, once she'd calmed from her mama-bear fury, was perhaps the most skittish woman he'd ever met. If she were a horse, she'd have to wear blinders to keep from jumping at her own shadow. Zane wondered if there was a Mr. Hunt in the picture.

Be sure to look for RESCUED BY A RANGER
by Tanya Michaels in September 2012 from
Harlequin® American Romance®!